"I'll mak

He paused _____ up
with the application fee, I'll do what I can to teach
you, Abby. But again, I can't guarantee—"

"I know, I know." She flew across the room,
grabbed his shoulders and kissed him full on
the mouth. A quick kiss. One of gratitude and
happiness with a touch of that electric excitement
he was fast becoming familiar with. In that
moment Jason also tasted fire and determination.

She must have surprised herself because she
rocked back on her heels and lifted her stunned
face to him. He clenched his fists to stop himself
from touching her cheek, from finding out if her
skin was as soft as he imagined it would be. "You
heard me, right? This is going to be hard work,
Abby."

"Sure. I hadn't considered it anything but."

Dear Reader,

I'm a believer in the butterfly effect—those ripples that occur with the simple beating of wings. Sometimes it's a person who gives us a gift we didn't know we needed.

My cousins Ron and Colleen lived a short drive away from my family. They had three children, all older than me and their house was always filled with the enthusiasm of living each day to its fullest. It was there that I first heard the words of Shakespeare. To listen to Ron utter the beautiful intricacies of language (he was an actor and Shakespeare professor) with clarity and affection touched my heart. He was one of my biggest cheerleaders and, in recent years, as his heath declined due to Parkinson's, he carried one of my books with him in his walker, showing it off at his care facility. I've joked it was the best book tour I could have ever gone on. But it's the truth.

With *Recipe for Redemption*, I knew Abby Manning would be struggling: her historic inn on the brink of ruin, the town's survival, finding where she belonged in the world and coming face-to-face with a hero who would push her emotional buttons. But then Abby's grandmother Alice (named for Ron's mother) arrived on the page fighting a battle of her own: the same battle Ron fought and, unfortunately, lost this past summer. Another butterfly effect? I think so.

Family connections, whether by blood or choice, are at the heart of Butterfly Harbor. How different my own life would have been without Ron quoting Shakespeare to me, or lending an encouraging ear when I needed it most. Just as Abby's grandmother and her friends do for Abby. Community, connections. Is there anything more important?

Anna J.

7/16

HEARTWARMING

Recipe for Redemption

—

USA *TODAY* Bestselling Author

Anna J. Stewart

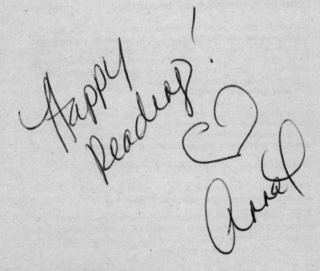

Happy Reading!

Anna

 HARLEQUIN® HEARTWARMING™

Recycling programs
for this product may
not exist in your area.

ISBN-13: 978-0-373-36791-7

Recipe for Redemption

Copyright © 2016 by Anna J. Stewart

Printed in U.S.A.

Anna J. Stewart says the greatest gift her mother ever gave her was never saying no to a book. A lifelong bookworm, Anna discovered romances early in high school and soon began writing her own. Hundreds of notebooks and reams of paper later, she writes "refreshingly unique, quietly humorous and profoundly moving romance" (*RT Book Reviews*). *New York Times* bestselling author Brenda Novak says, "The talented Anna J. Stewart never disappoints." Anna lives in Northern California with an overly attentive cat named Snickers.

Books by Anna J. Stewart

Harlequin Heartwarming

Christmas, Actually
"The Christmas Wish"

The Bad Boy of Butterfly Harbor

For Ronald Trouse

Cousin, teacher, father figure and kind, kind man.

Your brave battle will never be forgotten, and neither will you.

CHAPTER ONE

JASON CORWIN'S HAND stilled over the hotel registration form as he sniffed the air. "Do you smell smoke?"

A middle-aged woman with short-cropped gray hair passed through the reception area of the Flutterby Inn, Butterfly Harbor's main hotel, a stack of freshly laundered towels in her arms. The lack of concern on her face might have made Jason wonder if he were imagining things, but as a former professional chef, he was more than familiar with this particular smell.

"I have you down for three weeks, Mr. Corwin," Lori, the plump young woman who had introduced herself minutes ago, said. She leaned her hands on the whitewashed battenboard counter, lively green eyes devoid of concern as the air thickened. "Is that correct?"

"Yes." He scribbled his name, his eyes beginning to water as a thread of white smoke snaked out from under the double doors to his left. "I'm sorry, but shouldn't someone check—"

The deafening screech of a smoke alarm rent the air. Hints of gray puffed through the plumes of white smoke.

"It's nothing!" Lori waved her hand before turning to focus on the old-fashioned mailbox portals behind her. "That's just Abby in the kitchen. It'll clear in a few minutes."

The lobby became hazy. Jason's pulse kicked into overdrive as he wrenched open the sliding doors and got a face full. Coughing, eyes tearing, he hurried through the dining room, dodging the mishmash of tables and chairs. He tried to inhale but there wasn't any fresh air to be found, nothing to calm his nerves or stop the dread pounding through his body. Did it have to be the kitchen?

He'd kept his vow and hadn't stepped foot in a professional kitchen in over three months, but given the choice between burning to death in a hotel fire and breaking a promise to himself, he'd take choice number two.

He pushed open the swinging door and stepped into the kitchen, waving his hands in front of him to disperse the smoke. A stockpot of what he hoped was water boiled over and splashed into the too-high flame beneath it, causing bright orange flickers of fire to arch toward the ceiling.

"Come on, you stupid, plastic piece of crap!" A woman stood on the stainless steel worktable and banged the end of a broom against the smoke detector. "It's not like this is our first go-around." *Bang. Bang, bang.* "Stop. Making." She grunted and he could see her arms start to weaken. "So. Much. Noise! Ah!"

The kitchen went silent and she sagged forward, bracing a hand on her knee as she heaved out a sigh. "Got ya. Oh, sugar pots."

Before Jason could move, before he could utter a word, she jumped down and grabbed a thick orange towel, dragged out two trays of cremated somethings and tossed them onto the counter with a squealing "Ow!" The bang of metal hitting metal echoed in the room and in his head.

She shook her left hand as if she'd burned herself—how could she not—before reaching for the pot. The orange towel slipped dangerously toward the flames.

"Stop!" Jason yelled and dived forward.

She shrieked and leaped aside as the towel skimmed the still-flaming burners and ignited. "Who are you?" She flipped the towel onto the yellowed linoleum floor and did a little dance over it to stomp out the flames. "What are you doing in here?"

"Right now I'm wondering where the fire department is." He strode over and closed the oven door, flipped off all the burners and then shoved open the closest transom windows. "Hasn't anyone told you the kitchen's a dangerous place? It's not a playroom."

"I wasn't *playing*." She pushed the windows on the other side of the kitchen open and, as the smoke thinned, glared at him. "I was trying to make scones."

Jason looked at what seemed to be tiny shriveled briquettes. "You failed." He glanced up at the ceiling and saw the cover of the smoke detector hanging by a duo of thin battery wires. "Your detectors are not to code." No wonder he didn't hear sirens. It wasn't hooked up to anything but noise.

Now that he could see clearly, the entire kitchen looked stuck in the past. Only the refrigerator appeared to have been manufactured in the last decade, the stainless steel scarred and leaning toward tarnish. He could see rust forming in the tile grout around the cracked farmer's sink.

He bent down to grab the towel, but she

snatched the smoking fabric out from under his hand and tossed it into the sink overloaded with used bowls, spoons and...was that a tortilla press?

"I've got it, thanks." She shooed him away from the mess she'd made and toward the door. "All in a day's work. Nothing to worry about."

Must be the hotel motto. Was it too late to rethink his stay? Probably, considering he hadn't been the one to make his reservations in the first place. Fresh air collided with the smoke and thinned it out. He'd never been so grateful to fill his lungs before as he coughed out the remnants of her scone attempt.

Her mouth twisted as she peered at the charcoal briquettes scattered on the trays, counter and floor. "I don't know what happened. Our cook told me they were foolproof."

"You mean full proof."

"She said what she meant." She swiped a hand over her damp forehead and let out a long breath as she seemed to collect herself. "Not the way I like to greet new guests." She was choking as she tried not to cough and as she blinked, cleansing tears streamed down her face. "I'm Abby Manning. I run the Flutterby Inn. And you are—?"

"Jay Corwin." After three months, the lie came easily.

"Next floor show starts at five." Her laugh sounded strained as she planted a hand on her hip and studied the mess. Her doll-like face with a too-small nose and too-wide turquoise eyes eased into a smile that almost broke through his personal bank of storm clouds. How, with all those thick blond curls of hers tumbling around her shoulders, had she managed not to set herself on fire? He needed to keep moving, keep thinking, otherwise the walls were going to start closing in on him. Walls. Memories.

So many memories...

"You'll want to put some ice on your hand." Jason dropped his gaze to her reddening fingers. He headed toward the stainless steel refrigerator only to have her wave him off again as she dragged open the freezer door and sank her hand wrist deep into the ice tray with a relieved sigh.

"If you'd like to return to the lobby, Lori can—"

"Abby? Is everything all right?"

"Everything's fine!" Wincing, Abby pulled her hand free and shoved it into her jeans pocket, pressed a finger against her lips in a silent plea for his cooperation. "Just a little, um—"

The kitchen door swung open and an elderly woman entered. It was like watching night turn into day right before him as Abby's eyes brightened despite her fingers flexing in her pocket. "Good morning, Gran. How did you sleep?"

"As fine as anyone my age does these days. Hello. I'm Alice Manning." Alice bypassed Abby and headed straight for him, her steps short and slow. "This one here's my grand-daughter. I'm the former manager of the Flut-terby Inn."

"Jay Corwin, Mrs. Manning." He could see the family resemblance, the familiar soft fem-inine features right down to the same color eyes. He shook Alice's outstretched hand be-fore he bent down to retrieve a stray over-cooked scone off the floor and tossed it into the sink. The door beckoned him, offering freedom, offering relief, but he didn't see a way past Alice without being rude. Stuck. In a kitchen. Great. "A friend of mine recom-mended your hotel as the perfect getaway."

"Well, I hope you'll feel at home during

your stay. That's what we always aim for, right, my girl?" Alice glanced at Abby before she wagged a finger at him. "You'd be from the East Coast. New York, I'm guessing? Always could tell. Used to make a game of it when I checked customers in. I worked that desk out there for more than fifty years, long before this one was born. I know my accents." Gran angled her chin in Abby's direction. Something akin to pride shone in Abby's face as she watched her grandmother. "Nothing I like more than meeting people from all over this wonderful world, not that we get many visitors these days. Tell me, how long will you be staying with us, Mr. Corwin?"

"A few weeks." He couldn't remember exactly at the moment, because all he could think about was escaping the Flutterby Inn's kitchen. If he closed his eyes, he could almost hear the cacophonous symphony of the nightly dinner rush at JD's in New York.

"Good, good." Alice nodded and lifted a slightly trembling hand to smooth a curl above her ear. "Then you'll be here for the anniversary celebration. It's going to be quite the to-do, from what I hear. And what kind of work do you do?"

The truth froze in his throat and no matter

how hard he tried, he couldn't quite clear it. "I'm between jobs," he managed and avoided Abby's suddenly curious stare.

"Finding yourself, then?" Alice said with a solemn nod. "No place better than Butterfly Harbor to help you figure out life's big questions. Now, as for you."

Alice spun to face her granddaughter so fast, Jason held out his hands for fear the older woman would topple over. Abby reached out at the same time, shooting him a grateful look over her grandmother's stooped frame.

"Abby, tell me you haven't been cooking again." Alice shook her head and scanned the room, her rust-colored hair reflecting against the ceiling lights.

"You always told me practice makes perfect," Abby said in a tone that spoke of lifelong affection and commitment.

"I also taught you to accept your limitations. You should have learned your lesson when you were six and blew up your Easy-Bake Oven." She made a face at Jason, who kept his expression neutral. "Bet you didn't know one of those could fly, did you? Up and tried to launch itself out of the house on Christmas morning, I'm telling you."

"I thought we agreed it was a faulty light-bulb," Abby said without a hint of embarrassment.

"Your grandfather, bless him, and I thought it best to keep the truth from you. Now that you're almost thirty, I think you can handle it."

"You know me..." Abby stepped in and wrapped her arms around Alice and hugged her close. "I can handle everything as long as I have you. And I'm not going to stop trying to make Matilda's cranberry-orange scones you like so much."

"No scone is worth burning down our home." Alice clicked her tongue and patted Abby's back. "You always were an over-achiever, Abby girl, but it's time you wave a white flag and accept when you're beat. I'd like to go at least a week before hearing that blasted alarm again."

"I'll do my best," Abby chuckled. "Would you like me to drop you off at Eloise's this morning on my way to the hospital? I'm going to be leaving in a little bit."

"I'm ready whenever you are," Alice announced. "I'll go put my lipstick on and we'll zoom, zoom, zoom. A lady just isn't ready to go out in public without her red lipstick," she told Jason as she held out her hand again. "It was nice to meet you, Mr. Corwin."

"Jay, please. You, too, Mrs. Manning."

"Alice." She smiled, charming character wrinkles around her eyes appearing. "Welcome to Butterfly Harbor. I hope you enjoy your stay."

Abby's amused gaze faded as he caught her eye. "So do I."

"Mr. Corwin, there you are." Lori Fletcher, Abby's assistant manager and invaluable right hand, met them in the dining room as Abby led their new guest to the lobby.

She could feel the cool morning air brushing in through the front door Lori had opened to clear out the smoke. All the better to see Jay Corwin. Abby's gaze skimmed from his short-cropped, almost military-style brown hair to a neatly trimmed beard down to a myriad of muscles peeking from under a snug black T-shirt.

He seemed a bit more relaxed now that the smoke had dissipated. Or maybe it was a trick of the light. He'd stopped staring daggers at her and she was glad to see that frown on his face wasn't permanent. Not that he would win any points for a cheery disposition.

"Bonnie's doing a quick once-over on your room," Lori told him as she handed him the room key dangling from one of their trademark monarch butterfly key chains. "We have fresh coffee and pastries on the buffet in the lobby if you'd like to wait there."

"Thank you, Lori. Miss Manning." He bowed his head as if he were dismissing her. Abby gnashed her teeth. Storming into her kitchen to lecture her? As if she didn't know how inept she was when it came to cooking? Or that she didn't know how to silence a smoke alarm? Arrogant know-it-all.

"Abby, Matilda's going to have a coronary when she hears about this," Lori whispered once Jay Corwin was out of earshot. "She almost went on strike the last time you tried to cook spaghetti and over-boiled the sauce so it erupted like a volcano."

"If you don't tell her," Abby singsonged with a sweet smile as her face went hotter than the oven she'd been battling. She'd never understood how things got away from her so fast. "Then we don't have to worry, do we?"

"Uh-huh." Lori grinned, an expression that lit up her face as they returned to the desk. "I'd ask if this is the last time you plan to burn down the Flutterby, but now that you're attracting men who look as if they've modeled for a firefighters' calendar, I might start giving you my old matchbook collection."

"Not funny," Abby said. "I didn't think breakfast and dinner were going to be a problem."

"You had a good plan. Matilda's replacement didn't have any way of knowing his brother was going to die, and it's not like Butterfly Harbor is brimming with competent cooks."

Butterfly Harbor wasn't brimming with much of anything these days. "We'll make do," Abby tried to sound more confident than she felt. She was just going to have to make it work. "Meanwhile, we'll have to explain the situation to our guests and get by with them eating at the diner. Unless…"

"Unless what?" Lori's tone was hesitant.

"I could call Matilda and ask for some of her best recipes."

"Gee, Five-Alarm Manning, I can't understand why she didn't do that to start with."

"Are you guys really still calling me that?" Abby sighed as she headed to the über-organized registration desk and pushed aside all thoughts of sending out an SOS to Matilda. "Oh, no.

What's this?" She picked up the large metal showerhead.

"That," Lori said, "is a showerhead."

"Lori—"

"Room 206. It fell off when I was cleaning the bathtub."

"My own fault," Abby muttered. "I got sidetracked last week and forgot to check the rest of them." If it wasn't the showerheads taking suicide drops, it was leaky pipes under sinks or loose floorboards…everywhere. The Flutterby was falling apart, but she was determined to stay ahead of the collapse. She had to. She didn't have a choice. "Start me a list of any repairs we need to do. I'll get going on them after I visit Mr. Vartebetium." The Flutterby's owner had been in the hospital for several days now. Her fingers throbbed. It was all she could do not to run back to the kitchen and stick her hand in the freezer. "How are we coming on the reservations?"

"Working on them now," Lori told her. "It's been a while since we've had all twelve rooms filled, but we should have everyone's needs accounted for. That'll also leave two extra rooms for last-minute arrivals. That producer from the National Cooking Network is a picky one."

"New Yorkers," Abby muttered, casting a

glance to her newest arrival, who had taken a seat near the dormant fireplace. "I'm going to check with Matt about helping us get the last rooms in shape so we can have them as well." The recent Army vet had been doing odd jobs for her around the inn for a while, but his time was more limited now that he'd been hired as one of Sheriff Saxon's deputies. "It's going to be a crazy couple of weeks around here," she said to Lori. "We're going to need all hands on deck."

"We're ready."

Between the organizers of the By the Bay Food Festival and the production crew from the National Cooking Network, not to mention the out-of-town attendees, the Flutterby Inn was poised to be sold out for the first time in over two years. As much work as it was going to be for Abby and her three employees, it was their opportunity to make the Flutterby Inn shine in all its aging glory. And hopefully make a profit for their bedridden boss. "Nothing like going from a drought to a flood when it comes to guests." Abby inclined her head toward where their new guest sipped his coffee.

"We're in good shape. Besides, he paid for his reservation up front, so we can't exactly kick him out. I gave him the tower room, if that's okay? Kind of suits his knight-on-a-white-horse persona, don't you think?" Lori leaned her chin on her hand.

"The tower's fine." Abby ignored the question from the ever-romantic Lori along with the implication. Knight or not, she did not have the time or energy to invest in romance, no matter what her struggling online dating persona or her well-intentioned employee thought. Not that Jay Corwin was remotely her type. She liked her potential romantic partners to have fewer sharp edges to them. This guy was more prickly than a spiny jellyfish. "That leaves us with, what? Four guest rooms occupied through this weekend?" Lori nodded. Good. Not too much upkeep then, and at least two rooms would be vacated by the following week. "I'm going to drop Gran off at Eloise's for the day and then head over to see Mr. Vartebetium. I'll stop at the diner and pick up lunch. What do you want?"

"One of Holly's strawberry shakes would be heaven." Lori sighed, then looked down at her significant waistline hidden behind a full flowing skirt and oversize sweater. "But better make it a turkey on whole wheat. No fries."

What Abby wanted to do was remind the younger woman that depriving herself wouldn't help, but she didn't want to force Lori off the healthier bandwagon. Her friend's confidence had begun to climb and she'd even treated herself to a cut and color at the Bee Hive to tame her once brown, now nutmeg-highlighted brown curls. "You're doing great, Lori. Losing thirty pounds is nothing to sneeze at."

"It's the next thirty that has me worried. I'll hold down the fort, don't worry."

"Paige said to keep her on speed dial if we need extra help." But with her friend doing extra shifts at the diner, Abby didn't think it right to ask her to man the kitchen at the Flutterby as well. Not that Abby could afford to anyway, not with the way the business's finances were stretched these days. Not having an in-house cook was proving to be more of an issue than she'd anticipated. And it was only going to get worse with the influx of guests they were expecting.

She'd find a solution. She always did. She'd do anything to keep the Flutterby Inn running. It was the only home Gran had ever really known, and Abby wasn't about to have Alice spend her twilight years anywhere else. Especially now.

Abby rifled through one of her drawers for

the stack of meal vouchers for the Butterfly Diner. "I'm going to make sure our resident fireman is all set before I go."

"I'd say I saw him first," Lori said, "but you one-upped me with that fire of yours."

"It wasn't a full-blown fire." But it could have been. Gran was right. When was she going to learn her lesson? She and kitchens did not mix. Abby took a steeling breath and carried the vouchers over to their new guest, who was flipping through one of the anemic local tour books. "Mr. Cor—er, Jay?"

"Should I stay on alert for the duration of my stay, Five-Alarm Manning?" He didn't bother to look up from the booklet.

My, what big ears you have. She would not let him bait her. She couldn't afford to alienate paying—and from what she could tell, incredibly flush—guests. Some people, like this man, exuded money. "I'm afraid you've discovered my one weakness."

"Kitchens are dangerous for those not properly trained." The superiority in his voice obliterated the last of Abby's goodwill.

"Yes, I heard you the first time." Why did he make her sound as if she was a rambunctious five-year-old who'd dumped a container of flour all over her head? She bit her cheek.

She could tell her guest she'd been trying to save some money, that scones couldn't possibly be that difficult, that she hadn't wanted her guests to have to trudge to the diner. Or she could do as she'd done for the last seven years and keep her tongue in check to make sure her customers—even Mr. Jay Corwin— were happy.

"Since the kitchen is closed for the next couple of weeks—" she offered up a silent prayer that Matilda would return sooner than planned "—and your rate includes breakfast and either lunch or dinner, we're offering free meals to our customers down at the Butterfly Diner. I think you'll agree that's best while my cook is on vacation."

"You don't have a backup cook?" He frowned at her over the top of his coffee cup.

"We did. Matilda walked him through the paces before she left, but then his brother passed away. He had to fly back to Michigan."

"There's no one else available?"

"It took us weeks to find him. Besides, Matilda would throw a fit if someone she didn't know came in to work her kitchen." It was a joke. Kind of.

"You allow her to take time off and leave you high and dry during what could be a busy couple of months for you? Doesn't seem very responsible to me."

He couldn't have sounded any more judgmental if he'd banged a gavel on the sink. Life happened. And sometimes it had a cruel sense of timing. "Tell you what. If you're here when Matilda returns, feel free to let her know her annual long-distance breast cancer awareness fund-raising walk isn't smart business sense." So much for holding her tongue. "In the meantime, I hope you enjoy your stay. The diner opens every morning at six and what stores there are on Monarch Lane will open between nine and ten. If you have any questions or need assistance, let Lori know. She's more than up to the task, I'm sure."

Either he missed her sarcasm or he didn't care.

"Are the grounds around the inn open to guests?"

"Yes. There's a path down to the beach off the front parking lot. And if you give the Butterfly Diner a call ahead of time, Holly can make a nice lunch for you to pick up. Thank you again," she added before she pushed open the door. "I'm sorry your first few minutes at the Flutterby were distressing."

"Interesting, though." Jay gave her what

could have been interpreted as a smile. Such a shift from his earlier manner confounded Abby. "Have a good day, Miss Manning."

"Abby," she responded automatically, then, before she started to think better of him, headed off to collect Gran.

CHAPTER TWO

"WELL?" GARY CUNNINGHAM'S aged New York voice echoed through the Bluetooth as Jason hefted his suitcase and garment bag out of the trunk of the rented sports car. "Do I know how to find you the perfect hideaway or what?"

"It's definitely something." He'd spend some time later appreciating the lush landscaping that included thick, healthy red geraniums interspersed with critter-repelling oleander. He could hear the surf crashing against the shore and cliff line on the far edge of the property and smell that telltale Pacific Ocean combination of brine and open air. Nothing like an old three-story Victorian with beacon-bright yellow paint and peeling white trim to cut through the intricate groves of redwoods, cypress and eucalyptus trees. If the rest of the world ran out of oxygen, he knew where they could find some. "Hang on a second?"

The porch stairs creaked in welcome as he pushed through the etched glass front doors and gave Lori a quick wave of acknowledgment. He walked across hardwood floors in need of a polish, passing crisp white batten-board walls that displayed photographs of the inn throughout its extensive history. They provided a welcome distraction from the faded, out-of-date wallpaper.

At least he hadn't been inundated with the town's fluttering namesake. Not that he had anything against butterflies, but they did lend themselves toward a feminine aspect he didn't relate to. The creatures were so dainty, so delicate, like those lacy pastry swans he'd never mastered in culinary school, but at the same time butterflies were known to weather the most violent of hurricanes.

Reminded him of his current hostess, Abby Manning. He certainly wouldn't want to be a smoke detector in her presence. He tried to remember the last time anyone had surprised him. He unlocked his door.

Speaking of surprises...

The room was larger than he'd anticipated. He set his bags down on the feather duvet–covered California king situated amid a dresser, nightstands and a sizable flat-screen TV. The decor wasn't fancy but lent itself to practicality while skirting the far edge of stylish. The ceiling angled up from the walls into a point that he identified as the side tower that had poked into the horizon as he'd crossed into town.

"Okay," he said and heard the familiar rustle of papers and files as he spoke to his family's longtime lawyer and his personal confidant. Part mentor, part father figure, it was Gary he'd turned to over the years when it became clear his own father would remain emotionally unavailable. "So why did you pick this place?"

"Figured you had to be tired of four-star hotels and room service," Gary chuckled. "And the fresh air is a bonus."

"It seems Butterfly Harbor has plenty of that." Definitely not four star. He fingered the clean yet old-fashioned curtains draping the French doors to a small terrace. Three stars, maybe.

Pushing open the French doors, he stared out into the vastness of the Pacific crashing against the shoreline below. Even in mid-July, a chill coated the morning air, but that was the California coast for you: unpredictable yet peacefully welcoming.

The deep ocean breath he took eroded some of the tension in his body. He should have come here straight from New York. If he closed his eyes and concentrated, he could almost forget...

"Do you think you were followed this time?" Gary asked in that borderline boisterous tone a 1920s gangster might have used.

"No." He'd left Los Angeles in the dead of night. He'd have noticed if he'd been tailed. Besides, there hadn't been a car in sight for the mile and a half after he'd taken the Butterfly Harbor turnoff. "No sign of any reporters or cameras. I might finally be in the clear now that I stopped using my credit cards. Thanks for getting me in here so quickly." Not that booking a reservation would have been a problem.

"You call, I answer. Keeping you off the radar until you're ready to come back is what's important," Gary said. "So are you going to ask?"

"About Corwin Brothers?" Jason's stomach tightened into familiar knots as they fell into the months-old conversation about his family business. His *former* family business. "I don't know how many ways I can say it. I'm done with all of it. The board of directors made that perfectly clear when they ousted me as chairman." And that was after the National Cooking Network pulled his show off the air, the restaurant chain deal went into the toilet and his publisher decided to "wait awhile" on a new cookbook offer. The fact he'd lost all passion for the business, for the kitchen, for anything, really, since his brother, David, had died only added to his surrender.

"They ousted you because your father took advantage of your grief. He sold the board on the idea of a discount frozen food line when they couldn't think straight, and now it's tanking the company. This can't sit right with you, Jason. Your father's lack of understanding for what your grandfather wanted to build is the reason he left the company to you in the first place, and now what? You're going to let Edward swoop in and kill what's left?"

"You're forgetting that it was my mistake that started this slide to begin with." No, he didn't like the idea his father was in charge. Edward Corwin was a cold, calculating and profit-driven man—he always had been. And he'd never forgiven the fact he'd been ignored in his father's will. Jason leaned his arms on the railing and ducked his head. Frozen food. *Discounted* frozen food. Made with the cheapest ingredients from who knew what sources. Gary was right. It was a slap in the face to everything he and David had stood for, everything their grandfather had begun.

But Jason had sabotaged any hope of fighting his father and his arrogance and lack of sense. He didn't have any fight left in him. His brother's death had left him struggling. Depressed. Empty.

These days, Jason wasn't even sure if he was trying to escape the mess he'd made of his life...or himself.

"Sometimes I can't breathe, I miss David so much."

Like now, when there was more air than he knew what to do with and he still couldn't manage. It had been six months, and still, not an hour, not a minute passed when Jason didn't feel as if a part of him had died with his twin brother. His best friend. His anchor.

Jason wasn't supposed to be here without him.

He didn't know *how* to be here without him.

Jason scrubbed a tired hand over the back of his neck. If only he'd gotten on that plane with David like he was supposed to. If only he hadn't insisted on working late at the restaurant. Instead, he'd begged off the business trip that was meant to get the ball rolling on a deal that would have put JD's restaurants in dozens of Lansing hotels around the country. David could handle it, Jason had told him hours before the crash. He didn't need Jason and his acerbic attitude getting in the way of a potentially life-changing deal that would take them to the next level. The world had been opening up. Finally.

If only. If only...

Now everything they'd planned, everything they wanted was gone, and not only because David was. Because Jason had made mistake after mistake after mistake ever since.

Even now, six months later, his father wasn't letting anyone forget about David's death or Jason's fall from the pinnacle of culinary success. The added Edward Corwin spin on the truth had kept the media far more interested than they should have been, but that wasn't the worst of it. Whenever attention or headlines began to wane, his father gave yet another interview, another turn on the tragic loss of his son and the disgrace his surviving son had become. Somehow Edward had become the family martyr while Jason had done what he could to disappear.

Driving cross-country had helped, a little. Chopping off his trademark long hair and growing a beard, a little more. But Jason had never learned how to blend into a crowd. He hadn't had to, because David had always been by his side, guiding him, supporting him.

Jason had lost the only person he'd ever been able to trust, aside from Gary, and that, Jason was only now coming to realize, made living a whole lot more difficult.

"Grief takes time, son," Gary said in that fatherly tone Jason had spent most of his life wishing he'd hear from his own father. A tone reserved only for David, the son who could do no wrong. "People make mistakes," Gary continued. "You Corwins have the nasty habit of forgetting you're human. Crap happens. You'll find a way out of this, Jason. I have faith in you. We'll ride this out and you'll be back on top where you belong."

"On top or not, nothing's going to be the same." How could it be, without his brother? "You and I both know I never should have let Dad talk me into taking David's place in that cooking competition." And he never should have let himself get talked into using his sous chef's dish. "I've never liked those contests. They bring out the worst in people. But it was the only thing he's ever asked me to do."

Despite his anguish, Jason had felt so proud, as if his father had finally seen Jason after a lifetime of living in David's shadow. And what had Jason done? Surrendered to the pressure and screwed everything up royally by taking the easy way out. He'd wanted to win. Needed to win. By any means necessary.

And he'd destroyed his reputation in the process.

"Edward never should have asked you to do it. He knew you weren't up to it. David hadn't been gone two months…"

"But I did do it. Now I have to live with the consequences." Which meant he was left on his own, hip deep in the worm-ridden compost pile that was, at one time, a very lucrative career. Now his grandfather's dreams, his brother's dreams, were on the verge of disappearing altogether and he didn't have a leg to stand on. "I need to go, Gary."

"Before you hang up." Gary cleared his throat, an indication he'd been rehearsing whatever he was about to say next. "I thought you should know there's a food festival coming your way in a few weeks. You should stick around long enough to check it out."

His stomach rolled as if he'd eaten spoiled seafood. "There's a what?" Jason considered chucking his phone into the ocean as his hands went clammy.

"It's a new event they're using to drum up business in the area. They're calling it the By the Bay Food Festival. Coastal cuisines and wines, niche food companies looking to help small towns build up their presence in the tourist industry. Lots of local sponsorships. The National Cooking Network's covering it for a series of specials later this year about small-town celebrations."

"Suddenly Butterfly Harbor feels more like a setup than a hideaway." Of course. Now the three-week booking made sense. "When are they due to show up?"

"Not sure, but so you know, Roger Evans is heading up the production crew. He's, ah, been promoted. To assistant vice president of programming."

"Great." His former producer coming to town was the icing on the cake. *Only the Best* had been yanked from the airwaves days after word of Jason's cheating hit the internet and sent the crew into unemployment overdrive. Leave it to Roger to come out ahead of the game. No doubt elevating Jason's former sous chef to star status had assisted the producer up the ladder. "You do remember Roger and I didn't part on the best of terms."

"Maybe it's time to rebuild that bridge now that he's in a position to help you."

Even Gary had to get tired of tilting at windmills sometime. "No one with NCN is going to want anything to do with a scandalized ex-chef."

"You're not an *ex*-chef yet, Jason. Not as long as you're still answering your phone. We can salvage the book deal, and it's not as if they canceled your contract with the network. Suspended, sure, but there's always hope. Especially if you change your mind. If nothing else, let's get you back in the kitchen at JD's. Fight for what's yours. Fight for that future you and David wanted for yourselves."

"You still don't get it, Gary." Jason had to open his eyes to stop the ghostly image of David from appearing. "That future went down in the plane with David. Please don't ask again. I'll talk to you soon."

Jason disconnected before he said something he'd regret. He was already down a father and brother—he didn't need to alienate the last person still on his side.

He didn't have answers to much right now,

but he knew one thing for certain: he was done with the cooking world.

And nothing Gary or his father said would ever change that.

"DOUBLE MOCHA SHAKE, extra whipped cream, cheeseburger and fries, Holly. Stat." Abby slunk into a booth at the Butterfly Diner and dropped her head into her folded arms. Not even the comforting confines of her best friend's throwback diner decked out in hues of orange and black in honor of its monarch namesake were enough to lift her normally sparkly mood.

She gave a weak wave to Matt Knight and Fletcher Bradley as the two deputies dived elbow deep into drippy cheeseburgers of their own in the corner booth. It was nice to see the diner flush with customers, most of whom were longtime residents and business owners. Too bad none of them needed a room for the...year.

"Uh-oh." Holly Campbell set a coffeepot on the table and crossed her arms. "The last time you ordered like this you had just gotten dumped on prom night. All that's missing is the onion rings. What's up? Did you have another online dating disaster? You couldn't have found

someone worse than rented-bowling-shoe guy."
Holly tightened her ponytail and aimed a sympathetic gaze Abby's way.

"The newly engaged are not allowed to mock the emotionally unattached." Nonetheless, her best friend's teasing eased her mind. She honestly couldn't remember a worse day. "And for the record, I wasn't dumped. It was a mutual parting of the ways."

"Rewriting history, check." Holly grinned, but the concern in her eyes brushed lightly against Abby's bruised heart. "What's going on, Abs? You haven't been your usual shiny self for a few weeks."

"Oh, nothing much." Abby took a deep breath as she realized Holly, and not lunch, was the real reason she'd come to the diner. There wasn't anyone else she could confide in who would keep things quiet. "Aside from all the time-suck repairs the inn needs, I started the day by almost burning the kitchen to the ground—"

"Again?" Holly groaned. "You should come with a warning sign."

"Not you, too." It was bad enough to have Mr. Cranky Pants Corwin denounce her negligible cooking skills—she didn't need to hear it from her best friend. "Believe it or not, that was the highlight of my morning. I just came from seeing Mr. Vartebetium at the hospital."

"How's he doing?"

"Pretty good for an eighty-two-year-old man who's had his third heart attack." At least he was getting the break he needed. "They're still debating whether to send him to a transition facility before allowing him to go home. Remember all those months ago when I told you I thought maybe the Flutterby was in trouble? Yeah, well, I was wrong. It's in *huge* trouble with a great big *F* for financial. He finally confided in me how bad things are. His words? The Flutterby would be better off if we launched it off the cliffs."

"Oh, no." Holly sagged onto the bench across from her. "That can't be true. The Flutterby has been here forever. Maybe he's exaggerating. Do you think?" The hope in her friend's eyes didn't do much to bolster her own.

"He wouldn't come out with the details, but he gave me the keys to his filing cabinet," Abby said. "It must be pretty bad considering he stopped letting me oversee the books months ago." She'd assumed Mr. Vartebetium had wanted to keep as much control of his lifelong business as he could. Now Abby had to wonder if it was his way of keeping the truth about the finances secret. "How early is too early to crack open a bottle of pinot?"

She blinked back tears, which only made her mad. Abby Manning didn't cry. Abby Manning was the town optimist—she got things done, and if she didn't know how, she found a solution. Abby Manning never saw a gray cloud in the sky even when it was storming outside.

"The inn can't close, Holl," Abby whispered. "It's the only home Gran's ever known. It's her last connection to Gramps, and now with her Parkinson's diagnosis, ripping her out of that place will only make her decline faster." And it would kill Abby. The Flutterby was the first home *she'd* ever known. "I've got to save it somehow. I won't let it go without a fight."

"I wouldn't expect anything less," Holly said. "I wish I could help, but between this place and Simon's school tuition, not to mention Luke's and my wedding—"

"Do not make these stupid tears spill over, do you hear me?" Abby ordered, appreciating more than words could say how much she loved Holly for the thought. Holly had her back, just as Abby had had hers a few weeks ago when Holly hit a rough patch with her son, Simon. That was before Holly went and fell tail over teakettle in love with the onetime bad boy of Butterfly Harbor turned sheriff, Luke Saxon.

Looking at Holly's engagement ring glinting in the early afternoon sun made Abby's heart ache and sing at the same time. Her friend deserved to be happy, especially after all she'd been through.

"I don't suppose Simon is around?" Holly glanced at the half-filled diner. Whatever boost she needed, she'd bet her overly precocious eight-year-old godson could provide.

"He's at the community center with my dad and Charlie. I swear my son and Paige's daughter are tethered constantly, but at least they're staying out of trouble these days. Good thing, too, since Paige has been putting in extra hours here at the diner."

"As far as you know they're staying out of trouble," Abby mused, the idea of those two juvenile partners in crime roaming Butterfly Harbor on their bikes giving her heart a lift. "Tell him I'm up for a movie night anytime he's ready." But Abby figured her godson might already be aging out of sleepovers with his boring godmother. Well, boring when compared to seven-year-old Charlie Cooper

with her crooked smile, equally crooked pig-
tails and mischievous personality.

"Is there anything Luke and I can do?"
Holly asked, giving a nod of acknowledgment
to one of her customers.

"I'll let you know. But I should probably
get back to the Flutterby and dive into those
books. Can I get my order to go? Along with
a turkey sandwich for Lori?"

"Of course. You know Paige, though. Chances
are she'll throw something unexpected on your
burger." Holly patted her hand and headed for
the kitchen.

Considering Abby's luck today, it would be
a handful of jalapeños. Abby shuddered. She
hated jalapeños. She took a calming breath
and inhaled the familiar aroma—frying onions accompanied by hot sugar from Holly's
homemade pies.

How could some people make food sing
while others, like her, made it scream?

Abby plucked the pamphlet advertising
the By the Bay Food Festival from in front of
the laminated menu of Holly's desserts and
grasped a final hope. Her full reservation book
should bring in a good chunk of change for the
coffers. If Matilda came home in time to get
the kitchen up and running. If. *If, if, if.*

"Abby, what brings you by so early today?" Mayor Gil Hamilton, or Gil the Thrill, as he'd been known in high school, sidled up to her booth and leaned a hand on the table. With his longish blond hair and overbright blue eyes, Gil would forever be Butterfly Harbor's charmer in residence. He might have spent a good portion of his thirty-two years trying to distance himself from his father's financially irresponsible actions during his own term as mayor, but even benefit-of-the-doubt Abby had to admit Gil slipped too easily into the political swamp his father had polluted. Then again, she did believe his concern for the town's survival was genuine. So long as some of his ideas didn't strip the uniqueness out of Butterfly Harbor in the meantime. That was one of the reasons she was in support of the butterfly sanctuary he was trying to get off the ground.

"Errands," she said and painted on her trademark smile. She'd keep smiling even as the ship began to sink. "How are the plans coming for the festival?"

"Amazingly well, actually. Tents and banners should start going up around town and in Skipper Park sometime tomorrow, and Calliope has offered her empty property at Duskywing Farm for the open house on Thursday night. We lucked out with the timing. Being able to celebrate Butterfly Harbor's anniversary when we've got a town full of people gives us a chance to show off. One hundred twenty-five years is nothing to sneeze at. Plus, we'll get that national exposure thanks to all the media coverage."

"The Cocoon Club is anxious to expand on their success from the Pig in a Poke BBQ cook-off." The group of Butterfly Harbor seniors had their fingers in a lot of events these days. She only wished she could convince Gran to get involved with them again. Abby flipped open the pamphlet for the upcoming festival and immediately locked on the bolded wording on the second page. "Wait. This is an *amateur* cooking competition? As in no talent required?" With a hefty fifty-thousand-dollar first prize. Was this the universe's way of bashing her over the head with a skillet? "Who's sponsoring this? ShopMax Foods?"

"Hardly," Gil chuckled. "I told you, sponsorships have been rolling in. And NCN is footing most of it. They're hoping to find some new on-air talent. Since Butterfly Harbor pitched in a good chunk from our discretionary fund, we get to host the two-day competition while Pacific Grove and Monterey will pick up the other events. You know, now that I think about it—" Gil angled a look at her that told Abby his thought wasn't new at all "—it would be nice to have someone from Butterfly Harbor representing us to really get the community involved. I wonder if Matilda has any suggestions."

Why did he insist on asking questions he already knew the answers to?

"Last I heard she and Ursula were somewhere around Ohio." That motor home of theirs had more miles on it than the space shuttle, but the sisters' charity trek had become an annual event, one Abby wasn't about to get in the way of, not when both Matilda and Ursula were breast cancer survivors.

"What about you?" Gil asked.

"What about me?"

"You should enter, Abby. There's no one more amateur than you. Think about it. They're only allowing three competitors, so your chances of winning might be better than we think."

Was he serious? "Sarcasm aside, I doubt that's a good idea." Even if she had the inclination, by the time word got around town of her scone BBQ this morning, they'd probably start a petition to ban her from even owning a kitchen.

Still... She bit her lip. Fifty thousand dollars.

"Including one of our oldest businesses would look great in the advertising. Besides, you have the personality for it," Gil said. "Then there's the added advertising the inn wouldn't have to pay for. All you'd need to do is come up with the entry fee. Don't say no. Not until you check it out, but FYI, the deadline to enter is tomorrow." He rapped his knuckles on her table and headed out.

Temptation and opportunity knocked. That money could be the answer to her problems. Assuming she won, of course. And Gil was right about one thing: no one was more amateur than her. Oh, this was crazy, wasn't it? Even crazy for Abby, who wasn't known for always making the most reasoned decisions. The smoke detector was evidence of that.

She was getting ahead of herself. She couldn't make any decision until she got a look at the books. It could be she was worried over something a good couple of months could fix, in which case she had time to come up with a gangbusters promotion plan.

No reason to put all her expectations on a

competition she didn't have any hope of winning. Not until she knew what she was dealing with. But…she supposed it could be an option. A nuclear option, but still an option.

"Your order will be ready in about ten." Holly returned after filling her customers' coffee cups and clearing some tables. "What was that about?" She aimed a suspicious glance at Gil's retreating back.

"Possibilities." Abby shoved the brochure into her purse and smiled. "Do me a favor— add a small strawberry shake to that order? Lori deserves to remember life is all about enjoyment and taking chances."

Now all Abby had to do was remember the same thing.

CHAPTER THREE

ABBY MADE IT until five that afternoon before she uncorked that bottle of wine. The nuclear option was looking better by the second.

For the first time in memory, keeping a good thought had failed her. Not only had Mr. Vartebetium's fiscal warnings been shy of the mark, but they'd be lucky to keep the doors of the Flutterby Inn open through the summer.

Her employees and friends' jobs aside, she couldn't, wouldn't let Gran lose her home. Abby would go down swinging if she had to in order to make sure Alice lived out the rest of her life feeling safe and secure.

Meanwhile, Abby would start a list of words she didn't ever want to see in print again, beginning with *back taxes* and ending with *pipe replacement*. Even worse, the money she'd been assured had been set aside for a booth at one of the food festival's events didn't exist. There wasn't seventy dollars to spare, let alone seven hundred. She still had employees and bills to pay.

Not even the normally comforting waves of the Pacific worked their magic this evening. Nor did sitting on the bench in one of the more picturesque areas of Butterfly Harbor, on the hill outside the Flutterby. The cypress trees arched their branches in framed perfection while the frothy foam bubbled up and draped over the rocks below in the lazy tide. Every time Abby tried to find the bright spot, any bright spot, she floundered like a beached dolphin who had taken a wrong and very unfortunate turn.

What she did have, aside from a half-filled glass of wine and a too-thin sweater to keep the coastal chill off her skin, was a circling dread.

"I've learned one thing about your Butterfly Harbor today." Jay Corwin's voice scraped over her raw nerves as he approached from behind, his footfalls crunching in the gravel and sand. "You have a beautiful secret here."

Abby couldn't help it. She smiled, then hid the expression behind her wineglass as she sipped. "It won't be secret much longer. The new butterfly sanctuary they're hoping to build should put us on the map. So to speak," she added. Albeit probably too late for the Flutterby to benefit.

"Do you mind if I join you?"

She looked at him, trying to find a diplomatic way to say no, but she couldn't, especially not when she recognized the same tinge of tension and sadness she'd seen in her own reflection recently. Abby scooted over on the bench. "I'm sorry. I didn't bring another glass."

"It's fine, I'm not a big pinot fan." Jay glanced at the brass plaque on the back of the bench before he sat—a little closer than she'd expected, a lot farther than she wanted—and shoved his hands into the lightweight navy parka he wore. "Bob Manning. Your father?"

"Grandfather." Abby took in Jay's acclimated attire of jeans and flannel shirt. He struck her as a man who fit in wherever he went, especially with that assessing gaze of his. She'd never seen a color like his, with shimmering silver depths beneath the ocean blue. She didn't need to note his strong jaw to be reminded of his stubbornness or the permanent crease in his brow to make her wonder if he ever smiled. She hadn't really noticed before—probably hadn't been paying attention. He seemed incredibly sad. Now she wished she hadn't been quite so snippy with him.

"Grandpa Bob died five years ago," she said. "Right here, as a matter of fact. Came out to watch the sunset one night and went peacefully. Broke Gran's heart, but I can't think of a better way for him to go. The sunsets here are worth waiting for."

"It seems a nice place to grow up. What about your parents?" Perhaps if this friendlier, inquisitive Jay had appeared in her kitchen this morning, she might not have spent part of the day dreaming of putting itching powder in his bed.

"They died in a car accident when I was four." She pulled out a pair of gold rings and a diamond solitaire on a thin gold chain and held them between her fingers. "I've seen pictures of them, but I can't be sure if I remember them. Gran gave me these when I turned thirteen." She kissed the rings and tucked them away again. "Makes me feel as if I have a couple of guardian angels. Friendly ghosts, you know? It's why I never take it off." And wow, wasn't she chatty with someone she wasn't sure she liked. "Butterfly Harbor's been my home ever since."

He looked as if he wanted to apologize or

offer sympathy, but couldn't quite find the words. When he did respond, he said, "I've never really understood the appeal of small towns. I've always lived in big cities. Even spent some time in London and Paris. They're all busy. Loud. I didn't realize silence could be just as loud."

"So Gran was right?" Abby said, grateful for the distraction he provided. She didn't want to dwell on the red marks in the inn's accounting ledger. "New York?"

"Born and raised, then I traveled some." He leaned back and stretched his long legs out, crossed his ankles and sank into the late afternoon. "I like the peacefulness. Not sure for how long, though."

"I know a couple of kids who could shatter that silence in a second. Say the word. My godson and his best friend have been known to violate the town's noise ordinance."

Jay's brow furrowed. "Noise ordinance?"

"I'm joking." And not doing a very good job of it, for a change. Maybe she needed a nap. "We'd have to have a lot more residents to need an ordinance, and I don't think Luke would want that on his shoulders, anyway."

"Would that be Sheriff Saxon? I met him

while I was walking around town earlier. Nice guy. Nice dog, too."

Cash. How many times had she thought about ways to snatch that lovable mutt from the sheriff? "He'd better be, since he's marrying my best friend." As far as Abby was concerned, Luke was one of the most decent men she'd ever known, even though he'd be the first to shy from the compliment. "We're hoping he'll be done using the cane before the wedding."

The wedding. Abby closed her eyes, bit her lip. Darn it. Holly's early August wedding was scheduled to take place at the Flutterby. Add that to the list of things to worry about.

"What's that look for?" Jay shifted to face her more fully, something Abby appreciated as she went back to focusing on him. She'd never found beards particularly attractive, but on Jay it worked. Gave him a bit of a sophisticated air she'd bet would only be accentuated should he drop into a crisp white shirt and dark suit— "Abby?"

"What? Oh, sorry." Yeah, her thoughts really were getting away from her. "Just checking things off on my to-do list. That reminds me. I brought back more vouchers for the diner if you need them."

"Yeah. About that." He flinched as if she'd struck him. "I drove up to Monterey for lunch. Diners aren't really my thing."

There was that tone again, that authoritative *I'm better than you are* tone that proved she hadn't imagined his arrogance this morning. "Not your thing?"

"You know." He shifted his gaze out over the water. "Pedestrian. Boring."

Pedestrian? There wasn't anything *pedestrian* about Holly's diner. Or her food. "In other words, diners are beneath you and your New York sensibilities." So what had all the small-towns-are-charming comments been? Polite chitchat? Disarming her before he plunged the dagger in her heart?

"I didn't say that." But as he spoke, she heard the doubt in his voice.

"There's a reason why diners last through the ages. They're steadfast, sturdy." Holly's diner could be considered the spine of a shriveling town. A town she'd do anything to make successful again.

"Diners are also predictable and ordinary."

She shifted on the bench. "They're comfortable and homey."

"They're cheap and greasy."

"Wow." Abby shook her head, unable to

fathom his disconnect from reality. "I knew it. You're a snob. And fair warning, I wouldn't throw any of those adjectives around when Holly's nearby. She's likely to smack you with her grandmother's rolling pin." And if Holly didn't, Abby might. Who did this guy think he was, coming into town and passing judgment on everything she loved? Everything she'd fight until her last breath to protect?

"I'm not a snob."

Given the offense in his voice, you'd have thought she called him a serial killer. "Tilt your nose down once in a while, Mr. Corwin. Otherwise you can't see where you're going. Or where you are."

"I didn't mean to offend you."

"Well, you did. Maybe you weren't listening earlier, but this is my home. It's the only place on earth where I belong. The people, the businesses, the cracks in the pavement I used to ride my tricycle over. You don't get to come here to hide and judge anything you're not willing to experience for yourself."

"I don't need to experience something to know it isn't for me. And who says I'm hiding?"

"I run an inn, remember? I know hiding.

And boy, Gran was right. You are New York through and through. Oh, wait. I'm sorry, am I judging you on someplace I haven't been? Shame on me." She swallowed the rest of her wine and got to her feet. "If you'll excuse me, I need to take Gran to dinner *at the diner* before her bunco game. And FYI, you might want to get some earplugs, because believe it or not, we take silly things like bunco very seriously around here. Good night, Mr. Corwin."

How did "diners aren't my thing" lead to offending his hostess?

He really shouldn't talk to people. It never went well. He wasn't a snob. His father—now, *he* was a snob, and he didn't make any apologies for it. Jason gnashed his teeth at the thought of being painted with the same brush as his father.

He didn't get the impression Abby disliked many people—not after having witnessed her interact with her grandmother and those she worked with. He must have really pushed her buttons, which fascinated him. He wanted to think his interest in her was merely a result of having more time on his hands. He didn't have the pressure of the restaurant or contracts or budgets or…anything. He couldn't recall encountering anyone like her before, someone with more layers than an onion and the more he peeled away, the deeper he wanted to go.

Butterfly Harbor might not have the bustling activity of his native New York, but it had its own charm. He'd wandered around a good portion of it today, noticing the intricate puzzling of homes dotting the edges of Monarch Lane, what he assumed passed as Main Street, USA. He'd explored a couple of antique shops and the hardware store, even the throwback gift stores that reminded him of the old-fashioned five-and-dimes his mother had once told him about. He found their offerings eclectic, including all types of...yep, butterflies. The post office, reminiscent of a different era, sat wedged into one corner of a neighborhood grocery that had one of the best selections of organic meat and fish he'd ever come across. Truth be told, the selection of produce and food could have put the Chelsea Market to shame given a little extra push. Butterfly Harbor impressed him, but not nearly as much as the wide offering of locally farmed fresh produce.

David would have loved it here—the selection, the tight-knit community. If Vegas hadn't already been knocking on their restaurant door, they'd have explored the idea of opening smaller, more specialized restaurants in places like Butterfly Harbor.

Inspiration knocked featherlight against his mind. It might have caught hold if he hadn't been reminded every five steps of that blasted food festival. A weather-resistant banner proclaiming its start had been stretched across the entrance to Monarch Lane.

He'd watched trucks and trailers roll down the street and disappear around the hill. The rumble of engines and smell of gasoline took a bit of the small-town polish off the town, but he imagined an event like this would help keep businesses open and people employed.

Had he any inclination to dip his toe back in the water that was his former career, seeing Technicolor posters pop into windows as he passed was enough to make him want to scuttle back to the hotel and hole up in his room.

Even if he didn't plan on attending the festival, seeing the town explode into celebration over its one hundred and twenty-fifth anniversary would take the sting off.

A sting that had settled ever since he'd entered the kitchen at the Flutterby Inn. As exhausted as he was, he wasn't anxious to call it a night. Maybe it was the aftereffects of his conversation with Gary and reliving the last six months yet again. It didn't matter what his father was doing with the company, not when Jason couldn't do anything about it.

He'd destroyed his credibility with one wrong decision. No one was going to take him seriously in that world anymore. David could have, though. David could have survived anything.

Except a plane crash.

But Butterfly Harbor, despite its pending participation with his former colleagues, held his interest. He might not understand small-town appeal, but he didn't like the idea of places like this disappearing. Especially if it meant people like Abby and her grandmother, and maybe even the cutesy diner down on Monarch Lane, would vanish into the past.

The diner. Jason sighed. He supposed he owed it to Abby to try the Butterfly Diner before passing judgment. He relished saying *I told you so* about as much as she'd probably enjoy telling him *you were right*.

Jason shook his head, got to his feet and followed the sandy, rocky path to the Flut-terby. Maybe he'd keep his revelations, whatever they turned out to be, to himself. Unless it did turn out he was wrong.

In which case he'd have to find a way to choke down his least favorite dish: crow.

CHAPTER FOUR

"Bunco!"

Abby couldn't help but smile as celebratory cheers exploded from the dining room that overlooked the wave-heavy shoreline. The tides were rolling high tonight, crashing and cresting and echoing peacefully in her ears as she sat behind the registration counter, windows open, her fingers flicking the corner of the festival brochure.

"That's five buncos since they started," Lori said as she tugged on her coat. "That might be a new record."

"Let's hope Gran's one of them, otherwise she's going to be in a grumpy mood when the game's done. Hey, Lori." Abby had been putting this off all afternoon. "Are you good going full-time the next few weeks? Maybe even bunking in one of the smaller rooms until after the festival?"

"With my active social life?" Lori blinked wide eyes at her. "Whatever you need, I'm here. Something going on? Does it have something to do with that hot Mr. Corwin?"

"What?" Even the mention of his name was enough to set her blood to boiling. "No, of course not, and stop ogling our guests. I was thinking about entering that amateur cooking competition they're holding here in Butterfly Harbor."

"I'm sorry?" Lori's arms dropped to her side as she stared. "You're thinking about what?" That her friend was trying not to laugh should be confirmation enough Abby had gone and lost her mind, but she needed that money. She needed to do something to stop the Flutterby from failing. She needed to keep Gran in her home.

Not that entering was enough. She'd have to win.

But she'd worry about that later.

"For the advertisement?" Lori squeaked and fanned her face. "Sorry. I shouldn't be laughing."

"I know it sounds crazy." Abby went along with Lori's misconception. "The publicity could bring in a good chunk of business. And I figured Paige could give me cooking lessons."

"Um." The humor vanished from Lori's face. "Then you might want to decide now if you'd like to remain friends. That's not a great position to put someone in. It might make her an accessory when you torch the entire town."

"I'm not that bad." Maybe she needed that disclaimer tattooed on her forehead. "I get distracted. I can follow directions. They just get stuck somewhere between my brain and my hands."

"You do know you set the oven to five hundred fifty degrees this morning, right?" Lori bit her lip. "I checked when I cleaned up the kitchen. I wanted to make sure everything still worked," she added. "For when Matilda gets back."

"I was running out of time." But she kind of guessed that had been the cause. "I thought the scones would bake faster at a higher temperature."

"That wouldn't give the baking powder and soda time to activate. You took them from raw dough to rock hard almost instantly."

"So you do know how to cook?" Hope sprung like a fountain inside her. Maybe she wasn't crazy after all.

"I know how to watch the National Cooking Network," Lori corrected. "They do a lot of shows about the science behind food. Those competition things are scary. Like watching people's worst features being broadcast in front of your eyes."

"So you wouldn't be interested in being a contestant in the cook-off." There went that backup plan.

"I know things are stretched pretty tight around here." Lori frowned. "But this seems a little extreme, even for you. You sure you want to take this on with everything else that's happening?"

Abby bit the inside of her cheek. She wasn't ready to tell anyone other than Holly that the inn was in trouble. Not until she'd exhausted every opportunity to put a cork in the financial hole. "I thought it would be fun and a good way to promote the inn. Each contestant gets a ten-minute profile on NCN when they air their coverage." In a couple of months. Hopefully not too late.

"Sounds like you've already made up your mind," Lori said. "Whatever you decide to do, I'll be right behind you. *Behind* you, Abby. I love you, but not enough to get in front of a camera on national television. I'm going to go grab dinner before I drive the Bunco Babes home."

Abby smiled. "I don't know what I'd do without you."

"Let's hope we never find out. Night."

An end-of-round bell chimed loud enough to make Abby's ears ring.

The Bunco Babes—most of whom were significantly on the other side of Social Security—had been holding their monthly die games at the Flutterby long before Abby began working here. The group's themed get-togethers were both a pleasure and a pain, as inevitably something would get changed at the last minute, from the menu requests—tonight they'd ordered pizza from Zane's—to the decorations, but that was where Gran came in. Letting her focus on the group, both as a member and an organizer, gave her something to concentrate on other than the fact that she was growing older. Their continued patronage also brought in some extra cash, and right now, every penny counted.

And about those pennies...

Abby returned her attention to the online application Gil had steered her toward. Everything seemed straightforward enough.

No, she wasn't a professional chef. No, she hadn't had any professional training. Yes, she agreed not to use any employees of the Flutterby Inn during the competition. No, none of her employees or family were associated in any way with the National Cooking Network.

Her eyes blurred as she clicked the boxes. No wonder people didn't read the fine print in these migraine-inducing contracts.

"Okay, here we go." She hovered the mouse over Submit and caught the bold print below the button: "Application not processed until full payment of fifteen hundred dollars is received."

Abby sagged in her chair.

Fifteen hundred dollars?

Her heart lurched. She couldn't afford the seven hundred dollars for the miniscule promo tent the network would provide—how did she expect to come up with more than double that? Sell her car? Hardly. The ten-year-old clunker probably needed more than that in repairs, not to mention she needed a vehicle to get Gran to and from her doctors' and physical therapy appointments.

Asking friends was out of the question. Money and family—and to Abby her friends were family—did not mix. She didn't own anything of much value. Well, except...

Her stomach twisted as she pulled her parents' wedding rings free from her shirt. She bit her lip.

She couldn't be that desperate. Could she? Would it be worth it? Selling the only thing she had of her parents when there was no guarantee she'd win? If she did, she needed to rethink her strategy. She'd have to have help. Not financial. She needed someone to guide her, encourage her. She needed...

She needed a teacher.

Her thoughts spiraled around each other as she minimized the application screen and opened a new window, this time checking out the benefits of the upcoming festival on the NCN site. All those chefs, all those people who made creating meals look as easy as opening a door. How hard could it be if she really focused? Maybe it was as simple as reading as many cookbooks as she could get her hands on, and there was a library full of them in the kitchen. Matilda collected cookbooks like Mr. Vartebetium collected bills.

She clicked through the various chef bios, wishing she had their confidence, their talent. Their...

Abby squinted, leaned forward until her nose was practically pressing against the screen. That face. Her heart pounded. She knew that face. She recognized those eyes.

She gasped and looked toward the staircase. It couldn't be. Energy she thought she'd lost buzzed inside her like a frenzy of bees trapped for too long. He didn't have a beard and his hair was a lot longer, but there was no mistaking the attitude that exuded off the screen or those blue eyes.

She bolted through the dining room, lifting a hand in greeting as her Babes called out to her. She flicked on the kitchen light and headed for Matilda's overflowing shelves filled with her collection of signed cookbooks. Meticulously organized as Matilda was, Abby skimmed her fingers across the top shelf and yanked out the copy of *All the Best* by Jason and David Corwin.

One glance at the back cover was all she needed, except she almost didn't recognize him. So he could smile. He could even laugh. She could almost hear the brothers as the affection reached off the page and brushed against her heart.

David Corwin. He'd been killed, she remembered, trying to recall the details. Earlier this year in a plane crash. Ursula and Paige had talked about the tragedy at the diner, seen on the news how the entire food community had gone into mourning.

Along with his brother.

Jason. Now the sadness made sense, but she couldn't dwell on that.

Jay Corwin was a cook. No. She knew him well enough by now to lay odds he'd take exception to that term. *Jason* Corwin was a *chef*.

And he was right here. In Butterfly Harbor. At the Flutterby. Before a food festival.

Hugging the book against her chest, she wandered to the desk, dropping into the chair as her thoughts coalesced. She reopened the application, hovered the mouse over the final submission button.

Did she dare?

Her hand shook. No. Not quite yet.

She clicked off the screen, grabbed the brochure and hurried upstairs, turning the book face-out as she knocked on Jay's door. The TV inside his room went quiet a few seconds before he answered the door, a hesitant look of welcome on his face.

"Good evening, Abby."

Did he have to sound like Dracula welcoming her to his lair? Abby shook herself out of distracted mode and thrust the cookbook at him.

"I need you to teach me to cook."

OF ALL THE things Jason expected to find on the other side of his door—room service he hadn't ordered, an offer for turn-down service, a poisoned mint for his pillow—it certainly wasn't Five-Alarm Manning asking for cooking lessons.

He forced himself to resist the urge to glance at his and David's first bestselling cookbook. The book that had started them on the path to their dreams. "I'm not a chef anymore."

"Are, were, whatever. You can still cook." Abby pushed past him and took a seat in the wing-back chair next to the terrace doors. "I know, I'm being pushy and I'm sure you're still irritated with me over how I spoke to you before. Sorry about that."

"I really don't think you are." Clearly, she wasn't leaving any time soon. He closed the door.

"Yeah, okay, you're right." Her sneaky grin wrinkled the top of her nose and triggered an odd flutter in his chest. "But what are you going to do? Leave? You've paid for three weeks." Why was she looking at him as if she knew some big secret he remained clueless about? "I don't care about your employment status. What I need is someone to teach me. I thought about asking Paige since Matilda is out of town, but as Lori said, I'd rather stay friends with her, and, well, you and me? Not friends. Problem solved."

Jason crossed his arms over his chest and arched a brow. Another one of those layers, he supposed. "You got this spiel out of a self-help book, didn't you?"

"No, no." She waved a hand in the air. Her energy and enthusiasm flitted about the room like a rogue butterfly. "I just meant we don't have anything to protect. I already irritate you, and, well, the feeling's definitely mutual, but I need to know how to cook."

"And you want to hire me?" What grand epiphany could she have possibly had since her scone disaster this morning that would have her asking him for help?

"Not hire, exactly." Her face turned bright red but her expression remained determined. "I'm not exactly flush at the moment, so I was hoping you'd be willing to lend your expertise in exchange for my undying gratitude?"

"Your—what?" Had he missed the space-ship that had dropped her off? She wanted him to teach her *and* she was broke? "Okay, rewind. How about you start by telling me why you want to learn to cook."

"Oh." She held out a skinny pamphlet. "I want to enter this."

"The By the Bay Food Festival." Again. Everywhere he turned, he was reminded of that blasted festival. "Wait. A *televised* cooking competition?" How had he missed that little detail? He reviewed the dates. "You do realize this starts in two weeks." He'd been right. Gary's booking him at the Flutterby was on purpose. Tricky son of a—

"Yeah, I know," Abby said. "But you're good at this stuff. You said so yourself. It's in your back cover bio." She waggled his book in front of him like a red flag in front of a very irritated bull.

His mouth twisted. "Not funny. And not interested." Even if the idea of stepping foot in a kitchen again didn't make him twitchy, some people were beyond hope.

"Oh, come on! You're already bored out of your mind and you've been here less than a day. You need something to do. What else is there besides biding your time between sunsets?"

"Someone told me the sunsets are worth the wait." Clearly his refusal needed an explanation in order to wipe that puppy glimmer out of her all-too-tempting gaze. "Learning to cook in the best of circumstances takes time and patience." Something he was willing to bet she didn't have much of. "It's stressful and demanding." And required human interaction.

"I don't have to be able to cook for the president." Abby rolled her eyes. "I need to learn enough to compete and not set anything on fire. And maybe not poison anyone. Oh, and win, of course."

Yeah. Nothing to it. "After what I saw this morning? In two weeks? No, I'm sorry. It can't be done."

A bit of the fight drained out of her, but in its place, a spark lit her face. That same spark he'd seen when she'd battered that smoke detector. "Is that why you're hiding out in Butterfly Harbor? Did the stress of running a restaurant get to you after your brother died?"

"No." His lungs tightened. "No, it wasn't the stress." Exactly.

"Then what?"

"Leave it to me to find the one person in the hemisphere who hasn't heard." He plucked his tablet from beside the bed to search for himself, a humbling experience for sure, then skimmed past the links detailing David's crash. "Why don't you read this and then we'll see if you want to continue this conversation."

He held out the pad and ignored the unease circling in his stomach. At least Abby's dislike of him from the start had been genuine and not based on gossip rags and internet features.

She exchanged the pad for his cookbook that he set, cover down, on his bed. Needing some air, he pushed open the terrace doors and leaned his arms on the railing, waiting for the inevitable shocked and disgusted reaction he'd come to expect. Maybe paying for the room in advance hadn't been such a smart move.

Normally it took a couple of minutes for the facts to hit, but, as he'd begun to learn about Abby, she was ahead of the curve.

"I am sorry about your brother."

He squeezed his eyes shut until he saw stars. He hated the sympathy, the concern, the apology that accompanied the comment that was cursory at best. He'd heard hundreds if not thousands of them in the last six months. But none had been spoken in Abby's soft voice, with a gentleness that brushed over his ears as gently as if she'd touched his hair with the tips of her fingers.

"Thank you."

"Is this true? Did you really cheat in the last round of that competition?"

He didn't hear shock in her voice, or condemnation, but genuine curiosity. As if she didn't quite believe he was capable of sinking so low.

"It says you brought in a ringer to help you win this reality show thing."

Jason leaned over and stared into the bottomless surf. "I tried to pass off a dish my sous chef cooked instead of the one I attempted myself. I needed to win." Because losing hadn't been an option. Not with his brother's memory and his family's reputation on the line. Not with his father's expectations set so high he'd have to use a jet pack to reach them. "And then I lied about it." Which was, when all was said and done, his real crime. "On live TV. You can watch it on YouTube if you want. It's been viewed over two million times. How do you not know about this?"

"Do I strike you as an avid NCN viewer?"

Her sarcasm pulled a deeply buried smile out of him. "It also made national news. I was every media outlet's disgrace story for over a week." While Marcus Aiken, his sous chef, had been given his own show and a font of new endorsement deals.

"Big deal. So was the governor, and her approval ratings went up. So you made a mistake. People, humans, make them all the time."

She sounded so much like Gary she gave him a headache. "*People* are allowed to make mistakes. Celebrities, *Corwins* are held to a higher standard, especially in the food industry. Scandals like mine kill careers, Abby. Especially after you've been built up as some kind of icon. I'm proof of that. My own shareholders ousted me from the company my bro—" The word stalled in his throat. "The company we built."

"Icon. Wow." She sighed and shook her head. "Ego check on aisle seven. So, what? You ran? You're hiding out here because a bunch of people know you cheated and you were a jerk about it? You've been a jerk about a lot of things with me. What's the big deal?"

When had this conversation veered off the verbal cliff? He hadn't run away from New York, he'd walked away after it had been made abundantly clear he was too much of a liability for Corwin Brothers. "When you're one of the faces of a million-dollar brand, people—shareholders, specifically—shift into damage-control mode."

David had been the negotiator, the peacemaker. David had been the diplomat while Jason had been the moody artist few people wanted to deal with. Without David as a buffer, he'd had no patience or charisma to keep anyone on his side. He'd lost count of how many so-called friends had made the suggestion in less than understanding terms.

"Corwin Brothers is beyond my help," Jason continued. "And don't get me started on how my father plans to fix the company." By going against every principle their grandfather had held dear. But not even that was enough to push Jason back into the kitchen.

"Pfffh." Abby waved her hand again and shrugged. "What do network executives and shareholders know? On the bright side, if you tell me your girlfriend dumped you and then your truck broke down, I bet you could start a new career as a country music singer."

Jason marveled. She had the oddest view of the world.

"There was no girlfriend." That's all he would have needed to complete the equation. He faced her, part of him worried about what he'd see on her face, but all he saw was the same Abby he'd met in a billowing fog of smoke. Part energetic bunny, part warrior woman who would fight smoke and burned scones to the death. "I'm toxic to anyone and everyone in the industry. Nobody wants me."

"I want you." Abby jumped to her feet, then,

as her words sank in, her cheeks went that brilliant—and all too familiar—shade of pink. "I mean, oh, buttered biscuits!" She spun in a circle as if she could go back in time. "You know what I mean. I don't care about some scandal from your past or the fact you tried to cheat your way out of something or even that it sounds as if you ran away instead of fighting for your career. And I'm sorry, but what kind of father lets a bunch of shareholders oust his son so he can slither into his position? That's disgusting."

He stared. *Wh-what?*

"Okay." She plunged ahead. "So, yeah, maybe cheating was a dirty move, but are you sorry you did it? I don't mean are you sorry you got caught," she added when he started to respond. "If you had it to do all over again, would you?"

"No." That pressure valve he'd been waiting months to release finally did. Her question stunned him. No one had ever asked him that before. No one had seemed to care enough to, not even when he'd been so mired in grief he couldn't think straight. "Cheating was the worst mistake I've ever made and lying about it made it worse. It cheapened everything I worked for, everything my brother stood for.

I'll never take a shortcut again, no matter what it might cost me."

"So help me." She seemed bolstered rather than deterred by his admission. "I need to do this. The inn needs it. And maybe you can find a little redemption for yourself in the meantime."

The desperation in her voice wasn't something he wanted to hear, but he had the feeling she'd let something unintentional slip. "What do you mean, the inn needs it?"

She bit her lip, eyes darting around the room. He recognized that expression. He'd seen it on enough faces in the last few months to know it was someone's way of coming up with a story or plausible explanation.

"Finances are tight. If I do this, the inn will be featured in the network special," she said. "Butterfly Harbor needs all the word of mouth it can get, and we need guests. I'm sure you noticed we don't have many. It's an opportunity I can't pass up. Even if I am a hopeless cook."

"Not the best attitude or selling point when looking for a teacher." Jason stepped into the room and glanced over the rest of the pamphlet. "Hang on. You just said finances were tight and that you can't pay me. How are you coming up with the entry fee?"

She dragged her parents' rings across their chain, her smile tight. "I'll find a way."

As little as he knew about her, he didn't doubt it for a second. "I'm not saying yes." How could he, when it meant returning to the life that held nothing but dark memories and disappointment? "But if I were to agree to this, you should know up front you'll need to take time off work and it'll be long hours. I can probably keep you in the running long enough for you to get those ads, but fair warning, two weeks isn't enough to get you ready to win. Plus, you could hate me even more by the time we're done."

"You mean I'll get an even closer look at arrogant, egotistical, judgmental Jason Corwin?" She fluttered her lashes at him as if he were a teenage heartthrob. "Yay. He's so dreamy."

"He's also a class-A jerk with antisocial tendencies." He couldn't help it. Her teasing and calling things as she saw them amused him. How could anyone take himself seriously when she was around? "But since you know that going in..." She was right. He was bored and he didn't have anything else on his agenda for the foreseeable future. Besides, teaching someone to cook wasn't the same as cooking. "I'll make you a deal. If you come up with the application fee, I'll do what I can to teach you. But again, I can't guarantee—"

"I know, I know." She flew across the room, grabbed his shoulders and kissed him full on the mouth. A quick kiss. One of gratitude and happiness with a touch of that electric excitement he was fast becoming familiar with. He also, in that moment, tasted fire and determination.

She must have surprised herself, because she rocked back on her heels and lifted her stunned face to him as his lips curved. He clenched his fists to stop himself from touching her cheek, from finding out if her skin was as soft as he imagined it would be. "You heard me, right? This is going to be hard work, Abby."

"Anything worthwhile always is." She grabbed his book. "I'm going to start reading this tonight, but first, I'm clicking Submit on that application! How about you meet me at the Butterfly Diner for an early lunch tomorrow, say, eleven o'clock, and we'll go from there?" She set her jaw and grinned at him, challenge issued.

"The diner, huh?" His stomach rolled at the thought of it. What was it she'd said earlier?

Holy hamburgers? "Has anyone ever tried to say no to you?"

"Once or twice. Didn't work. Good night, Jay. And thank you."

He caught her arm as she passed, looked into her eyes for a second longer—not long enough. "My name is Jason."

She nodded as if she was coming out of some sort of trance. "Jason, then. I'll see you tomorrow." She hugged his book like she was an anxious freshman headed off to her first day.

He opened the door for her, waited until she disappeared down the stairs before he closed it again. The doubt crept in, slow and slithering, working its way into his overwhelmed brain.

Whatever desire, whatever passion he'd once held for his profession was gone. He'd lost his appetite for all of it. The idea of diving back into that world that haunted him was enough to freeze his feet to the floor. Which left him with one question.

What had he just gotten himself into?

CHAPTER FIVE

"ABIGAIL MANNING!" HOLLY glared at Abby as if she wanted to crawl over the counter and strangle her. "Things cannot be so bad at the inn you had to sell your parents' wedding rings."

"I know." Except they were. Abby forced a smile. The ache in her chest remained and she could still feel her hand burning from when she'd handed over the rings, but she refused to look behind her. Sometimes it took sacrificing the past to try to save the future. At least that's what she kept telling herself.

If anything, spending three hours early this morning replacing another two showerheads, tightening valves under sinks and touching up chair-rail paint in the soon-to-be-occupied rooms was all the reminder she needed of how much there was to do. "I don't think my parents would want me to have to put Gran in a home, which is what's going to happen if the

Flutterby closes. This is the only way out I can see."

Holly moved aside for the ever skinny, fashion boundary–pushing server Twyla, who grabbed a fresh pot of coffee and warmed up the late-morning customers' cups. "And for what?" Holly lowered her voice. "To enter a cooking competition. A *cooking* competition? You know that means you'll have to cook, right?"

Abby inclined her head and pressed her lips into a hard line. Sometimes Holly's sarcasm rankled her nerves.

"Oh, wow." Holly crossed her arms. "I thought maybe you were exaggerating yesterday."

"That was before I looked at the accounting records. Mr. Vartebetium has been using his personal savings to balance the books for over a year. He's also neglected to pay the property taxes for the last four, which that prize money would cover. The inn is hemorrhaging, Holly, and Gran needs stability, especially since her diagnosis." *Abby* needed stability.

"And what's Gran going to say when she hears you sold those rings?"

"Gran won't say anything, because *no one* is going to tell her," Abby warned Holly. "I did what I had to, Holly, and I sent in the entry fee forty minutes ago." No turning back now. All those rules. No wonder she'd woken up with a headache. "It's a done deal." She was locked in tighter than plastic wrap over a steaming bowl.

Hey. She jolted in her chair. She'd learned something from Jason's cookbook last night after all.

"On the bright side." Holly shifted her gaze out the glass door. "You found yourself one handsome cooking teacher. Nicely done."

"Yeah, we'll…" Abby spun on her stool as she saw Jason bending down to give Cash, Luke's beautiful golden retriever, a hearty pet of greeting. "We'll see," she croaked. He'd certainly never smiled at her like that, and was that a chuckle she heard as he stood up and followed Luke into the diner? If anything she seemed to put his face in a permanent state of disapproval.

"Ladies." Sheriff Luke Saxon in all his uniformed finery led the parade of his overactive soon-to-be stepson, with Jason bringing up the rear. Cash remained outside the front door, peering inside with a look of resignation.

"Am I too early?" Jason slipped his hands into the pockets of his oh-so-nicely fitted jeans. Abby nearly toppled off her stool but then covered by grabbing hold of Simon and yanking him in for a hug.

Holly straightened to her full height, an amused gleam in her eyes as she glanced between her best friend and Butterfly Harbor's recent arrival. "Abby's always early. A good thing for any instructor to know about his student." Holly strode around the counter and held out her hand. "You must be Jay. Nice to meet you."

"Thanks. It's Jason, actually." He cleared his throat, inching his chin up as if accepting a challenge. "Jason Corwin."

"Welcome to Butterfly Harbor, Jason. Tell me something." Holly leaned in as Luke slid an arm around her shoulders and squeezed. "Will you be videotaping your cooking lessons with her? I'm thinking they'd make great holiday entertainment—ow!" She glared at Abby, who had yanked hard on her ponytail. "Seriously?"

"Very seriously," Abby said as she hugged the stuffing out of her godson until he squealed. "You, sir, have been MIA for too long. I miss my movie and pizza buddy."

"Sorry." Simon grinned up at her, those big brown eyes of his even bigger behind thick black-rimmed glasses. "Charlie and I have been busy."

"I knew it." Abby sighed and spun him around so she could lean her chin on the top of his head. "I've been replaced by another woman. You two aren't trying to take over the world again, are you?" She peered over his shoulder at the haggard notebook clutched against his chest. Simon and his notebook. A dangerous combination.

"Not the world," Simon said with a little too much seriousness, that jolted Abby's nerves and was reflected in Holly's suddenly attentive expression. "Just Butterfly Harbor."

"Don't worry. The sheriff is on full alert." Luke shifted on his feet, barely leaning on the cane in his hand. "His school starts soon, so we stopped in for a quick snack before heading out to find the perfect backpack. Jason, good to see you again. Remember that poker game I told you about."

"Sure. Yeah. Sounds great."

Abby wasn't entirely convinced Jason thought so.

"Give Paige your order." Holly patted a hand against the front of Luke's khaki shirt before she lifted up on her toes to kiss him. "But I'll make your mocha shake."

"You realize that's why I'm marrying you, right? No one makes a mocha shake like you."

Holly eyed him with suspicion. "Hmm. And here I thought it was my homemade pies. Simon, let's leave Aunt Abby and Jason to their *lunch*, shall we?"

Abby would not blush. She would not... *Too late!*

"Back corner booth is free." Abby hopped off her stool by the register and hurried off, hearing the muted rumblings of manly farewells and fellow customers' conversations.

"Tell me something." Jason slid into the booth across from her. "Is Butterfly Harbor a news dead zone, or does no one care about my past?"

Abby eyed him as she sipped the water she'd set on the table when she'd first arrived. "As far as scandal rankings, I would put cheating on a national TV show somewhere between Mrs. Greely's penchant for pilfering neighbors' flatware and whoever's been snipping buds off Mr. Rondale's prized roses. Someone will probably say something at some point, but if you're looking to have that past held against you, the last person you want to talk to is Luke. He's a big believer in second chances."

"Sounds like there's a story there."

"If you ask, he'll give you the abbreviated version. Growing up we called him the bad boy of Butterfly Harbor." Abby's heart still ached for the life Luke led growing up. Between his abusive alcoholic father and an accident that had nearly cost Holly's father his life, Luke had worked hard to overcome his past. She still admired the courage it had taken for him to come home after all those years away. "It was rough going when he first showed up, but then he stopped letting his past define him. Now look at him." She nodded to where Simon had all but superglued himself to the sheriff and Holly stroked a finger down the center of her fiancé's chin. "Happily ever after."

"Nice to know things work out for some people."

"Things work out for a lot of people." How sad he didn't realize that.

"But not you." Jason glanced uneasily at the laminated menu behind the ketchup bottle. "You're not married."

"Blunt and charming as ever." Yet somehow she was getting used to it. "Maybe I'm waiting for some tall, handsome, scandal-ridden ex-chef to sweep me off my feet." She grabbed the menu to push into his reluctant hands. "Meanwhile I divide my time between a genius eight-year-old and, most recently, a bowling alley tech with a penchant for shoe rentals."

"I never know whether you're joking or not."

"I wish I was joking. Read the menu already, Super Chef. It's not going to bite, and look." She swiped her fingers over the top of the black-and-orange Formica table and showed them to him. "No pedestrian grease."

"Darn straight there's no grease, pedestrian or otherwise." Holly frowned at her as she set a glass of water down for Jason and tapped her fingers against the rolling pin sticking out of her apron. "This diner might be old, but it's my second baby. It was my grandmother's for almost forty years."

"I'm beginning to think I should have worn protective gear." Jason glared at Abby, who grinned in response.

"That remains to be seen." Holly placed a firm hand on her hip. "It's not often we get celebrities in here, let alone chefs with best-selling books and award-winning restaurants. I'm hoping we'll surprise you."

"I'm sure you will," Jason said. Abby was certain he was trying to find the means to inch out of arm's reach of Holly's weapon of mass destruction. "Can I have a minute with the menu?"

"Absolutely. Twyla will take your order when you're ready. And you." Holly pointed a stern finger at Abby. "We're not done with our conversation. I'm not happy with you."

"Love you, too," Abby sang as Holly waltzed away.

"What isn't she happy about?"

"Nothing important." Abby pinched her lips shut and tried not to dwell on the rings she'd sold. Good thoughts. Positive thoughts. They weren't gone forever. Yet.

"Did you have to tell Holly what I said about diners?"

"I tell Holly everything." Abby shrugged. "Have ever since the sandbox."

He set the menu down. "You've been friends that long?"

"You sound surprised. You were friends with your brother, weren't you? What?" She couldn't decipher the odd expression on his face.

"We were. But we were also competitive. I figured that's all people saw."

"Then people weren't looking very closely." All anyone had to do was look at the photos from David Corwin's funeral to see his twin brother had been devastated by his death. She'd bet that arrogant and rude demeanor Jason wielded like a weapon was his shield against the grief. One thing about grief: the more you struggled against it, the tighter its grip became. "You look like him, you know. Since you cut your hair and grew the beard. Was that on purpose?"

"Maybe. He was a good man." Jason's voice dropped as he ducked his chin to focus on the menu, but not before a flash of surprise crossed his face.

"I'm sure he'd say the same about you." Abby leaned over and attempted to catch his gaze, but he might as well have become an ostrich with his head in the sand. "You haven't talked about him with anyone, have you?"

"It doesn't matter. Nothing changes the fact David's gone." He tightened his fists as if he wanted to punch something. Or someone.

Yeah, he was dealing with his loss. Sympathy edged in and eased her hostility. "Maybe you haven't talked to the right person. Friendships like mine and Holly's make life so much more fun, not to mention there's a built-in support system when things go wrong. Or when you lose people. Maybe you should work on that. Now try *reading* the menu this time and order." She tapped her finger on the laminated card. "I'm all paid up. I'm ready to start my classes."

CHAPTER SIX

"How LONG ARE you going to make me wait before admitting I was right about the diner?" Abby blinked overly innocent eyes at Jason as she pushed open the Flutterby kitchen's door. "You devoured that steak sandwich like a carnivore after a vegetarian sabbatical."

"Listen to you, all culinary talk." He stood in the doorway, bracing the door open with his hand and waited for his heart to stop racing. He scanned the room as his hands went cold, his cheeks turning icy, but he'd made a deal. Jason Corwin was many things: a disappointment to his father, a twin without a brother, and he was a cheat, but he was also, first and foremost, a man of his word.

At least Abby's special way with words kept him on his toes. Her irritating penchant for levity could bode well for his state of mind. He scrubbed his hand over his beard, the whiskers rough against his palm as he forced himself to step inside and take charge. "You were right."

About a lot of things. "Holly's diner might just be the exception to a lifelong prejudice."

"I should be recording this conversation on my phone so I can play that admission over and over." She patted a hand against her heart before she clapped and then rubbed her hands together. "Okay, Teach. What's first?"

"First, you go and change into something less flirty."

"You think this is flirty?" Abby plucked at her knee-length coral-and-pink flowered skirt, white tank and coral sweater and wiggled her toes in her flat slipper shoes. "Really?"

"It might be hotel attire, but it's not suitable for the kitchen." Whatever uneasy truce they'd called wasn't making his life easier. If anything, he had the feeling his life was about to get very complicated now that Abby Manning was a part of it. "Jeans and T-shirt are just fine."

"That wouldn't be professional."

Battling over her clothes wasn't an ideal beginning. "I know you're on emergency call for managerial issues, but you're also a student learning how to operate in this room. Up to you."

"Just so you know, passive-aggressiveness

only enhances that jerky quality you've got going on."

He refused to be baited. "Does this hurt?" He pressed the tip of his booted foot against her toes.

"Hey!" She scrambled away.

"Now imagine dropping a knife, which I'm sure you will. Would you want to be wearing those when it hits your foot? Besides, no arch support, and cooks spend a lot of time on their feet. Go change. Hard-topped shoes if you have them. And tie your hair up." Nothing worse than hair in your food.

"What are you going to do?"

"I'm going to get your first lesson ready." Once he got his blood pressure under control. One deep breath and he might pass out. "The faster you change, the faster we get to it. Scoot."

Scoot? Jason's hand froze on the refrigerator handle. When was the last time he'd said *scoot* to anyone?

"You can't see me, but I'm—"

"Sticking your tongue out at me? Yes. It's a stainless steel fridge, Abby." He stared at her reflection. "Go, please."

He could do with the cheek. And he hadn't been kidding about the flirty skirt. She was so feminine, so girly and so out of control with that mouth of hers that he should want to cover his ears every time she approached him. Instead, he found himself thinking about other ways to keep her quiet. Like kissing her...

He frowned. He had enough on his plate these days without adding *that* into the mix. But now that the thought was there...

His hand gripped the bundle of celery as he realized Abby could well be the first person who'd ever been completely honest with him. Did she really not mind what he'd done? Had all the drama and scandal in New York been blown out of proportion in his mind? Or was it that Abby didn't care who he was or what he did that she didn't have an issue commenting on his rude behavior. When was the last time anyone had called him a jerk to his face?

Aside from his brother.

Having someone new throw his own observations back at him was monumentally better than having the person blow smoke up his... exhaust pipe, as was the case with most of his friends and coworkers in New York. Everyone had been so concerned about not offending him or saying the wrong thing; most of them had said nothing.

He took a deep breath as he unloaded what

he needed out of the fridge, his pulse picking up speed the closer he got to having to hold a knife. He clenched his fists, as if he could control the shaking, and pushed aside memories of the last time he'd cooked a meal. The walls pulsed, heavy and hard in his ears, and he thought he saw them throb toward him. He squeezed his eyes shut and crouched down for a slow count of ten. Focusing his thoughts, he forced himself free of the panic he'd been convinced would settle the second he returned to this space.

The clanging of pots, the staccato sound of knives hitting a cutting board, the shouts and orders flying overhead as they scrambled to get the meal on the plate in time for the judges. Nothing he'd cooked, nothing he'd prepared would be anything but a disgrace to his brother's memory. The empty plate mocked him. Whispered to him…

"Stop." He pounded his fist on the stainless steel counter before stalking over and yanking open one of the large wooden drawers. "This isn't then. This isn't that. Get your head in the game."

Still, his hand trembled as he hovered over the hilt of the blade shining up at him. A flash, so quick he wondered if he'd imagined it, and he saw David's face in the reflection of the steel, identical blue eyes narrowed in that silent manner he had of challenging Jason every day of their lives. *You can do this*, he seemed to say. *You've got this. You've always had it. Now suck it up and get to work.*

Jason squeezed his hand tighter, willing David's image to vanish. Willing him to stay. Sweat broke out on his forehead as he stared into the drawer and stepped aside. The knives could wait. There were other things he could do.

Once Abby returned, clad something like the uniform he'd suggested—although he wasn't convinced the sneakers on her feet were going to last long—he'd familiarized himself with Matilda's kitchen. One of the first lessons he'd ever learned was you didn't mess with anyone's space without their permission. From the few comments he'd heard from Abby about the inn's longtime cook, it seemed like sage advice.

He could also tell whatever kind of cook Matilda was, she didn't skimp on organization and preparedness. Impressive. Especially considering the stove she had to work with was about thirty years out of date. Only four burners? How did she manage that?

"Do I pass inspection, sir?" Abby curtsied.

"Better." Better than better. That orange shirt of hers brightened her face and showed off curves he now realized had been hidden beneath the flouncy skirt. As if he needed any added distractions. "Next time salute. Okay, step one, always step one, wash your hands, please. Then we'll get to know these knives."

He pointed a finger at the drawer in the worktable he'd left open.

"Awesome." She did as instructed and joined him at the spacious island. "Ooh, I like this one." She pulled out a twelve-inch carving knife and poked her finger against the end. "Sharp, too."

He pushed her hand down to the work surface and reconsidered the idea of protective gear. "Let's begin with this one." He indicated the more flexible six-inch vegetable knife with a forgiving blade. "Hold the hilt in your palm." He waited for her to pick it up, then arranged her grip into the proper position. "See? You don't want to hold it too tight. Ease up." He put his hand on top of hers, then shook. "Relax. Too tight and your hands will cramp up. Nice and easy hold, thumb in." One of the most common mistakes amateurs made. "With your thumb out, it limits your mobility. Keep it in and you can move around easier." He rotated his wrist, combining the movement with a slow slicing motion. "Okay?"

"Yep." She turned her head and grinned over her shoulder at him. This close, he could smell lavender and the ocean clinging to her skin and hair. "Do you think I'll ever be able to cut air as well as you do?"

He was not going to laugh. "We'll start slow and easy. No rushing, remember?" He placed the bamboo cutting board in front of her and handed her a stalk of celery. "Curved side up. The knife goes in easier. And hold the other end of the celery with this hand here, fingers tucked under your knuckles."

"Like this?" She chopped a good chunk off the end.

"Smaller. And we want pieces to be as uniform as possible so they all cook evenly."

She tried again, putting too much arm into it.

"Stop. It's good, but you're making this too difficult."

"You said cooking was difficult."

"You're cutting, not cooking. And no sassing, please."

"Sassing?" She grinned at him. "Oh, am I helping you expand your vocabulary, Scooter?"

"You know this will go faster if you stop playing around, right?"

"Fine." She heaved a sigh. "Forget the fun. If I'm doing it wrong, then show me, Super Chef."

He took a deep breath and moved in behind her again, wishing he had the courage to take hold of that knife himself so he wouldn't have to deal with…her. All those curves and softness, how she held her spine so perfectly straight. "Together." He covered her hands with his, placed her fingers in the correct position. Their close proximity didn't do anything to help him keep a mental distance, but he stepped closer, trapping her between him and the counter as he eased the blade down. "Feel that? Nice, easy movements." Familiar movements, familiar sounds. All the things that used to bring him such pleasure now felt like torture. "Not too far, just enough to… there. Good." The knife slid through the stalk with that anticipated crunch, and he loosened his grip.

He peered over her shoulder, craning his head slightly to watch her face. He grinned as she stuck the tip of her tongue out of the corner of her mouth, as if cutting celery was as complicated as deciphering nuclear codes.

"I think I've got it." She let out a surprised laugh. "Look at that, I made celery."

"You cut celery. Let's do another. This time on your own." He released her hand as if touching her set his skin aflame.

"And the training wheels come off. Yes!"

Jason ducked as she did a fist pump with her knife. He grabbed her hand as his good mood evaporated. "Guess what I'm going to say now?"

"Knives shouldn't be waved like magic wands?" But he saw her flinch. "Sorry. It's like I told Lori last night. I get distracted, moving on to the next thing while I'm still on the first, you know?"

"I'm beginning to." He could relate to distracted, but he couldn't afford to be. Especially with Abby waving sharp implements in front of his face. "I'm going to get a bowl to put these in. Keep the knife down, please, and pull off another four stalks."

"Right." She set his mind at ease by leaving the knife on the counter. She had bunched all the stalks together when he returned.

"What are you doing?"

"Saving time." And didn't she look proud of herself. "It takes so much to cut up one, but if I use this knife here…" She grabbed hold of the large carving knife she'd first held. "I can get it done in less than half the time. See? Watch."

Before he could stop her, she gripped the knife as he'd taught her and chopped her way through the stalks. What she didn't do, however, was curl the fingers of her other hand under, something he was about to mention when...

"Um, Jason?" She squeaked his name as he let out a long sigh.

"Yes, Abby?"

"Does celery bleed?"

"No, Abby." A headache pounded behind his eyes. "Celery does not bleed."

"Oh." Her face went white as blood dripped onto the celery and cutting board. "Then maybe this wasn't the right knife after all."

He grabbed hold of her wrist and dragged her over to the sink, the knife clanging on the countertop. She swayed against him as he stuck her sliced fingers under the cold water.

"Ow."

"Saw that coming," he muttered. Part of him had wanted to warn her, correct her in time, but lessons had to be learned the hard way. Then they weren't forgotten. "Lesson two— no shortcuts."

"Got ya." She leaned her head back and

rested her cheek against his chest as he held her hand. "I don't feel so good."

"Lesson three? Get used to blood."

"Mine?" she gasped.

"And others'. The kitchen is a dangerous place, Abby. Those shortcuts you want to take, all those distractions you admit to, they can cause real harm. Not only to yourself but anyone else you're working with."

"Um, Jason? About that blood?" She was squeaking again.

"I'll get some bandages. Where's your first aid kit?" He should have gotten that out right away.

"Under here." She hopped to the side and pointed. "Jason, um, we might have another problem."

"We do?"

"Yeah. I'm going to be sick."

It was all the warning he got as she leaned over the sink and threw up.

He sighed and knocked his forehead against the cabinet as he pulled the first aid kit free.

This was going to be harder than he'd thought.

"I CAN'T BELIEVE I did that." Abby moaned as Jason pressed a second cold rag into her hand

and lifted it to her forehead. As if yesterday's fire hadn't been embarrassing enough, now she'd almost puked on her teacher. "I never thought I was squeamish."

"You're just learning all kinds of things today, aren't you?" He finished cleaning up the sink and the counter, erasing all traces of blood—and celery—from the workstation before wiping everything down with bleach. "We agreed I'd tell you what to do. Until you're more confident in the kitchen, I don't want you making any food-related decisions on your own, hear me?"

"Uh-huh." Her stomach rolled as she nodded. It was like all the aftereffects of a hangover without the enjoyment of drinking. "I'm sorry."

"There're no apologies in this room." He tapped a wooden spoon in front of her non-bandaged hand. "And you're done for the day."

"What?" Abby dropped the rag and, despite her relief, gaped at him. "But we only just started. I don't have time—"

"Your head's not in the game and I need to reevaluate my plan. We'll go again tomorrow, first thing, so you might want to tell Lori and your staff that you'll be busy. All day."

"I'll try to do better." Like maybe wearing a pair of steel-lined gloves.

"Don't try, do."

"Ah, man, don't try quoting the little green dude to me, Jason. I'm not ready to like you yet. Come on." She waved her hand in a circle. "Say something rude. That'll make me feel better."

He didn't look amused. "You're a menace in the kitchen."

"Oh, ouch." She rolled her eyes. Shocker. "You can do better than that. How about I taunt you? Um." She scrunched her nose as she considered her options.

"Don't tell me you've lost your edge already."

"I think it's over there." She pointed at the sink and then felt as if she'd located a long-buried treasure when he grinned. Finally. One for her. "Can I ask you a question?"

"Apparently you can."

She flashed back to Mrs. O'Riley's eighth-grade grammar lessons but refused to correct herself. "Why did you become a chef?"

"Why?" The befuddlement on his face when he looked at her might have been comical if she didn't think it sad. "I've never really thought about it. David and I just…decided.

We spent so many years at the restaurant with our grandfather there was never any question."

We. Interesting. "You didn't ever want to be anything else?"

"No. Never thought about it."

And yet he'd walked away from everything as if it didn't mean a thing. "Do you like it? Did you, I mean?" No need to poke the bear too hard.

He shrugged. "Sure."

Wow. Could he have sounded any less enthusiastic? When she'd gotten her first job at the Flutterby, she couldn't wait to get to work in the morning. How did he make professional cooking sound so…boring? "Matilda's always cooked for me when I didn't eat out or gorge on peanut butter. But she banned me from this room when I was ten."

"I'm afraid to ask, but I should probably know. What did you do?"

"Have you ever noticed that salt and sugar look exactly the same?"

He didn't seem surprised, which could be either good news or bad. "I did that. Once."

"Was it your grandmother's birthday cake? And did you neglect to tell anyone you'd gotten creative with the recipe before it was served to over fifty guests?"

He folded up the dish towels after drying the last of the knives. "This would be one of those distraction things, right?"

"I wanted to help. And Matilda was always so busy in here, it seemed like fun." She reapplied the rag and sighed as the coolness sank into her skin. "I'm not getting the same feeling now."

"Because you're putting too much pressure on yourself. You need to relax and not take it so seriously."

"But it is serious," Abby said. How could she not put pressure on herself with everything that was at stake? "You've been saying so, so it must be true. I know I said I was okay not winning, but I really need to, Jason. We need that money." He had to understand that...without her giving too many details.

"What you're expecting of yourself is impossible. I'm not saying winning isn't possible, but expecting to be perfect right out of the chute isn't. Especially since you don't even know who you're competing against."

"Would it make a difference if I did know?" She sat up straighter, an idea forming. "Because I bet I can find out."

"Find out what?" Jason stopped putting the

bleach away and popped up from the under-sink cabinet, his expression turning wary.

"Who my competition is. I'm friends with the mayor. I bet he'd tell me if I—"

"No." Jason planted his hands flat on the counter and leaned toward her, any humor vanishing from his face in what felt like an arctic blast. "There will be no cutting corners and no, I repeat, no cheating, do you hear me?"

"That's not—" The vehemence in his voice unsettled her.

"Giving yourself an advantage people you're competing against don't have is cheating. And I'll pack my bags and leave right now if that's how you plan to try to win."

"You don't think you're a little oversensitive about this subject?" When he'd cheated it had been out of ego and pride, at least according to what she'd read. She had more riding on this competition than he did, including her employees', not to mention her own and her grandmother's, livelihoods.

"I'm certainly more in tune with what the consequences are when you're caught. Trust me, Abby, cheaters and liars are eventually exposed. It's not worth the risk. Or the fallout."

"Fine." Her dramatic sigh seemed lost on him. He was so odd. So different from anyone else she'd ever known. Maybe that was why he irritated her so much. She couldn't figure out how to deal with him.

"You're better than that, Abby," Jason said in that superior tone of his. "It might have felt like fun and games last night when you asked me to help you get ready for this, but looking to skirt the rules the second you hit a speed bump is not going to get you what you want. You want to win that badly, do the work and make it happen. If it helps, I have faith in you."

"You do?" She glanced at the sink before looking at her bandaged fingers. "Why?"

"Because you're motivated. You're doing this for more than yourself. You have a purpose. You might not be ready for the Cordon Bleu or even the burger shack outside town—"

"One minute he builds me up, the next he tears me down." She tried to ignore that slimy feeling of shame slipping over her for even thinking about asking Gil for a favor. "Admit it, you were never a cheerleader, were you?"

"There's the insult I've been waiting for. And no, I wasn't a cheerleader. I dated a few, though."

"What a surprise. I was the high school mascot," she said with more pride than she should feel. "They stuck a bird mask on my head. Smelled like chicken, oddly enough. Is there anything I can do before tomorrow that will help prepare me for what you have in mind?"

"As a matter of fact there is." He pulled a hardcover cookbook off Matilda's shelf, one with pictures of bowls, a whisk and, heaven help him, knives on the cover. "I want you to study this tonight. It's basic and has photos, which should help with developing your technique." He placed it into her hands, although it felt like another fifty-pound weight added to her shoulders.

"Shouldn't this have 'dummies' in the title?"

"I'm not a fan of that word." Jason returned to peruse the other titles on the shelves. "It shows a lack of confidence and pride. You want to fail? Then fail spectacularly while trying. There's no shame in that. But you are not stupid, Abby. If I thought otherwise I never would have agreed to help you."

"Gee, I'm feeling all warm and fuzzy inside." She got up and grabbed a lemon-lime soda out of the fridge, popped it open and felt her stomach ease with the first sip. Ah. Much better.

"I'm going to test you tomorrow on what you read tonight. I also want you to consider real-life meals you'd want to cook for Alice or your friends if they came over for dinner. Nothing fancy, whatever food you like. Then we'll move on to round two."

The preround had burned her hand. Round one had sliced her fingers. She'd probably have to amputate something after round two. "You're putting me back on the horse, aren't you?"

"You can do this, Abby. You just need to remember why you want to."

As if she could forget. She'd gotten exactly what she'd wanted. She was in this mess.

If only she didn't have to cook her way out of it.

CHAPTER SEVEN

FOR THE FIRST time since he'd left New York Jason didn't wake up with that cloud of dread hovering over him. The heaviness that had been his constant companion for longer than he cared to admit had lifted, and he rolled out of bed looking forward to what the day might bring. A day he decided to start with a run. He tossed on his running clothes and was out the door before the Flutterby Inn had its first decanter of coffee steaming in the lobby.

The brisk morning air welcomed him as he started a slow jog down Great Copper Way toward Monarch Lane, letting his body readjust to physical activity that required more than shifting from one chair to another.

He didn't bother with earphones or music, choosing instead to let the crashing waves and squawking gulls accompany him through the winding hilly roads. He had the morning, and seemingly the entire town, to himself as he jogged to the newly opened youth center at the far end of town.

He stopped, jogging in place for a few minutes as he took in the sleepy site, the thick, damp sand of the beach, and listened to the rattling of rocks and pebbles as the water shifted in and over.

Welcoming the familiar and long-absent burning in his lungs and legs, he pulled out his water bottle and drank down the contents.

The past six months faded as if he were forgetting a bad dream. His thoughts, while still jumbled with regret and frustration, melded with the early sun as he headed back to the inn at a leisurely pace. He wasn't ready for his quiet solitude to end. He wasn't ready to surrender his hold on Butterfly Harbor.

"Morning, Jason!" Holly Campbell waved to him from across the street as she scrubbed down the diner's windows. "Coffee?"

Jason hesitated. He figured he'd grab a cup at the hotel, but the aroma of roasting beans led him toward the diner like an entrancing spell. He might be a morning person, but a people person? He'd always been more content to stay behind the scenes, letting first his grandfather and then his brother run the show. David had thrived in the spotlight while Jason had withered. Not that any of it mattered now. Those days were gone. But that didn't mean he couldn't become more sociable. Besides, it would be nice to hear Abby call him something other than insufferable and rude.

"You're out early today," Holly said after she flipped the sign around to Open and went to the brewing coffee to pour him and herself a cup. "Have a seat."

"Thanks." At least he'd cooled off some due to the crisp bite in the air. He sipped tentatively, then nodded approvingly as the bitter notes slid over his tongue. "That's great."

"Someday I'll stop surprising you." Holly grinned over her shoulder at him. "It's one of my splurges. An African roast I combine with a more popular restaurant brand. Gets the blood singing and creates loyal customers."

"Appreciate it." He checked the clock as it ticked to 6:00 a.m. "I'm not the only one who starts early."

"Requirement of the job. We diner owners have our regulars who have been known to beat the sun. But they aren't here now, so we have a few minutes to talk."

"Do you have a subject in mind?" He should have known the coffee wouldn't be free. But so far it was worth whatever the price of admission.

"How about Abby and her whackadoo plan to win this amateur food competition? Do you honestly think she can compete with those other cooks?"

"Remains to be seen" was the best he could come up with without lying. But Holly had things about right with *whackadoo*. He'd heard of people reaching for the stars before; it would have been more realistic if Abby's stars were in the same universe she occupied. "She had a bit of a bumpy start yesterday." Bumpy? What an understatement, but part of him was anxious to see what his student was going to throw at him next. "She has drive. She wants to win. That's a good motivator."

"That's a very diplomatic answer." Holly sipped her own coffee.

"I've been told I'm arrogant and rude, so diplomatic sounds like I'm making progress."

Holly chuckled. "Abby tends to call things and people as she sees them. You always know where you stand with her."

"You don't strike me as someone who beats around the bush, Holly. If there's something you want to ask, go ahead. Trust me, I have very thick skin." Over the years, if his father hadn't been ignoring him, he'd been criticizing him. Jason had considered it a good training ground for restaurant reviews.

Holly angled her head and pinned a piercing brown gaze on him that had him shifting on the counter stool. "I'll admit it, I read up on you when Abby told me what's going on."

"Is this the part where you inform me that I'd better not hurt your friend or you'll find a way to serve me to your customers?"

She smiled. "They only do that in movies or Broadway shows, so consider yourself safe on that front. I'm also not one to pass judgment on anyone's life or choices. Anymore, at least. That said, I wouldn't be thrilled to see Abby get sucked into the vortex of your mistakes or their repercussions."

"I wouldn't wish that on anyone," Jason said and meant it. "I'm still a walking disaster, so be sure you keep your distance."

"We've all made bad decisions, Jason."

"Most people don't make them on national television." Or drag their innocent dead brother into the fray. Or end up tanking a company because of it. "Gotta admit, this is the most polite warning I've ever received."

"This isn't a warning, Jason. It's a conversation. I have a lot of respect for what you do. What your brother did. Owning and running a four-star restaurant in New York is a bit more pressure filled than operating, say, an ordinary old-fashioned diner." Holly waved a hand around her establishment. "I can't even imagine how hard you had to work for what you have and how difficult things must be now that your brother's gone. I'm sorry about that."

Jason glanced away before he saw any sympathy in her eyes. "Thanks. But this mess is my own fault. I took a chance I shouldn't have." He'd let his father goad him into something he hadn't been comfortable with and then let the pressure get to him. Maybe he'd done it for David—maybe that's what he'd convinced himself of. Or maybe he'd done it in an attempt to finally win his father's approval.

"You're interesting. There's something about you." She paused, but used her finger to draw a circle at him. "Can't quite put my finger on it, but I'm sensing there's a lot more to you than anyone gives you credit for."

That observation didn't make him uneasy in the slightest. He took another swallow from his cup. "Does your coffee have magical powers?"

"Only the power to wake people up. Which

you'll need if you're teaching Abby to cook. Do me one favor?"

"Okay." *Here it comes.*

"Be careful with her. She puts on a good show, but her heart is about three times the size of the rest of ours. That means it's a bigger target."

Was anyone ever going to say what he expected them to? That he was poison, that he'd disappointed everyone in his life, including himself. Was everyone in Butterfly Harbor genuinely this nice, or was it a matter of waiting for the other shoe to drop? "They're only cooking lessons, Holly."

"Well, in case it turns into something more, tread lightly, okay? She's got a lot going on and life's been kicking her around. I'd hate for her to have to add you to that list. As someone who can relate, I just wanted to put it out there."

"Noted." He didn't know what else to say. He didn't have any designs on Abby Manning. How could he? He'd never met a woman he had less in common with. Yet he'd often found himself dwelling on that flirty, bright smile of hers or the way she put her hand through her thick blond hair when she was nervous. Not his type. But that didn't mean he wasn't tempted to find a pleasurable route to keep her from that incessant chattering of hers. Healthy male appreciation, he told himself. That's all it was. Wasn't it?

The bell over the door chimed as a sleepy-eyed woman strolled in, her eyes brimming with that familiar glaze of caffeine dependency. She held out her hand for the mug of coffee Holly passed to her. "Mmm. Thank you." Her long ash-blond ponytail draped down her back as she drank, looked up to the ceiling and sighed. Her jeans and bright-colored T-shirt matched Holly's similarly casual uniform.

"Charlie's going through one of her late-night phases," the woman explained. "I had to tell her three times to turn off the light and go to bed, but that's what happens when she discovers a new series of books. Don't know what I'll do once school starts. Oh, hi." She smiled at Jason. "You're Jason Corwin. It's great to meet you. I'm Paige Cooper."

"Nice to meet you."

"Confession time." Holly held up her hand as if about to swear an oath in court. "I have to admit I lured you inside under false pretenses, Jason. Paige is a big fan."

"Are you?" Jason gripped his mug tighter as he offered his other in greeting. "I can say the same. Your steak sandwich yesterday made me admit to Abby I had the diner pegged completely wrong."

"Oh, wow." Paige smiled as her cheeks brightened, although not in the same enchanting way as Abby's. "Careful. Abby won't let you forget that."

No kidding.

"Your opinion makes me feel like I just won a James Beard Award," Paige continued. "I'm sorry about everything you're going through. Losing your brother like that and then, well, the rest. JD's is on my bucket list of places to eat. I just have to hit the lottery first."

Jason nodded as he wondered when the mention of David would stop feeling like an arrow to the heart. Not to mention what he was waiting for... Were people in this town purposely avoiding calling him a cheat and liar in front of him?

"I know the restaurant's expensive," he said. "That's something we were working on before he died." The idea of smaller, more affordable eateries where the focus would be on the food rather than the ratings and profit still held more appeal than the craziness of upscale Manhattan. Since they'd been so successful, they'd thought it a risk worth taking, one that, because of its narrower profit margin, their father had been adamantly opposed to. Not that Edward had had a say while David was alive.

"I started carrying this around when I heard you were in town." Paige dug into her bag and pulled out a worn, tattered soft-cover copy of *All the Best*. "Would you mind signing this for me? You and your brother have taught me a lot."

"Good to know, for Abby's sake," Holly said.

"Um, sure." He patted his shirt, his hands tingling at the thought of holding another tangible token of his and David's past. "I don't have a pen—"

Holly set one on the counter as he took the book from Paige. The other night, a copy of this book was the last thing he'd wanted to see. He remembered the day of the photo shoot six years ago. He'd hated every minute of it, couldn't find a smile that didn't make him look like some psycho out of a stalker film. It wasn't until David had started nudging him, trying to break his focus, even put him in a headlock and mussed his hair that he'd loosened up. The photo they'd chosen for the back cover was his favorite, hands clasped on each other's shoulders as they'd doubled over in laughter.

It had ended up being a good day.

He flipped through the wrinkled and stained pages, a pressure building in his chest he couldn't define. "You have used this book a lot."

"And experimented with your recipes," Paige admitted with a nervous laugh. "I'm sorry it's so messy and spattered. I probably should have bought a new copy for you to sign, but..."

"No, this is great." He didn't see a bunch of bound pages of information that had hit the bestseller lists. This book, their book, meant something to Paige. "Those stains feel like a badge of honor." One that was stabbing him right in the heart as he flipped to the dedication he'd written.

For my brother, my friend, David Corwin. Thank you for helping me learn to fly.

And beneath...

For Jason Corwin. For always catching me when I fall.

When he handed the signed copy to Paige, he did it with a hand he couldn't stop from shaking. He got to his feet to prevent them from seeing; he didn't want to watch Paige flip through to what he'd written. He didn't want to dwell on the fact that he'd walked away from everything his brother had stood for and believed in. Everything Jason could never do on his own. "Thanks for the coffee, Holly."

"It's on the house," Holly said when he reached into his pocket. She mouthed a silent thank-you as he left. He pretended not to hear Paige call out her thanks, choosing instead to lose himself once again in the crashing shore of a small town that was quickly becoming too large for him.

AFTER AN EARLY-MORNING meeting with her staff that included bolstering their anemic work schedules and covering her own backside, Abby felt much better about turning the inn over to them under Lori's supervision until the festival kicked into high gear.

Matt Knight had come through and finished up Abby's to-do list around the inn, so she could breathe a sigh of relief. Except the less she had to focus on, the more she worried about the upcoming competition and how much was riding on her winning. This was her one shot at pulling the inn out of the financial fire. She had to succeed.

Knowing how the accounts stood, she'd have to dip into her savings to cover everyone's expanded hours, but after giving herself a stern talking-to, she decided to fully commit to the contest. Otherwise she'd always wonder if there was more she could have done.

Item number one that morning, however, had been to restock the first aid kit as a precaution.

"I don't understand this food competition thing of yours," Gran said as Abby gathered up her files and notes while Lori headed into a follow-up meeting with Bonnie and Judy, her two invaluable Jill-of-all-trades employees. Abby found Alice standing at the bay window overlooking Grandpa Bob's bench. "What purpose is this going to serve other than give you more to do?" her grandmother asked.

"Free advertisement, Gran." The lie came easier every time she told it. "The participating cooks each get some publicity on a national network," Abby added. "We'll also get mentions in print ads in some big travel magazines and blogs."

"Time was, all we had to do was send out postcard reminders to our former guests to fill this place up."

"Yeah, well, time was Butterfly Harbor had more to offer than a handful of stores and the ocean." They would have been enough for her.

"What about that new butterfly thingama-bob Mayor Hamilton's been working on?"

"The town council wants to make sure Gil's following proper procedure."

No doubt to make sure he wasn't taking any kickbacks or payoffs for the project. She couldn't blame them. Gil hadn't stuck to the straight and narrow with the council members as much as he could have. Making arbitrary decisions he should have consulted them on hadn't won him many fans. Gil had not only his own past working against him, but his father's as well. The shine of the Hamilton name had been seriously tarnished over the past decade. Abby frequently wondered if the new mayor was trying so hard to distance himself that he didn't realize it was at a serious expense, like trustworthiness.

"Last I heard they'd narrowed down the decision to three possible locations."

"And what's it going to be again?" Alice frowned.

"A butterfly sanctuary, research station and natural history museum." Abby loved the idea, especially if the project did as was promised and brought more families to town and made Butterfly Harbor a tourist destination. Not that they'd be able to rival the spectacular and expansive Monterey Bay Aquarium, but a project like this could be an addendum to anyone traveling through the area. "I believe the TrueLane Academy is going to be one of the sponsors, which makes sense since they're a school for gifted students." The same school Simon Campbell would be attending in a couple of weeks. "It's going to be good, Gran. You'll see."

"And this food festival will help with all this?"

Abby sighed. "The town needs an event like this. They're looking for volunteers to help organize it. The Cocoon Club has been working with the mayor's office. You should join them."

"I thought maybe you'd like me to stick closer to home. In case you and Lori need my help."

They were drifting into familiar territory and an area she wanted to steer her grandmother clear of. "Everything's covered here, Gran, and the doctors have told you keeping active will do wonders for you."

"I'm active enough. Eloise and I have a good time together." Her grandmother's hand tightened around the window frame. "Your grandfather started that club."

Abby's heart twisted. She couldn't imagine anything more wonderful than the love her grandparents had shared for over four decades, but it had been five years since Gramps had passed. Abby knew some people got mired in grief longer than others, but it had to end sometime, didn't it?

She hoped it did. For both Gran and for Jason.

Abby set her papers down and went to her grandmother, wrapping her arms around Alice's increasingly frail form, resting her chin on her shoulder. "Is that why you stopped participating in the Cocoon Club after he died? Because it reminds you of him?"

"I see him everywhere. Feel him, too." Abby could feel her grandmother trembling. "Even now, I can remember how he'd sit on that bench and marvel at the ocean. He said it never failed to remind him what mattered. Of how small we are when compared to the rest of the world. He loved this place. I miss him."

Abby tried to block the fear of failure, that she'd be forced to take Gran away from her last connection to the man she'd loved. "Gramps was a good guy. He wouldn't want you to stop living. He'd worry. It makes me worry."

"Time's coming you won't have to worry

about anything but your own life." Alice squeezed Abby's hand. "I'm scared of what comes next. Not dying. That's when I'll see my Bob again. I don't want to lose myself before then. I don't know that there's anything worse."

"I don't want that, either." Abby's throat went tight. "Your doctors are optimistic, although they probably wouldn't approve of you locking yourself away for the last few months. There's so much you can be doing. And your friends will help."

"It's been a long time since I've been to one of their meetings. Aside from Eloise, I didn't exactly leave on the best of terms."

No, she hadn't, but that's what mourning did to some people. They lashed out at those closest to them.

That her grandmother, once the life and heartbeat of Butterfly Harbor, feared she wouldn't be accepted by her lifelong peers and friends broke off a little piece of Abby's heart. All the more reason to do whatever it took to keep her grandmother in the home—and town—she knew and loved.

"I bet your friends would love to see you again. How about you give Eloise a call and talk to her about it? Maybe find out what they're planning for the festival. I'm sure it's something big, since it's including the town's hundred and twenty-fifth anniversary celebration." Something Abby was hoping to capitalize on whenever she could.

"I still have all those old photo albums your great-grandmother kept from when they'd come here on vacation. Maybe the club could use those."

"It can't hurt to ask. Come on. Let's get you on the phone. I've got cooking class in about an hour." She tugged her away from the dining room window and Grandpa Bob's bench.

"You're a good girl, Abby. My boy and your mother would be so proud of you."

"Thanks, Gran." A pang of regret struck as Abby thought about her parents' rings. "I had a good example to follow. Now how about we start mending some fences with your friends?"

CHAPTER EIGHT

"I'M DOING PRETTY well for my second day at boot camp, aren't I?" Pride swelled within Abby at the mildly impressed expression on Jason's face when she finished naming all the cooking utensils and equipment he'd lined up on the counter. "I bet you thought you'd trip me up on the food mill." She tapped a finger on the handle of the stainless steel appliance that could pass as a medieval torture device.

"You're stalling. You still haven't told me what you use it for." He spoke in the same tense tone he'd started the day with. The smile she'd begun to get used to had gone into hibernation. Abby was carefully contemplating unexpected ways to blast him out of his sour mood.

"Soups, mashed potatoes." She ticked them off on her unbandaged fingers. "And tomato sauce."

"At least now we know you won't get lost

in the kitchen without me." He busied himself putting items away.

"Are you going somewhere?" Her stomach dropped. He wasn't abandoning her already, was he? Not after she'd stayed up until 1:00 a.m. reading the book she'd dubbed *Cooking for the Culinarily Challenged* and aced Name This Utensil right down to the lemon zester and garlic press. "Did you decide to go back to New York?"

"Hardly," Jason scoffed in a tone that told her she'd hit the nail on the head with her second question. "I'm not going back. But I'm not always going to be with you, Abby. I've read up on the competition. You'll be on your own. No sous chef, so the more you know, the more you learn now, the better prepared you'll be for whatever they throw at you."

"A sous is a cook's assistant, right?"

"A *chef's* assistant, yes."

"What's the difference?" She ignored her promise not to touch anything without permission and slipped her recently burned hand around the handle of a whisk. Not even she could do much damage with that. "A chef and cook both cook."

"There's about a hundred thousand dollars' tuition worth of difference."

"Could you possibly say that with a touch more condescension?"

"That's the second time you've called me a snob." Finally, some life sparked in his eyes as his jaw tensed. She could see where he'd intimidate people, but where some withdrew when attacked, he struck out. "I might not act how you think I should, Abby. I might not see things how you do with those rose-tinted glasses of yours, and I might not be great with folks, but that doesn't mean I'm turning my nose up at everything."

"Not everything, no." She'd certainly tapped an overly sensitive nerve, hadn't she. A nerve he didn't want touched. One that needed to be exposed. She should back off and let him deal with things on his own. She didn't need this, didn't need his problems on top of hers, but Abby had never been able to turn away from someone in pain. Whether Jason Corwin wanted to admit it or not, he was hurting. She moved closer. Pushed harder. He needed someone to. "Remind me again how much dinner would cost me at your restaurant."

"That's—different. That's not here." He slapped a dish towel onto the sink. "New York's a different world."

"A world you miss."

"Yes. No." He dropped his head forward for a moment before he seemed to shake himself free. "No, I don't miss it. I don't have the drive anymore."

"I don't believe that." Abby moved up behind him, a hand poised to reach out, to comfort, but she closed her fingers and kept her distance. "You come alive in this room, Jason. You're almost a different person. I've seen it, even in the few days you've been helping me. Yes, you're fighting it and no, you may not want it, but cooking is a part of you. It's who you are. So maybe you're not ready to go home to New York and maybe you won't be for a long time, but it would be a real shame if you closed that door forever."

The internet had given her more information than she needed about the infamous Corwin brothers. One charming and energetic, the other—the one standing in front of her—brooding and brilliant and now oh so alone.

She saw that now that she'd watched some of their shows. How she'd love to meet the Jason she saw on-screen with his brother. Their affection for one another was palpable; it made her as the viewer want to be part of their family, part of their lives, even if it was only making a meal from a recipe they'd created.

She'd fought the temptation to watch the video showing Jason's brutal decline in front of millions of viewers. When his pride wouldn't allow him to own up to what would be a life-altering mistake.

He'd looked so...lost.

He was still lost.

"I know all about the seven stages of grief, Abby," Jason said. "Why do you think I'm standing in the middle of a hotel kitchen in Butterfly Harbor when everything that's ever meant anything to me is all the way across the country?"

"Because you've found yourself inexplicably drawn to the hotel's manager?" She fluttered her lashes at him when he looked at her. "Ah, there's that irritable super grouch I've come to appreciate. You're here in Butterfly Harbor because you haven't decided whether you want to fight for what you have left."

"First a snob, then a grouch, now a coward." He went to the fridge and pulled out a large glass bowl filled with eggs. "Am I moving up or down the food chain?"

"Depends on your point of view." Good. Anger, even irritation, was an improvement over wallowing. "I get that you're working through a lot of stuff, Jason. And I totally respect that, but I have to tell you, you're draining my energy." She tapped her fingers on the counter as she waited for him to respond. "You can't talk to your family, you can't talk to your friends. Do you even have friends?"

"I never had the knack David did when it came to making them."

That explained so much. "Well, you can talk to me. Use me as a sounding board. Get all this emotion out so you can do something other than brood in my tower room like the Phantom of the Kitchen. Or is it something else? Did one of those nasty reporters write another snarky article about you? Do you need your Super Chef ego stroked? Cook me something, oh, honored one."

"I'm curious." He stared at her. "These things you say, do they pop into your head on their own or do you keep a notebook somewhere? We're in a kitchen, Abby. Boundaries need to be set. This isn't the place to get personal."

She stared at the ceiling and let out an overly dramatic sigh. "The jaws of life couldn't get you to open up. This isn't *personal*. It's a conversation and advice from someone who's trying to be your friend. I thought you went for a run this morning. Should I send out a search party for your missing endorphins?"

Did he have to look at her as if she'd sprouted a second head? "I have never met anyone like you before. Where do you come up with this stuff?"

"I read books. Come on, Jason. Friends talk to each other. Let me help."

"You really think we're friends?"

"You watched me puke. Trust me, we're friends." She grabbed hold of his arm with both hands and shook him hard. "Do I need to give you a time-out? Talk to me! Or shove that bad mood of yours aside and let's get back to—oh." She looked down at the broken eggs on the floor.

She pressed her lips tight as a giggle escaped. She covered her mouth, but the laugh must have shown on her face.

"That's not funny," Jason said, but as he looked down, too, his lips quirked. You'd think he'd hurt something if he cracked a smile.

"Give it a couple more seconds." The laugh escaped, and soon, she had to drag in a breath to stop from choking. The more she stared at his face, the more she saw him struggling to figure out how he should react. Her giggles got worse. "Come on. You're almost there. There's nothing wrong with laughing in the kitchen, Jason." She nudged him again and sent another egg crashing to the floor. "Come on! Laugh!"

"Okay." His chuckle felt like she'd been presented with a gold medal. "That's enough." He retrieved a handful of paper towels, hesitated and then pushed them into her hands. "Your mess, you clean up."

"Fine." She swiped at the dampness on her face and crouched down. "What happened this morning, Jason?" She mopped the floor and soon discovered raw eggs weren't exactly easy to scoop. Yuck. "Did someone in town say something to you? About the cheating thing?" She was beginning to think they needed a code name for it.

"Even if they did, it couldn't be any worse than what my own father said. He couldn't remember being more disappointed in me. Which is saying something, given our history. Especially since he's the only reason I entered that stupid contest to begin with." He slid down the side of the workstation, bracing his arms on his knees as he watched her struggle with the eggs.

"I read somewhere that it was your brother who was supposed to compete."

"Which is why I stepped in. My father convinced me that I'd be honoring David. Instead, I disgraced both of us and the company. And made it ripe for a takeover."

"And all this was a while ago, right? So what happened today that set you off?"

He hesitated, as if discussing this morning's events was more difficult than something that had happened months ago. "Paige asked me to sign her copy of *All the Best*. It brought back… memories. Of David."

"Good ones?" Abby sat back on her heels as his grief washed over her.

"One of the best." He steepled his fingers, his elbows resting on his knees. "First time in a long time I've thought of the good times."

"Good memories put you in a bad mood. And you think I'm odd." Her teasing tone triggered a flicker of amusement in his sad blue eyes.

"Yesterday you asked me why I became a chef. I became one because it was David's dream. We did everything together. Same schools, same jobs, same girls. Not at the same time," he added when Abby groaned. "I never wanted to do anything else, because I knew whatever we did, we'd be great together. He loved the family business and he was so good at it. He could charm anyone, any occasion.

The two of us with our grandfather, it was the perfect fit, even though I always felt as if I were more along for the ride while David drove."

Unease uncurled in her stomach as she finished swiping up gooey egg yolks and dropped them into the garbage can. "That can't be true. You might think it is, but given how well you two did, there's no way it wasn't a team effort."

"Yeah, but that's the problem, isn't it? There's no more team. There's nothing, and I don't know if that's ever going to change."

"So let nothing happen for a while." She took another swipe with a new batch of towels before throwing them away and crouching down in front of him. "Maybe it's time you stop focusing on everything you've lost, on all those things you can't change. The past is the past, Jason. It always will be. There's no fixing it, but you can move beyond it. Maybe the road you were on with David isn't meant to be traveled alone. It's time you find a new one."

"Now who's channeling the little green guy?"

Her entire body jolted when Jason took hold of her hand, twirling his fingers around hers. He stared at her in such stark concentration she could see the grief mingling with sorrow in his eyes.

This shouldn't feel right. She shouldn't want him to touch her, to hold her. She shouldn't want to comfort him and help him get through his loss. And yet...

At this moment, she didn't want anything more.

"I've always been David's little brother. By six minutes," he clarified when she frowned. "He had six minutes on me and never let me forget it. I don't know that I know who I am without him."

"I'll tell you who you are. You're Jason Corwin." She lifted her other hand and touched his cheek, her fingers tingling at the feel of his beard. It was softer than she'd expected, especially given he wore it like a shield. "Maybe for now that's enough." She hoped she had something to do with how the heaviness seemed to be lifting off him. "You don't have to decide anything today. Or tomorrow. Or even next week. There's nothing you have to do except be you. And maybe help me kick some cooking butt. So stew on that."

He arched a brow.

"I've decided my new goal in life is to torture you with puns. Skewer you with tomatoes? Maybe fry you in oil? Or we can get back to my cooking lessons, because our time is running out. What was next on your agenda?"

His smile returned. "Scrambled eggs."

"Oh! Hmm." She gripped his fingers tight and leaned in, inhaled the scent of ocean air mingled with roasted coffee on his skin before she plucked up an errant eggshell. "I'm ahead of the game with cracking the shells. What's step two?"

THERE WAS NO way on this green earth Jason would tell Abby she'd been right two days in a row. It would set a precedent he had no intention of sustaining.

Doing nothing had never sounded more productive. He'd never not done something before. He wasn't sure he knew how. His entire life was in flux. Walking away from everything he'd helped to build over thirty-one years was a loss unto itself, and that was on top of David's death.

It was as if Abby giving him permission to grieve had unlocked a door he couldn't pry open. She seemed to understand everything. And now, because of her sledgehammer personality and dogged determination, the floodgates in his head—and heart—had burst open. He was thinking more clearly, as if a fog had lifted.

Nothing about his visit to Butterfly Harbor had gone as expected. Everywhere else he'd managed to avoid...people, but apparently even he had his limits when it came to a lack of socialization. Finding something as productive as teaching Abby to cook—and, yes, he had to admit it had an element of fun—felt far better than dwelling on all those things he couldn't do anything about.

His father had given an interview to yet another tabloid show this morning, but this one hadn't had the same explosive effect as the previous ones, either on the internet or with him. With each day that passed, Jason was finding it easier to put the past where it belonged: behind him. And Butterfly Harbor was helping him do that. The people here truly didn't care about what he'd done. They did, however, seem inordinately curious about what he was doing now. He'd met so many people and shaken so many hands in the last few days, he was beginning to feel like a politician. Plenty of Abby's fellow residents were interested in his thoughts about the festival and wanted the inside scoop on Abby's participation in the cooking competition. Butterfly Harbor felt like another world, far removed from the real one that was obsessed with success, celebrity, headlines and ratings.

Except the real world would soon be coming to town. The coverage for the By the Bay Food Festival could kick up all the dirt that was finally beginning to settle.

He'd done his research. It wasn't only his former producer who would be overseeing the production and Abby's cook-off, but a number of his former colleagues, not to mention at least one judge who had been sitting on the other side of the table when Jason had been exposed as a cheater.

He couldn't risk tarnishing Abby's chances in the contest by publicly showing his support. Even staying in the shadows might be dangerous for her. He couldn't risk whatever burning embers of scandal might reignite and take Abby and Butterfly Harbor down with it.

This place didn't deserve to be put in the spotlight for the wrong reason. He didn't want to become the story. Again.

Abby had sounded panicked this afternoon when she'd thought he was leaving, but her protests had gotten him to thinking she should be made aware of his plans. He couldn't stay much longer. Which meant he needed to hurry her lessons so he could break away free and clear. And soon. Before the festival began. Before his past caught up with him.

A quick inquiry at the front desk had him forgoing the complimentary wine and cheese offering to follow the darkening path around the Flutterby's extensive property. The earlier breeze was a bit chillier now as his feet crunched in the thick covering of dead leaves coating the overgrown trail.

He should have done more exploring. This patch of acreage felt as if he'd stepped into some sort of secret garden, complete with run-down cottage dwellings, black iron fencing and yards screaming for attention. He went left at the fork in the path and headed up the small hill, a garden exploding with midsummer color that glowed even in the starry moonlight.

There was nothing overgrown, run-down or depressing about this little house.

A dim light glowed from inside the curtained window as he pushed through the trellised gate. Wide mismatched flagstones led to her front door, which was flanked by a collection of equally dissimilar potted plants that he realized had been a tad neglected.

He knocked on the door, wincing as the sound exploded into the silent night. She pulled the thin lace aside and Abby's pixie-perfect face peeked out at him.

"Jason, hi." She opened the door. "Everything okay at the inn?"

She'd gone totally relaxed in her yoga pants and sci-fi sweatshirt, her hair pinned to the top of her head with what looked like wooden chopsticks. He could hear the muted strains of Stevie Ray Vaughan at his guitar-playing best and...was that burned garlic he smelled? "Everything's fine. But I do have something I need to talk to you about." He couldn't help it. He sniffed. "You're cooking."

"You caught me, Teach. I gave myself homework so I could get a jump start for tomorrow. Come on in." She waved him inside. "You want some wine? I have something other than pinot around here."

"Is that code for I'm a wine snob?" He closed the door behind him and cast an appreciative glance around her small but comfortable home. A small beige sofa and matching chair cuddled in the corner, opposite a rather large flat-screen TV situated against the peaceful blue walls that mimicked the ocean mere steps away. A casual dining area led into the galley-style kitchen that, while filled with smaller appliances than he was used to, seemed serviceable.

"Listen to you, working on that sense of humor." She pointed to the wooden shoe rack she'd converted into a wine rack. "Choose your poison. Unless you want beer? I keep some for Luke when he and Holly come over for takeout."

"Wine sounds great." He dropped into a crouch and examined her selection. "These are pretty good."

"Again with the surprise. I might not know kale from collards yet, but I take my wine very seriously. I like the Australian shiraz myself. Kind of goes with everything."

"Works for me." He grabbed the corkscrew from the counter as she retrieved a second glass from a cabinet. "Nice place."

"It's cozy." Abby shrugged as if dismissing his compliment, but he could see she loved it here. "Mr. V—that's short for Vartebetium— and his wife gave this to me when I took over as manager, um, seven years ago? Right before she passed away."

"And Alice lives in the hotel?"

"In the same suite she and Gramps shared," Abby said. "It's not huge, but I suppose by your New York standards, it would be. She's comfortable there and feels safe. That's all that matters."

"My New York standards might surprise you."

Abby grinned as he poured. "Let me guess, penthouse apartment? No!" She stuck out a finger when he narrowed his eyes. "Loft. You live in some obnoxiously large one-room stainless steel monstrosity."

Was he that predictable? "In my defense, the monstrosity has a huge kitchen."

"Better than my dollhouse one, you mean?"

"It's different," he agreed. "Not better." This place was all...Abby. "So what are you making?"

"Pasta carbonara." She set her own glass beside his and pushed her hands in her back pockets. "I was feeling pretty good about my egg success today, so I did a recipe search. Bacon, pasta, eggs and cheese. Sounded like a sure bet."

"But?"

"Well, I haven't set off the smoke alarm. Yet." She returned to the small four-burner stove and showed him the singed pan. "I put the heat up too high, didn't I?"

"Looks like." Wine in hand, he switched

on the burner and tested to see how high the flame went on low, medium and high. "Not your fault. Your pilot needs resetting. Do you mind?"

"Are you kidding?" She shifted her pot of water and frying pan to the other side of the kitchen and moved aside as he pulled the stove out from the wall.

He bent down and, after a few adjustments, tried the burners again. This time when they clicked to life, the flames were more manageable. "Should help." He pushed the stove back into place, found a new pan and replaced the pot of water on the burner. "Why don't you try the recipe again?"

She didn't look so confident now.

"I'll be hands-off, I swear." He lounged against the cabinet behind him as she drank down a good portion of her wine. "I'll be here in case you have questions. Take your time. In fact, this will be a good lesson in distraction management. There's always something going on in a kitchen. Always someone else, tons of noise and banging and yelling. Might as well get used to it. That stage you'll be on is going to be chaotic."

"Would you like me to provide you with a

metal pot and a wooden spoon for your personal enjoyment?"

He was pretty sure she was teasing. "I think my presence will be enough to keep you on guard."

"You're telling me." She planted her hands on her hips, let out a long breath. "Okay, let's start over. Only this time I'll cook for two."

Either he was that good a teacher or Abby had finally gotten her mind in the right place, because when they eventually sat down at the small round table, he didn't have any qualms about eating what she'd cooked. He might have a lot to say about her pot and dish management—her kitchen looked as if a bomb had gone off—but one battle at a time.

"Well?" She twirled her pasta around her fork.

He did the same, using his spoon to catch the loose strands of spaghetti. He bit in, the silkiness of the egg combining with the garlic and crispy bacon mingled to make an excellent bite. He nodded enthusiastically as he chewed. "It's good, Abby. The pasta probably could have done with another two minutes, but it's really good."

"You mean it?" He'd never seen anyone appear so relieved before.

"Do I strike you as the type of person to flatter falsely?"

"Not at all." She dug in and grinned. "I can't believe I cooked this."

"Is there a local paper we could call to put the word out?"

"Ha-ha. Oh! I forgot the garlic bread." She dashed back into the kitchen and let out a low groan. "Well, that didn't last long."

She carried a cutting board with a slightly burned loaf of sourdough to the table.

"Believe it or not, bread can be tricky," he said.

"Yeah, right." Whatever happiness she'd embraced thanks to the pasta faded as she dropped into her chair. "Who ruins bread?"

"My first job out of cooking school was in a four-star restaurant in Chicago. My job, my *only* job, was to bake their signature rolls they made during the day." He couldn't ignore the skepticism on her face. "I swear. Take a lump of dough, roll it into a ball, tuck the edges in and bake them. That's all I had to do. I can say without hesitation your scones were better than my first batch of rolls. I walked away from the oven."

"Does bread need babysitting?" She started

eating again as he sliced through the charred end of the loaf.

"No, but you shouldn't let it cook for ten extra minutes. Batch two, I was so paranoid, they were still raw in the middle. Finally, one of the sous chefs came over and guided me through it. He also noticed I hadn't put the bread in the center of the oven; it was too close to the burners, so…" He shrugged, took a bite of bread and smiled. "This tastes like that night, which, believe it or not, isn't such a bad memory. Good job not overdoing the garlic."

"Could use more cheese."

"No apologies or excuses, remember? Whatever you put in front of anyone is your work. Be proud of it. Don't give people something to criticize. If they find it on their own, fine. Just smile, nod and say, 'I appreciate your feedback.' Otherwise, every plate you serve, consider it a masterpiece."

"Maybe you can write a companion book— *Cooking Wisdom from Jason Corwin*."

"Want to bet how many copies that would sell?"

"One, at least. Thank you." The smile on her face was one he'd remember for nights to come.

"For what?"

"For helping me. Believing in me. For not making me too much of a nervous wreck in there when I wanted to try something not on your agenda."

She made him sound like a drill sergeant. "Your kitchen. Besides, you're off hours. I see you brought some of Matilda's cookbooks home with you?"

"Mmm-hmm." Her appetite picked up, as did his, and, surprising them both, he took a second helping. "That okay?"

"More than. I'd like you to go through and pick out a bunch of recipes that appeal to you. We need to start building your style."

"My style?" She drank more wine. "I thought this was cooking, not fashion."

"Every artist, cooks included, has a distinctive style. It would help if you had some go-to techniques that you're comfortable with, ingredients you like using. The more you can enjoy what and how you're cooking, the more natural it'll feel when you get thrown a curveball."

"What's your style? Don't tell me, that French stuff that sounds all stuck-up."

He laughed. "Okay, you caught me. We have some nouvelle cuisine on the menu. I know, it sounds snobby." It sure did now, anyway. "But David and I were transitioning. Going more field-to-table, good, local, organic ingredients. Hopefully at more affordable prices. We still needed to keep our current clientele happy, though, so we decided on traditional American with Italian and French inspirations."

"Was that English? Because you've lost me." She pointed her fork at herself. "Food illiterate, remember? Burger. Salad. You know, diner lingo."

"Now who sounds like a snob? I'm known for my pesto-infused escargot."

"Snails?" Abby dropped her fork and grimaced. "I'm taking cooking lessons from a guy who could find dinner in my yard?"

"Ever tried them?" Telling her it was one of his favorite meals probably wasn't a good idea. Neither was telling her about the sweetbreads.

"No. And rest assured, I never will. Blech." She shook her head and reminded him of a five-year-old refusing to eat her green beans. "At least tell me you do something fancy like soufflés and stuff."

And *stuff*? "We do. Seared scallops are a specialty. Lots of seafood, especially papillon en croute." He could only imagine the fresh fish they had available to them in Butterfly Harbor and the surrounding seaside towns.

"I'm going to need a hundred more lessons after all if you keep this up."

"Ratatouille."

"Oh!" She brightened. "That sounds nice. On Fridays, Calliope Jones opens Dusky-wing Farm to host a local farmers' market. We should check it out. You would lose your mind at her garden."

"We'll work it in. Do you like to garden?"

"I used to. When I had more time."

He could tell she missed it. "You've got a great space for it in your front yard. You should think about it."

She shrugged. "Maybe I will." She picked up her plate and headed into the kitchen, leaving Jason at the table. When she took her time coming back, he followed her and found her standing at the sink, staring into space.

"What did I say?"

"Nothing." She shook her head and turned on the water. "It's nothing. Sometimes it's easy to forget everything I've got riding on this. You just reminded me why I'm in this competition in the first place."

"You mean it's not for the free advertising?" he asked with too-wide eyes.

She faced him, irritation evident on her face. "Do I ever fool you?"

"You're not the world's best liar, Abby. I figured you'd tell me when you were ready." He'd had the feeling it wouldn't take much to nudge her in that direction.

"The inn needs money. A lot of money, not to mention attention. Me competing gives us at least half that, and if I win, well, then I win all around. Not enough to get us in the black, but enough to get us over a serious hump."

"How serious?" He didn't like the sound of this at all.

"My boss informed me the other day this place is ready to close its doors. If that happens or even if Mr. V sells, I don't have enough saved to buy any kind of house for me and Gran, and I refuse to put her in some facility where I'll always have to be traveling to see her. She's mine. End of story."

"Wait a minute, hold on." Jason rested his hands on her shoulders for fear she'd take off into orbit. "You're getting ahead of yourself. Why would you have to put Alice in a home? She seems pretty lively to me."

"She's in the early stages of Parkinson's." Tears spiked her lashes and blurred her vision. "It's manageable and the doctors believe it'll stay like that for a while, but keeping her comfortable and positive about things will help. Which is why I can't tell her about the money issues. But in the end, she won't get better. Oh, shoot. Now I'm blubbering all over you." She stepped away, grabbed a napkin and blew her nose. "How about that? Dinner and a show."

"Why didn't you tell me all this from the start?" He should have known there was more to her desire to learn to cook than earning a little publicity for the inn.

"I haven't told anyone. Except Holly."

"Of course." As he would have told David if he was in trouble.

"Word gets around Butterfly Harbor faster than the speed of light. I've got employees who rely on me to keep things stable, and I don't want Gran worrying—plus, the Flutterby is like an anchor. If something happens to it, if it goes under, what's to stop it from taking the rest of the town with it? I need to fix this. So." She shrugged. "I took a chance." She touched a hand to her throat as if reaching for something, then clenched her fist until her knuckles turned white.

"You don't have to defend yourself to me, Abby. I get it." He only wished he didn't. But it did put more responsibility on his shoulders. He'd figured before he left he could teach her enough to get her through the first round. Maybe. But one or even four or five solid recipes weren't going to win her anything other than bonus points. Working with her to ensure she'd have a shot at winning? That was going to take a different strategy. "If I thought for a second you'd take it and if I had any liquid funds at my disposal, I'd help you. Everything I have is still tied up in Corwin Brothers."

She sighed and dropped her head back. "I don't know whether to be irritated you'd offer or relieved you understand me." She wrapped her hands around his forearms and squeezed. "I appreciate the thought. And it means a lot that you'd offer, but honestly, what I really need is for you to help me win. I can do it." Perhaps by sheer will alone, from what he saw. "I just need you by my side to make it happen, even if you're in the shadows. Believe it or not, I feel better in the kitchen when you're around. Tonight proves that. That reminds me, didn't you come here to talk to me about something?"

"Oh, that." He'd come to tell her he'd have to leave soon, that he couldn't be here during the competition and risk reigniting the scandal that was finally dying down. But as he looked at her now, all that glossy blond hair, her red-rimmed hope-filled eyes and pouty lips, he wasn't sure he'd ever seen a prettier sight. He shook his head. "I wanted to let you know some people aren't going to be happy to see me around here. During the festival. I didn't want their reactions to come as a nasty surprise."

"Trust me, nothing anyone does or says these days surprises me. I run an inn, remember?"

"How about I help you with the dishes before I go?" He needed a distraction, but found himself leaning over to press a kiss on her forehead. Chills raced down his spine as he heard her soft gasp. He stepped back and touched her cheek. Her skin felt as soft as he'd imagined it would.

Abby Manning had just become a major problem. But what was worse?

He wasn't going anywhere.

CHAPTER NINE

"IF THERE'S ONE thing I've learned about you in the last week," Abby said Friday morning as she and Jason headed up the hill and over to Calliope Jones's Duskywing Farm, "it's that you tend to go all quiet when you've got something up your sleeve."

"No sleeves today." Jason pointed to his well-formed biceps, which Abby had been taking more and more notice of.

They'd fallen into an easy rhythm the last few days, and hour by hour, Jason seemed to relax. Who knew he had an edgy sense of humor or that he was capable of talking to people without the threat of bodily injury?

He still got on her nerves and the feeling was mutual. Her continued tendency to leap without thinking remained an issue, especially for someone as straitlaced and controlled as Jason.

Her attempt at deep-frying fresh herbs had almost set off the smoke detector for the first time since the day they'd met, something she wouldn't have done if he'd told her to make sure the herbs were bone-dry before they went into the oil. But of course that information had been in the cookbook he'd told her to refer to, so...

Yeah. Her bad.

"I have to admit, I've been wanting to check out this farmers' market ever since you mentioned it," Jason said.

"Why didn't you say something sooner?" Abby asked. "Calliope's a friend. The market might only be on Fridays, but she would have given you a tour anytime."

"I was waiting until you were on more solid footing with what you've learned."

More likely he wasn't up for adding even more people to his expanding social circle. She'd never met anyone so reticent when it came to making friends. "Well, you haven't yelled at me in the last two days, so I'm feeling pretty good about my odds." Abby didn't mention the fact she'd been staying up until all hours poring over cookbooks, chef biographies, internet sites and anything else she could get her hands on to try to get a better grasp of what her style was. So far she was going with…edible. As long as she had a guide, a recipe, she was gold. It was when she ventured off on her own that she ran into trouble.

At least they finally had a schedule of events for the competition. The three rounds would be held over two days with two events on day one. With no eliminations, each of the three contestants would receive a cash prize, but the fifteen-thousand-dollar second-place award barely ticked her radar. She needed to win the entire kit and caboodle to keep the Flutterby solvent. For Abby, there was no second place. "I kind of miss you yelling at me, now that I think about it."

"I've never yelled at you," Jason said, and she caught a frown wrinkling his brow as if he wasn't so sure.

"Maybe not. But I bet you wanted to." She'd become an expert in identifying his varying expressions of irritability and frustration. He'd definitely wanted to.

"Oh, well, wanting to is an entirely different thing." Jason chuckled, a sound she never tired of hearing. "No one learns well under negative instruction. One thing's for sure, Abby Manning. You have done wonders for building up my patience."

"And maybe reminding you where you started?"

He pushed his hands into his pockets. "Maybe."

He still wasn't overly chatty when it came to talking about New York or his brother, so she'd stopped pushing. He'd get there. Eventually. When he was ready.

Abby loved mornings like this when the chill burned off early and the sun beat down in tempting warmth. She'd purposely pushed him out the door ahead of schedule so he wouldn't make a big deal about the detour she wanted to take.

He hadn't been kidding when he'd said he'd be a taskmaster. The hours had been long and her feet had definitely hurt—she'd even ordered new chefy shoes with extra-padded insoles—but she no longer felt like breaking out in hives when she walked into the kitchen. And she'd stopped dropping eggs and stabbing herself with the knives.

Little things like that made her happy.

She was planning on taking advantage of every free minute she got today, especially since Matt Knight had managed to put another serious dent in the fixes and repairs around the inn. Abby wasn't entirely convinced of

Matt's willingness to play handyman. She had a suspicion that his hanging around the Flutterby had more to do with Lori. No matter how many hints Abby dropped, Lori still wasn't picking them up. She really had to work on that girl's self-esteem.

"Hang on." She touched Jason's arm when they crested the hill on Skipper Way. "There's something I want you to see."

He looked at his watch.

"For once, can you ignore your schedule?" Abby groaned and pushed his hand down. "You're so predictable. It's a beautiful day, and besides, how can I be a sponge for information if you don't give me a chance to let things soak in? Another day in the kitchen like yesterday and I'm going to boil over. Everything's going to spill out."

"You are getting pretty good with those cooking puns," Jason said. "Fine. What is it you want me to see?"

"One of the things that makes Butterfly Harbor so special." Even a brief bout of impulsiveness invigorated her. She held out her hand, waited the extra beat of five for him to remove his hands from his pockets to wrap his fingers solidly around hers. "It's still early, but…"

Abby lifted her chin and felt the morning warmth bathe her face and neck, a sure sign they were in time for the magic awaiting them under the eucalyptus grove. The uneven road had seen better days, but its cracks and pot-holes, while making driving a hazard for even the sturdiest vehicles, meant fewer visitors. Due to budget cuts and reassessments, the underbrush was overgrown, and she stopped long enough to expose the rickety picket sign at the beginning of the footpath.

"Just a little ways down here." She glanced at Jason and smiled as the tension in his hand and arm melted away. He gazed up at the thick trees, that sense of peace she always felt washing over her evident on his handsome face. "It's early in the year. The real magic starts in late October through the winter, but I'm betting there are some eager arrivals hanging around. Shh." She pressed a finger against her lips, tempted to tap another against the brow he arched her way as they stepped under the thick canopy of the natural butterfly habitat.

The smell of damp earth and thick leaves drifted into her lungs. Their feet rustled in nature's debris as she pushed vines and branches out of their path. She couldn't wait for the town council to finally approve the mayor's plans for the sanctuary. This place needed tending if they were going to continue to have an impact when it came to keeping the monarch butterfly off the endangered-species list. The thought of these creatures becoming extinct hurt her soul. What would the world become without butterflies?

"This used to be my secret hideaway," she whispered, grabbing hold of his arm to hug it against her as they picked their way through another overgrown section. "Here. Sit down."

She released his hand and brushed her own over the rough seat of the weathered wooden bench.

"What are we looking for?"

"Wait. You'll see." He didn't strike her as someone who stopped to smell the roses or, in this case, to watch the butterflies. "There are some things you need to see to believe." She gazed up into the thicket of eucalyptus as thin beams of sun shimmered into the grove.

"I don't see anything."

"It's not a scheduled TV show," Abby said. "There. Do you hear that?" A rustle, ever so slight, for a fraction of a second. And again. "They're waking up."

Jason fidgeted, as if he couldn't get comfortable. Abby slipped her hand to her side and covered his, squeezed his fingers in a silent order to relax.

"Give it a few minutes, Jason. There's nothing so urgent that you can't enjoy something not a lot of people experience."

That rustle and fluttering sound increased, as did the spread of the sun's rays as morning fully blossomed. As light streamed through the openings, the leaves began to shift, to move.

And come to life.

"Are those...?" The disbelief in Jason's voice brought a smile to Abby's lips. "There's so many of them."

A flicker of wings, black obscured by the awakening orange, dainty lives fluttering into the new day as they launched, one by one, two by two, arcing in and around the other clusters as if giving their fellow butterflies a wake-up call.

"I used to come here all the time growing up." Abby leaned her head on his shoulder. "Gran told me it was magic, watching the butterflies wake up. Sitting here makes me realize how powerful nature is and how insignificant all those things we stress about are." Like money and bills and looming property taxes. Broken showerheads and blaring smoke alarms didn't belong here. Not for these few minutes in her grove. With Jason. "How can anyone worry about anything when they're surrounded by...this."

She waved her hand in front of her as if in slow motion and felt her heart expand as a monarch landed on her finger. "That's good luck, you know." She kept her arm and hand steady, watching in amazement as the thread-thin legs twitched and grasped, lacy, tissue-like wings pulsing against the infinitesimal life force coursing inside it.

Jason lifted his hand toward the insect with more hesitation, or perhaps it was reverence, that she'd seen him use. Having had enough human interaction, the butterfly pushed away and disappeared into the thicket.

The butterflies continued to swirl around them, darting close to them before they flew away. A few dropped silently to the forest floor like drifting pieces of discarded paper.

"Are they dead?" Jason asked, pushing off the bench. Crouching, he held out a hand.

"Maybe. Then again." She joined him, cupping her hand under his to scoop the butterfly into his warm palm. "Maybe they're not awake yet. It's the warmth of the sun that does it. And if that doesn't work—" She arced her hand and covered his, leaving enough room to incubate the insect.

The smile that spread across his mouth entranced her and lit up his eyes as if he too were being awakened. "I can feel it. It tickles."

Abby pulled her hand away and the butterfly righted itself, as if shaking off the shock of its gentle fall. "See? Magic," she whispered. "There's not a more perfect place on earth as far as I'm concerned." She watched as the butterfly took flight. "There used to be thousands upon thousands of them clustered on the leaves. Draping over one another like a protective curtain after their migration from Mexico. The numbers have dwindled significantly, but as long as there's one, there's hope."

Jason rose, brushing his palms against his thighs before holding out a hand for hers. She took it, feeling, for a moment, at least, like a princess in a fairy-tale garden that only the two of them knew about. "I think I am beginning to understand," Jason said as he drew her hand close to his heart. "About how special this…place is. Thank you, Abby."

"Anytime." She blinked faster than the butterflies around her fluttered their wings. "But let's keep it our secret, okay? At least while we can."

"Agreed." He stroked a finger down the side of her face as a frown marred his forehead. She swallowed, losing herself in the ocean depths of his eyes as quickly as a ray of sunlight could bring a butterfly out of slumber. "Our secret."

"I HAD A TEACHER at cooking school who suggested I should meditate," Jason told Abby as they rounded the corner and stepped through a large trellised gate. Overhead a sign with uneven lettering said Duskywing Farm. The dirt parking lot had more cars in it than he would have expected, which explained the sounds of laughter, conversation and…was that flute music coming from inside the property? "I need to tell him about your butterfly grove." Until today, he'd wondered who had time to meditate. With the calming effect Abby's secret had on him, however, he added yet another item to his *I've been wrong* list.

"I only hope the plans for the new sanctuary won't change it too much," Abby said. "It doesn't need more than basic upkeep."

"I've heard plenty of people talk about the sanctuary, but everything still sounds up in the air." As opposed to the big-city politics he was familiar with, where everything seemed a done deal well before it should have been.

"Mayor Gil's been tweaking his original plans and the town council isn't happy about it." They headed across the thick lawn, following the staked signs toward the market. "Originally the project wasn't supposed to include any chain stores or big businesses, but it seems Gil's changed his mind and started making deals for new tenants and owners."

"Big business would strangle this place," Jason said. He'd seen it before. The idea that the charm of this town would be swallowed up by capitalism and commerce felt like a crime against society.

"Maybe his ideas have stopped the exodus of folks for now. People want to see how things play out before they commit to selling up, but what price will we pay in the long run? We want places here no one else has. That should be the attraction, not the same old restaurants, the same old stores people have in their own towns. That's what makes the Flutterby so special. There's no place on earth like it.

"The sanctuary and research facility fit perfectly. The rest?" Abby shrugged. "Who knows what we're in for. Morning, Calliope!"

Abby stood up on her toes and waved to someone in the throng of tents and stalls.

"Abby, hi!"

The visual punch that was Calliope Jones spun in a rainbow of colors, from her tie-dyed maxi dress to the bright red of her hair. She favored intricate beaded braids worthy of a production of his favorite medieval fantasy novel.

"She's...unique," Jason said.

"You have no idea," Abby sang under her breath, holding out her hands as a barefoot Calliope greeted them.

"Last time I saw you here you were buying up all the eggplants for Matilda." Calliope wrapped her arms around Abby in a big hug before turning a blinding smile and excessively twinkling amethyst eyes on him. "Jason Corwin. Welcome." Calliope grabbed hold of his hand, the tangle of bracelets and yarn around her wrists jangling and shining in the sun like a mutant form of butterfly. "I'm Calliope Jones. You've been making a name for yourself around the harbor."

"Have I?" Jason's stomach dipped and that tension he thought he'd left in Abby's grove returned.

"Taking on this one in the kitchen? You're a man who appreciates a challenge. I like that."

"She's been a very eager student." The need to defend Abby sprang to life on its own.

"Ah, that would be Abby Manning working her magic, I take it? Tell me something." Calliope stepped closer and angled her head in one direction, then the other. Jason smelled jasmine and honey with a touch of lavender. "Has she shown you the secret grove yet?"

"She has," he answered. "But she said your garden and market are even more spectacular. I've been trying to convince Abby to start a garden in her front yard."

"That's a spectacular idea." Calliope looped her arm through his before doing the same to Abby's. "I've always told her I thought she had a green thumb. She's never had the proper motivation to put it to use. Right, Abs?"

"Mmm-hmm." Abby shot Jason a wide-eyed panicked look behind Calliope while he marveled at the fact there was someone even more bubbly than Abby. But he wouldn't call Abby eccentric. Not when the dictionary definition was currently leading the way around the back of her fairy cottage of a house.

"Tell me something, Jason," Calliope said.

"If I can."

Calliope tightened her hold on him. "That competition you were a part of. The one where you tried to pass off your assistant's dish in place of your own. I'd like to know——"

"Calliope!" Abby turned furious eyes on her. "That's none of your business."

Jason couldn't speak. Not because of Calliope's question. It was refreshing someone came right out and asked him about it. But no one had ever defended him so vehemently before, especially not to one of their friends.

"I haven't asked my question yet," Calliope said as if she didn't get the message. She turned her full attention to Jason, who was trying not to kick himself for thinking his past would stay in the past.

"Go ahead," he said in what he hoped wasn't too hostile a voice. "Ask."

"What was it you fixed that day? Because honestly, I thought it looked far superior to that slop your assistant made."

Jason blinked. "Ah." What was it with the women in this town short-circuiting his brain? "Roasted lamb with a rosemary butter and peppercorn sauce. But it was the popovers that had me worried."

"That was your mistake." Calliope smiled warmly at him. "You didn't have faith in yourself. Lost your way, didn't you? Before that show and since."

Jason had to stop walking so he could process what Calliope was saying. "I wanted to win."

"Pah!" Calliope got them moving again, the beads in her hair clacking against each other like dull wind chimes. "Didn't have anything to do with winning and everything to do with losing who you are. You, sir, are a master at what you do. An artist. You've lost your light. Bet this one will help you find it again, right, Abby?"

"Sometimes you give me a headache, Calliope." Abby looked as shell-shocked as he felt. "He wanted a tour of your garden, not a psych evaluation."

"Oh, the eval is a bonus," Calliope said. "But the garden." She pushed open a small wooden gate and led them inside. "That's my pride and joy."

If Calliope Jones was a surprise, her garden could qualify as another wonder of the world. "This is—" His breath left him as he pulled free of his guide and wandered down the narrow path. He moved past billowing bushels of kale and green leaf lettuces and went into the fragrant, elegant-patterned herb garden that not so long ago he would have killed to have had at his disposal.

The extensive acreage behind her house was completely encompassed by every color of the rainbow, and as he took an inventory, provided every possible offering a yard in this part of the state could offer. It was all he could do not to drop to his knees and dive his hands into the rich soil. "Are those beehives?" He couldn't decide which direction to head in first, but found himself entranced by the seven, no, ten white hives buzzing with activity. "You make your own honey?"

"Of course. Allergies." Calliope grinned and stepped out of the way of a chicken pecking toward its elaborate cage. "Family's been cursed by them. Mom and Stella especially. And the bees have done wonders for my vegetables. So does this pass your inspection?"

"Pass?" Jason bent down and snapped a plump green bean off the climbing stalk of a trellis nearby and broke it apart, popping one half in his mouth. "Calliope, I've been to some of the finest gardens in France and every market in New York and Chicago, and I can tell you, I'd use your garden in a heartbeat over theirs. This is incredible."

"Calliope's always had a way with nature," Abby agreed as she snagged a handful of mini tomatoes and devoured them like candy. "Milk thistle, especially."

"For the butterflies," Calliope explained as she wandered in the other direction, lifting her hands out in front of her.

"She's like their dealer." Abby laughed.

Jason stared as a flock of butterflies swirled around Calliope, topping her hair and dancing across her arms and fingers as if they were coming home.

"Calliope, Mama needs her tea and we're out of mint."

"You know where it is, poppet," Calliope called to the young girl who raced around the corner into the garden, her paisley dress whipping around her knees.

Jason looked from Calliope to the girl, who, as far as he could tell, was a carbon copy of Abby's friend. Bright red hair, open, freckle-faced smile and the same radiant, unaffected glow.

"Hi, Abby!"

"Stella. I haven't seen you in ages." Abby gave the girl a quick hug and dipped down to meet her eye to eye. "You have to stop growing so fast or you're going to be taller than your big sister."

"Mama says I'm Calliope's mini me."

"Let's hope in that Mama is wrong." Calliope relinquished whatever effect she had over the butterflies and strode to Jason's side. "I'm glad you like the garden."

"I'd take you back with me to New York if I thought you'd go." Jason felt a pang in his chest. He'd gotten so caught up working with Abby these last few days, he'd barely thought of the city and the possibility of returning home. "I tried to start a rooftop garden at the restaurant after my brother died, like a memorial? All I managed were weeds."

"Your heart has to be in something to make things flourish." Calliope cast him an eerie, knowing look. "You'd be surprised what the right attitude will bring you."

"Any time you'd like to leave my head alone would be great." As unnerving as her statements were, he couldn't find any anger toward her.

"I say what I see. No filter, my mama says. I'm hoping Stella will have a bit more tact when it comes to interacting with people. Careful, Stell," she told her sister over her shoulder without looking. "Don't bruise the leaves too much."

"I know, I know." Stella rolled her eyes.

"Ten-year-olds think they know everything," Calliope said.

"Who's to say they don't?"

"Well, now." She nodded slowly and tucked a thick red curl behind her ear. "I'll have to take that into consideration for the future. Let me get you a basket." She ducked inside a whitewashed shed and retrieved a large woven basket that she pushed into his hands. "You and Abby fill it to your hearts' content. A welcome gift. You should fix that girl a special meal. Maybe pick up one of those knives yourself and remember what made you fall in love in the first place."

"With cooking?"

Calliope smiled and twirled away, a tiny daisy clasped in her fingers. "With whatever."

ABBY STEPPED OFF the elevator on the third floor of Southern Memorial Hospital the next day, the small potted African violet she'd bought at Calliope's farm in one hand, a small container of chocolate chip cookies she'd triumphed over in the other.

She and Jason had spent the rest of yesterday afternoon and most of the evening in the kitchen, getting her up to speed on properly cooking chicken and fish, which resulted in something resembling dinner. She'd done pretty well with the chicken, but when it came to cleaning and gutting the fish, she'd almost reverted to her first lesson with her head in the sink.

With the excitement about the festival picking up steam around town, she'd been inundated with calls of encouragement and offers of support and more than a few orders for her to show them what Butterfly Harbor's best could do. Since she'd talked herself into this crazy plan she was finally beginning to think she had a decent shot at winning.

Room 316 had been cordoned off by privacy curtains. She opened her mouth to call out to Mr. Vartebetium, but stopped when the elderly man's voice sounded first.

"Gil, I told you, I'm not ready to talk about selling the Flutterby yet."

Abby froze. Selling the Flutterby?

"Mr. V, surely you have to see the practical points of selling." The familiar, condescending voice of Gil Hamilton told her the mayor wasn't thrilled with Mr. V's response. "I've spoken to the bank holding the mortgage."

"My business isn't any of yours!" Mr. V blasted with such vehemence Abby considered intervening, but she resisted. "I don't care that your daddy owned that bank or not. You've got no right."

"Your privacy issues aside, I need to be kept informed when one of this town's landmarks is in danger of closing. They're considering foreclosure proceedings and we both know those property taxes you owe aren't going to disappear anytime soon. Besides, shouldn't you be retiring?"

"The Flutterby isn't some willy-nilly job, young man," Mr. V said, and the spark of life in his voice gave Abby a bit of hope. "The Flutterby Inn's been part of my life since long before you were born. I'm not about to walk away from it on your say-so. Besides, Abby is aware of everything, and from what I hear, she's got plans."

Abby's face flushed. Word really had gotten around town if Mr. V had heard about it even while he was in the cardiac ward.

"We both know Abby doesn't have a prayer of winning that competition," Gil said.

Abby's heart stuttered. So much for having the mayor's support.

"At least two of her competitors have won other contests," Gil continued. "Abby's barely got boiling water down."

Abby's confidence took a nosedive. Which

cooks? Which contests? She wanted to ask but thought of Jason and his insistence such knowledge would be cheating.

"I realize how much the Flutterby Inn means to both you and the town," Gil said. "But I wanted you to be aware of your options. I've been in touch with a friend of mine at Clover Hotels and they're seriously considering making an offer. A substantial offer, Mr. V, one that could set you up for the rest of your life."

"And how long might that be?" Mr. V snapped. The curtain shifted and Abby saw Gil's feet move in her direction. She darted to the side. "I'm eighty-two years old and on my third heart attack. What do you think I'm going to use the money for? Skydiving lessons?"

"Mr. V, this is a serious conversation," Gil said and she heard the rustling of papers. "I've got some information here for you to look at…"

"I'm not selling out to some big chain that doesn't understand the concept of personal service," Mr. V told him. Abby smiled, relief sinking through her. "And you best not be taking any kickbacks from these businesses you've been pushing on Butterfly Harbor, or else we'll be holding another special election to rid ourselves of the Hamiltons once and for all."

Pride swelled in Abby's chest. Good old Mr. V. He was on her side. He was willing to fight for the Flutterby after all.

"At least look at what they've done with other businesses throughout the state." The resignation in Gil's voice told her he wasn't completely immune to criticism. "There's no harm in getting an idea."

"There's harm in giving up, and I'm not doing that. Not yet. Now you get your big ideas and your big head out of my room, Mr. Mayor. Before I sic my nurses on you and have them poke you with one of their needles."

There was a long moment of silence. "I'll just leave these here."

Abby dashed to the doorway and made as if she were entering as Gil stepped out from behind the curtain.

"Oh, hi, Gil." She kept her voice as sweet as possible and nearly gave herself a cavity. "Nice of you to visit Mr. V. All ready for the festival?"

"Nine a.m. next Thursday," Gil said, looking a little green around the edges. "Good luck with the contest. We're all pulling for you."

"So I hear. Sounds like my competition is going to be pretty stiff. Hope I can get that water-boiling technique locked down." She didn't regret her words as comprehension slid over his face. "Your voice carries, Mr. Mayor. You should work on that. Mr. V, I brought you some presents."

She stepped around Gil, part of her bidding a silent farewell to the boy she'd known growing up. All these years she'd given him the benefit of the doubt because they'd been his father's misdeeds, but there was a time to outgrow your circumstances. Something it seemed Butterfly Harbor's mayor didn't have any intention of doing.

Abby poked her head into the room and tried not to gasp when she saw Mr. V reach for the manila folder beside his bed.

Mr. V made to look as if he were trying to sit up straighter, but with the way he avoided her gaze, they both knew the truth.

"Wasn't expecting you today, missy." Mr. V patted the significant space beside him on the bed. He didn't take up much room these days, but despite his frail appearance, there was still steel in those gray eyes of his. His hair might have thinned in the nearly thirty years she'd known him, his body might be stooped, but he'd always be the kind innkeeper who used to sneak her lollipops when Gran wasn't looking.

"Gran's in physical therapy." She lowered herself onto the thin mattress. She'd been grateful for the day off and she thought Jason was, as well, as he'd headed out for Monterey before breakfast this morning. "I thought I'd make the best use of my waiting time. This is for you."

"Isn't that pretty." He held out his hand for the flowers as she passed the pot to him. "This must have come from Calliope Jones. No one grows blooms like that woman." He flicked a crooked finger against the delicate petals. "And what's that?" He angled a look at the plastic container in her other hand.

"Practice cookies," she said. "I've been taking cooking lessons. But I'm guessing you heard about that."

"Been hearing a lot of things lately, despite my bad hearing," Mr. V attempted to joke, but as he pulled off the lid, he cringed. "How much did you hear?"

"Enough to know Mayor Hamilton probably won't be leading my cheering section." She couldn't resist temptation. She picked up the envelope. "May I?"

"I don't want you frettin' just yet," Mr. V

said as he chose a cookie and examined it. "You make these?"

"I did." It had taken three tries to get them right. She'd kept getting distracted, first by the news the NCN crew would be arriving sooner than expected, then by an overflowing toilet in room 105. Fortunately she'd already blocked off that room because of the faulty air that made a ruckus whenever it was switched on, but Matt was waiting on parts for the final fix. "Feeling dangerous?" she teased her boss.

"A bit. It's not on my approved food list." He peered around Abby before nibbling on the edge of the cookie. "Abby." He took a bigger bite. "My goodness. These taste like my Maisy's. Hard to believe she's been gone eight years." Tears flooded his eyes. "What a gift. Thank you." He closed the container but held the solitary cookie in his hand as if it were gold.

"I found her recipe in one of Matilda's cookbooks. I looked at the accounts," she added before she lost her nerve. "I understand how bad things are."

"I can only imagine how disappointed you are in me." He seemed to shrink into himself. "You and I both know the Flutterby was

Maisy's dream. When she died, my heart went with her. I've lost any fight I had for the place."

Just like Jason losing his brother. Like Gran without Gramps. Each of them had lost their rudder. "I wish you'd told me sooner. I might have been able to do something." That's what bothered her most. The lost time, the lost potential. Maybe it was her fault. She should have been paying closer attention.

"Abby, to be honest, you and your grandmother are the only reason why I've kept things going this long. I owed it to both of you and your grandfather. I promised him you two would always have a home at the inn, but I've been thinking about selling for a while."

"But you told Gil—"

"You think I'd let that son of a reprobate dictate who I'd sell to? I'm not about to put any more money into the pockets of those Hamiltons, and mark my words, there are a lot of others in town who feel the same. No." He patted Abby's hand and tugged the envelope out of her fingers. "Whatever this offer is, it wouldn't be good enough for me to accept."

"But it could give you bargaining power for whoever does offer to buy the Flutterby." He might be old, but he was still as cagey as ever. In his position, she might do the same thing. Except she wasn't in his position. Hers was even more impossible. "Has an offer been made?"

"It has. I haven't accepted. But the time's coming. They want an answer by the first of the month."

"Not yet." She breathed a sigh of relief. Three weeks, though. She wasn't sure what she hated more, the tears that clogged her throat or the calendar for moving so fast. "Were you ever going to tell me?"

"When the time was right. Abby, I've handled this badly and I owe you and your grandmother so much, but the time has come."

"No. No, it hasn't, Mr. V. Not yet. Despite what Gil said, I really do think I can win this competition. And the money would be enough to get the tax people off your back. Would that be enough to change your mind?"

Mr. V shook his head. "There's so much more to it than that. You're a smart girl. You must see that."

"I do." And it was keeping her up nights. "But it's Gran's only home. It's been my only home and it's Butterfly Harbor's crowning glory. You have to see selling it to some big corporation, or even a small one, would change it forever. Please let me try."

"You always have been its biggest cheerleader." Mr. V patted her hand again. "I can't promise anything, Abby. Not with my health the way it is and no heirs to speak of. Anything happens to me, the state's going to get its hands on it, and that would be a real tragedy."

"Can you give me those three weeks?" Maybe she'd missed something. If she didn't win the competition, maybe she could take out a loan...except she had no collateral. All she had was the Flutterby Inn, and even that wasn't hers. This first step had to be enough to kick things in the right direction. "Please let me see what I can do. At least until the festival plays out. Who knows? I might just win after all."

Mr. V ducked his head and looked at the cookie still in his hand. "You've always done whatever you set your mind to doing. Ever since you were little. And you've never once wavered in your loyalty to me or the inn. I'll give you your three weeks."

Abby let out a sharp breath and nodded. "Thank you."

"But that's all. The old girl doesn't have much fight left in her. Neither do I."

"That's okay." Abby got to her feet and hefted her purse over her shoulder. "I have enough for all of us."

"IT'LL BE NICE to have a full house again," Alice said as Abby helped her up the porch stairs of the Flutterby. "All those people. All those stories."

"I'm sorry I haven't been around for you very much." She held onto Alice's hand tighter than normal. "I hope you don't think I'm ignoring you."

"You've been in the kitchen with that good-looking chef of yours." Alice grabbed hold of the porch post and pulled herself up the final step. "There are worse ways to spend your days."

"Gran." Abby chuckled. "Don't get any ideas in your head."

"Too late. Handsome son of a gun. Not nearly as good-looking as your grandfather was, but to each her own."

"He's a friend, that's all."

"Friends make the best lovers."

Abby's face went hot. If Jason wondered where she came up with stuff, exhibit A wobbled her way inside the Flutterby.

"Don't you go worrying about me, Abby girl. Eloise and I are meeting with the Cocoon Club this afternoon—"

"Are you sure you're up to it?" Abby pushed

open the door and let Alice in ahead of her. "You're usually tired after physical therapy."

"Nothing a nap won't fix. And make up your mind, young lady. Either you want me to get out more or you don't. Don't go changing your mind on me. I get confused enough these days."

"Yes, ma'am. I did fix you some lunch before we left. It's waiting for you in the kitchen."

"I was wondering when I'd see evidence of these so-called cooking lessons of yours," Alice teased. "Wasn't sure if it was that or if you were up to some hanky-panky."

"Gran, you know me better than that." As if she had any time for hanky-panky. Then again, Jason did manage to turn her thoughts to...

Alice smiled. "Yes, I do. And I believe some hanky-panky would do you and that chef of yours some good. At least give me some peace of mind and tell me he's a good kisser."

"Gran, enough."

"Ha! I knew it." Alice patted her cheek and gave her a look of such tenderness, Abby's heart twisted. "That's my girl. It's time you broke a heart or two. Life's not meant to be lived working, Abby. It's meant to be lived, period."

Who needed the little green guy when she had Gran around?

As Gran tottered slowly toward the kitchen, the screech of brakes and car doors slamming had Abby turning to the window. "Lori, you ready? Looks like the NCN crew is here even earlier than they said."

"Their rooms are good to go." Lori stood up behind the desk and smoothed the front of her striped dress. "Bonnie and Judy got everything in order and Matt did a quick run-through to check all the pipes, fixtures and air units."

While Lori had overseen a thorough cleaning of the halls and floors. What would she do without them?

"Remember, whatever the guests want, they get. We need them happy."

"Understood."

Apprehension pinged in Abby's stomach. They didn't know it, but their new arrivals had become make-or-break guests. Her conversation with Mr. V had lit a fire under her renewed determination to save the Flutterby. Independence was vital to her grandmother's well-being. Take that away and she'd decline at warp speed.

That meant grabbing hold of every opportunity that came flying at her in the next three weeks. She'd save the Flutterby if it was the last thing she did.

She pushed open both doors and welcomed her guests with a professional smile. "Hello and welcome to the Flutterby Inn."

"Miss Manning?" The middle-aged man with bright white teeth strode up the stairs and held out his hand. Was that a smile or a sneer on his wrinkle-free face? "Roger Evans. Assistant VP of programming with the National Cooking Channel. Pleasure to meet our first contestant." His handshake felt like a floppy fish, limp and cold. She really needed to stop hanging out in the kitchen so much. Everything was becoming about food.

"Nice to meet you." She counted five, no, six additional guests coming in the front door. "We have your rooms all ready for you. We'll take care of registration and keys and you can start enjoying Butterfly Harbor. We have your dinner vouchers for the Butterfly Diner set aside—"

Roger stopped short. "I'm sorry, our what?"

Yep, definitely a sneer.

"I was told our accommodations included breakfast and dinner here at the hotel." Roger Evans's face contorted as he yelled, "Emily!"

The young woman standing almost directly behind him cringed, tucking her thin brown hair behind small ears as she cleared her throat. "Ah, yes, sir." She tapped open her tablet and said, "I was certain I told you that the Flutterby's dining room was closed until further notice. Yes, here it is." She showed him the registration confirmation. "We were notified ahead of time." She cast Abby an apologetic glance.

"And I told you if this was the case to make other arrangements. I pay for the convenience of in-house dining. If that's not possible, perhaps we need to look at alternative accommodations outside Butterfly Harbor."

"There's no need for that," Abby said as Gran emerged with the sandwich and salad Abby had fixed for her earlier that day. "I'm sure we can come to some agreement—"

"Our guests have arrived." Alice's face lit up as she set her plate down on the counter and approached the group. "Alice Manning. Former manager and grandmother to this charming young lady." Her right foot shuffled slightly as she moved toward Abby and Mr. Evans.

"Roger Evans." The politeness returned, but only barely. "And the rest of my staff from the National Cooking Network. We were informed the kitchen was closed."

"Oh, no. Well, yes, I mean it has been." Alice glanced down at her plate. "Our cook is out of town for a charity event, but Abby's hired—"

"Excellent, problem solved. All the better."

Abby felt the color drain from her face. "I'm sorry?" she squeaked. "How, exactly?"

"Your grandmother just said you've hired someone to fill in. We don't expect much, only what your website promised."

"But—" Abby couldn't stop her mouth from dropping open. His reservations hadn't promised the dining room. If anything, they'd warned...

"Emily, it appears as if we'll be checking in after all." Roger smirked in Abby's direction as all the color that had flooded her face over the past few minutes drained away. "I look forward to seeing what one of our contestants is capable of in her own kitchen. Miss Manning, is there someone who can take care of our bags?"

"Yes, of course." How could so few people have so many bags? She couldn't recall the last guest who had requested bag delivery, but, as she'd told Lori, whatever they wanted. "Lori,

would you mind getting everyone checked in
for me? I need to make sure the kitchen is
ready for dinner service."

"Would you like me to call—" Lori started
as she frowned past Roger Evans.

"No, that's okay." Abby's head went light
as she steadied herself. Dinner. For... She
counted the number of people again. Oh, who
was she kidding? But she'd have to figure
something out. If she had to send Holly and
Paige an SOS for takeout, so be it. "I'm good."
She slid a sympathetic smile to the relieved-
looking Emily. The poor little thing seemed
as if she could use a good meal, something
she wasn't likely to get from Abby. "Ah, dinner service is at seven." She fell into her usual
Matilda-inspired spiel. "We'll open the dining room for wine and appetizers at six thirty.
Any questions or concerns, please let us know.
Gran?" She watched her grandmother retrieve
her lunch and, with a surly expression aimed
directly at Roger Evans, Alice sat in one of the
chairs by the window overlooking Gramps's
bench.

"Eloise is picking me up in an hour," Alice
said. "I'll poke my head in before we leave."

"Great." Anything they wanted, she'd told
Lori. Time to do whatever it took, she told her-

self. Abby checked her watch. Three hours.
Should be plenty of time. The question was,
to do what?

CHAPTER TEN

Jason pulled his rental into one of the few remaining spaces in front of the Flutterby Inn and stared at his past. The oversize white panel van with a satellite welded to its roof was an upgrade from the last one his former producer had used. The custom hubcaps and silver striping along the sides were a dead giveaway Roger Evans had arrived, probably driving in from San Francisco, where NCN had a satellite office. Early. As usual.

There wasn't anything Roger Evans liked more than keeping people on edge. Especially in front of the camera. Last-minute script changes, missing implements, even replacing ingredients on a whim or creating conflict between on-screen personalities made for good TV, he'd told Jason and David multiple times.

David had been able to roll with the punches. Jason had just wanted to punch Roger.

He grabbed the gift bags containing the presents he'd picked up in Monterey that afternoon and imagined the look on Abby's face when she saw the monogrammed chef's jacket for her to use during the competition. A graduation present, he told himself. Nothing more. She'd been working hard and deserved it, and, okay, maybe she needed a confidence boost. She might have become more comfortable in the kitchen, but he wasn't convinced her mind-set was where it needed to be to win. Every little bit would help. But to be safe and to make certain there was no mistake as to his motivation, he'd tempered the gesture with small tokens for both Alice and Lori.

He thought a day away would help clear his mind. Leaving behind the kitchen, the reminders, all those thoughts Calliope had managed to plant in his head. Whether he needed it or not didn't seem to matter, not when his mind wouldn't stop spinning around all the ways he could incorporate those beautiful ingredients into various dishes.

He imagined a grilled summer vegetable salad topped with balsamic and a sprinkling of goat or feta cheese. A chilled sangria spiked with apples and oranges. Berry-vanilla short-cake and orange liqueur whipped cream.

He clenched his hands around the steering wheel.

How many endless hours had he and David spent tweaking and finalizing seasonal menus to make the most of whatever was available to them? It didn't seem to matter David wasn't helping him this time. His brain was perfectly content to take over the task all on its own, despite Jason's determination to resist.

Before coming to Butterfly Harbor, he hadn't had any intention of returning to the kitchen. He didn't want to be reminded of the life he'd walked away from. The life he didn't see as possible without his brother by his side.

But now…

Maybe Abby was right. Maybe something *different* was possible.

Abby with her radiant smile and teasing eyes. Abby and her verbal battles interwoven with a language all her own.

Abby and her desire to do whatever it took to protect her family and her livelihood.

He'd missed her. Not having her with him today felt strange, as if he'd left something behind. Except all he had to do to find it again was return to the Flutterby.

Between dodging Gary's increasingly pleading phone calls, the festival and now Roger Evans's arrival, how many more hints did Jason need to finally stop running and move forward?

He dismissed the inclination to sneak inside and avoid the crew. It wasn't as if he had anything left to lose by having to deal with them. Besides, avoiding them would only make his connection to Abby and the Flutterby all the more suspicious. Not that he planned to do much socializing outside the inn once the festival started. If anything, he was hoarding a stash of crime novels to dive into so he could avoid it altogether except when it came to Abby's competition.

He'd promised to be there for her.

Time to step out of his comfort zone.

Familiar faces swam past him as he headed inside. Fragments of names of those he knew tried to grab hold as they worshipped the coffee cups in their hands, marveled at the view and coughed the fresh air. All this time, all these months, and they'd stuck it out working for Roger. Brave souls. It wasn't until he got inside without having been acknowledged that he realized he wasn't being ignored; they hadn't recognized him with his short hair and beard.

Emily—he thought that's what her name was, a petite dark-haired girl who couldn't look more stressed—sat chatting with Alice while Abby's grandmother held her purse in her lap.

"Hello, Alice." Jason bent down beside her and touched her arm. "How did your PT appointment go this afternoon?"

"Oh, Jason." Alice beamed at him, breaking into a chuckle as she touched his hand. "I'm waiting for Eloise to pick me up. It's nice of you to ask. It went fine, dear. Although between you and me, I'm not sure I need them."

"You let Abby and your doctors decide that, okay?" He offered Emily a smile and when she blinked, he could see her begin to reason things out. "I bought you something."

"A present?" Alice gasped as Jason handed her one of the bags. "Oh." She pulled out the filmy scarf and held it against her wrinkled cheek. "It's lovely, Jason. And it's my color." She tucked it around her neck and shone. "Bob loved for me to wear color."

"Your Bob was a smart man." Jason heard the muted conversations begin to wane. "It's as perfect for you, as I thought. Have a good time with Eloise, okay?"

"Jason?" Emily asked in her soft tone. "Jason Corwin?" She shifted forward in her chair and held out her hand. "I'm E—"

"Emily, yes, I remember. Nice to see you again." She couldn't have looked more surprised if he'd jumped out of a birthday cake. "Is Roger still keeping you hopping?"

"Faster than a jackrabbit." Emily's Texas twang came out. "It's good to see you, too. Ah, are you here for the festival?"

"I hear it's sure to be a great event." He avoided the question.

"We hope so." Emily didn't sound convinced. "You know Roger. He's all about the drama."

"And where he doesn't find it, he'll make it up. Speaking of." He rose to his full height. "I'd best say hello. I'll talk to you later. Alice, don't go breaking any hearts tonight in that club of yours."

"Go on with you." Alice laughed, but he enjoyed the tint of pink in her cheeks that reminded him of her granddaughter.

"Good afternoon, Lori." Sidling up beside Roger, Jason leaned a casual arm on the registration desk and mentally counted down the seconds until Roger paid attention to the world around him. "Can I get my room key?"

"Of course, Jason." Lori looked grateful for the break as Roger scribbled his name on the registration printout. "Did you have a good day?"

"Quiet," he replied without going so far as

to admit to being lonely. "This is for you. A thank-you for your hospitality the last few days."

She grasped the bag in both hands. "That's so nice of you. Give me just a moment and—"

"If you don't mind, she's helping me—" Roger glanced at him. Jason watched recognition take hold and Roger's attitude shift. Slightly. "Jason? Well, this is certainly a surprise."

"For both of us," Jason lied. Seeing Roger again in his painfully familiar chinos and polo shirt reminded Jason of how he'd always compared him to a weasel with his beady dark eyes and shifty personality: charisma when it worked to his advantage, temper and bluster when it didn't. Not the best for forging relationships, but more than adequate for producing ratings.

Unless one of his star talents got busted for cheating.

Maybe Jason had found a silver lining after all.

"Probably more for you. Not sure if you heard, but I was promoted to assistant VP of programming."

"I did. Congratulations." The word scraped

like a razor in his throat. "So this festival coverage idea is your baby, then."

"We're hoping to discover some untapped natural talent now that space on the schedule's opened up."

Jason pretended that wasn't a veiled reference to his current on-hold status.

"You're different, Jason," Roger said, his critical gaze skimming over Jason's short hair and beard. "For a moment there I swore I saw David—"

"New start," Jason interrupted, ignoring the comment he knew was intended to stab. "New look."

"Everyone's been wondering where you've been hiding. It was like you dropped off the face of the earth. And now here you are. What a coincidence."

It was, but not because of Jason's machinations. "Not hiding." Not anymore. "Recharging. This is a good place to do that." He gestured to Alice, who, along with the rest of Roger's employees, had given up any pretense of conversation so they could listen. Everyone always loved a show. Too bad Jason wasn't up to giving them one. "Enjoy your stay." He pocketed his key and moved away.

"Mr. Evans, you're in the Monarch suite,

room 207." Lori slid a key toward Roger. "I'll bring your bags up as soon as I get the rest of your party checked in."

"Thank you."

Jason glared at Roger's back as he headed toward the stairs. He slipped into kitchen commando mode so easily, his heart thudded heavy against his chest. To the remaining group he said, "Anyone who's incapable of carrying their own bags, please feel free to leave them here so *I* can deliver them later."

Murmured apologies and cringes of regret accompanied the reclaiming of bags.

"You didn't have to do that," Lori said. But he could hear the gratitude in her voice.

"You do more than enough around here," Jason told her as he realized how often he'd acted like Roger: as if the world owed him something because of what or who he was. He tasted bile in the back of his throat. As if he were better than...everyone.

"But Abby said to give them whatever they—"

"I'm sure she did." Because that's what Abby did. She kept everyone happy no matter what price she had to pay. At least he wasn't held to those same restrictions. "I'm overriding her on this one. Speaking of Abby, where—"

The smoke alarm shrieked from the kitchen.

It took him a second to process the sound before he dropped his chin to his chest and sighed. "Never mind. I know where to find her."

"OH, NO. No, NO, NO." Abby slammed the smoking oven closed, turned the dial to off and grabbed the broom and hoisted herself onto the work counter amid the jumble of bowls and knives, along with half the items from the refrigerator.

She used the broom handle to smack the plastic cover. "Come on. Off. Off, you stupid—" The alarm chirped, screamed, chirped again and fell silent with what to her sounded like an exhausted whine.

In her haste to scramble down, her foot caught a bottle of chardonnay and sent it crashing to the floor. Wine exploded everywhere. Her hands slipped as she tried to grip the edge of the counter and she toppled backward and landed in the midst of wine and shattered glass. "Son of a biscuit—"

"You've made progress." Jason's voice boomed from the doorway as he stared up at the detector. "You didn't kill it completely this time."

"You're back." Abby sagged, partly out of mortification, partly out of relief. Could the man have a worse sense of timing? "I wasn't sure when you would be—"

"Obviously." He swung the door shut and set a purple gift bag on the counter. "What happened?" He headed over to the stove, opened the door and ducked down. "There's nothing in here."

"I know." Only she could make an empty stove smoke. "I was preheating it."

"To five hundred?"

"I guess I wasn't paying attention," she grumbled.

"Abby, this stove is ancient. It needs caution and care, remember? You overloaded it taking one of your shortcuts."

"I didn't have time to think about it." She slapped a hand down on the floor and yelped. Glass shards stuck out of her palm. Tiny beads of blood exploded on her skin. "I have to fix dinner for all those people."

"Why?" Jason left the oven door open, probably to finish airing it out. "The dining room's closed until Matilda—"

"Because that...that *man* out there threatened to take his entire crew to another hotel if he didn't get food service." She plucked the glass out of her palm and winced. "Ow. Even though his reservation clearly stated the dining room wouldn't be available during his stay. I can't afford to lose the business. So."

"Typical," Jason muttered. "Roger managed to find your weak spot and you took another of your flying leaps."

Abby flinched. "I'm on a slow learning curve. What's wrong with me? And what weakness?" Wine seeped through her clothes, straight through to her underwear until she felt as if she'd squish when she moved. She dragged her jean-clad legs in under her and tried to stand, but her feet slipped. "I thought I had all this cooking stuff under control. Then I got in here and panicked."

"You had your lessons under control. I don't recall setting you free to work on your own just yet. Give me your hands."

She shook her head. "I can do it." Except she couldn't. All she managed to do was completely soak the rest of her jeans and butt. She felt like a struggling beached whale. "Okay, fine." She held up her hands.

He moved in and leaned down, locked his hands around her forearms and hauled her up.

"Thanks," she sighed as she flew off the floor before being dumped over his shoulder. "What are you... Jason!"

He carried her out of the kitchen, through the dining room and out the side door to the wraparound porch. Then he set her down.

"Well, that was unnecessary," she grumbled.

"What did I tell you about sandals in the kitchen?" He loomed over her, nudged his foot against hers. Her backside hit the railing.

"That they're dangerous." She bit her lip. "But—"

"There are no *but*s, Abby. It's like everything I've taught you this last week disappeared into the ether. Now tell me what's going on. You've stood up to plenty of people before—why not Roger? What possessed you to think a week's worth of cooking lessons means you can prepare dinner for a dozen or so people?"

"Desperation." She crossed her arms over her chest. "I told you, I couldn't risk losing the business."

"He wouldn't have gone anywhere else," Jason told her. "He needs to be in town to work. Commuting thirty minutes every day isn't an option."

"And how was I supposed to know that?" Her energy drained. "I'm running out of time, Jason. The festival's less than a week away, and if today's any indication, I'm never going to win, and now Mr. V's talking about selling and—"

He moved in as if he were about to throw her over his shoulder again, but instead, he kissed her.

Solid, firm, hard and quick. Or it would have been if she hadn't gripped her fist in the front of his T-shirt and held on. She heard herself whimper in the back of her throat when he placed his hand on her hip, as if making sure she wouldn't try to run.

As if she would. As if she could. Her knees wobbled. Her head spun. And every word poised to flow out of her lips vanished.

"So that's how to shut you up." He stroked a finger down the side of her face before he stepped away. "Now. Back up. What's this about Mr. V selling the inn?"

She grabbed hold of the railing. "You should patent that move. It's like you put the whammy on me." Abby blinked to get her focus back. Except he was still there. Close. Too close. She planted a hand against his chest and shoved him away. There. Better. Somewhat.

"Some big hotel chain's made Mr. V an offer on the inn and they want an answer in three weeks. And they aren't the only ones." She sighed. "When I got to his room, I overheard Gil trying to convince him to sell to another corporate chain interested in the property. But that was before he told Mr. V I didn't have a prayer of winning. Clearly he's onto something, given what just happened." She swiped her stinging hand over her thighs.

"He's not right, he's an idiot." Irritation flashed in Jason's eyes. "Why didn't you call me?"

"Why would I call you?"

"For help, Abby. With dinner."

Was he serious? "Because—" She broke off. It didn't occur to her to lie. "Because you don't work here. And—" She hesitated, then found she didn't have the energy to lie. "Honestly? I didn't think you would."

"You didn't think—" He scrubbed his hands down his face and let out what sounded like a primal growl. "After everything we've gone through the last week, you thought I'd abandon you now? Abby, you're the only reason I'm still here."

Her heart stuttered. "I'm the what?"

"Well, you and the competition." He paced

in front of her. "I'd planned to be long gone before any of *them* showed up." He pointed a finger over his shoulder. "I told you, I don't want this world anymore. I don't belong in it, and in case I didn't mention it before, Roger Evans is one of my least favorite people on the planet."

"Okay." Where was this going? What was he saying? The frustration wafting over and off him fascinated her.

"Given all that," he said, "why else would I be here except for you?"

She wasn't following. "If I had called you it wouldn't have been about the *competition*. It would have been about cooking dinner. For people. In a restaurant. And as helpful as you've been in instructing me, it's not as if you've been whipping up some miracle meals around here. You haven't cooked anything yourself since you got to town. You've barely picked up a knife."

He shoved his clenched fists in his pockets. "That doesn't mean I can't."

"No, it means you won't. And I understand that, Jason, I do. But you can't get upset with me for assuming you wouldn't want any part of the mess I've made. Do you think I don't see how much it hurts you every time you step foot in my kitchen? I don't want that for you, no matter how much I might need your help."

"That's what you think? That I'm not ready to cook again?"

She raised her hands as if to strangle him. "It's like talking to cement! Listen to me, Jason. Of course I think you're ready. But I also think *you* don't think you're ready. You fight it every step of the way. I didn't want to add to your burdens, which is why I dived in." She flung her arm out, pointing toward the kitchen as he stopped pacing and looked at her. "Without thinking things through. As usual. And now everything's screwed up, so unless you've suddenly had some great self-awareness epiphany—"

"Do you want my help, Abby?"

"Yes." But more than anything, she wanted him to be okay. With cooking, she reminded herself. "Yes, I want, I *need* your help. But not because you feel obligated to. Not even because you want to. I want you to start cooking again because you need to. It's who you are, Jason. Doing nothing isn't working for you. But maybe this will."

"You mean you were wrong?"

"Really?" She kicked out a hip and tapped

her fingers against her waist. "That's just rude."

"It might help to hear it. One time, please. Say it. 'I, Abby Manning, was wrong.'"

"Will it put an end to this inane conversation?" Inane, maybe. Enlightening? Definitely. Fun? She almost grinned. Absolutely. "Fine. Yes, I was wrong."

"It's like a magic spell." His handsome face broke into the biggest grin she'd ever seen. "I feel all tingly now."

"I should have made a bigger mess in the kitchen." She would not laugh.

"Messes can be cleaned up. And that's what I'm going to do. I suggest you do the same."

"Of course." Mop duty again. She was getting good at it. He caught her arm when she attempted to pass. "I mean go home and change. I don't need you smelling like wine and..." He moved in closer and sniffed. "Rosemary. What were you doing with rosemary?"

"Experimenting." It had also been the first herb she'd seen in the fridge. "It looks like a tree."

"Interesting. Gives me some ideas."

"You have ideas?" That was fast.

"Abby, I've been having all sorts of them since I met you. And as for you!" he yelled as he leaned over the railing and stared up at the sky. "Is this your version of a cosmic kick? How many signs are you going to send me?"

Abby hesitated before she tracked his gaze. "Who are you talking to?"

"David." Jason shook his head, and for the first time since she'd known him, she didn't see the sadness hovering at the mention of his brother. If anything, he looked at peace. "I'm pretty sure he's been talking to me. I just wasn't ready to hear him before now. I'll meet you in the kitchen. Hurry up. We've got a lot of work to do."

CHAPTER ELEVEN

JASON MIGHT NOT have met Matilda, but something told him if she got a peek at her kitchen right now, she'd walk off the job permanently. Abby hadn't just dived in without thinking, she'd reverted to being a five-year-old who'd thrown a *what can I get into* party. What a mess.

So this was the push he'd needed, was it? Abby and all her craziness had finally forced him out of complacency and back into the world where he belonged.

Only this time, he wasn't in it for success, or fortune, or reviews, or accolades. Abby's business, her home, was at stake, and after a bit of prodding, she'd admitted she needed his help.

That part of himself he'd kept locked away for the last few months stirred to life, and where days before he'd found only fear and trepidation, a fire caught and roared to life.

A fire he continued to stoke as he got down

to work and cleaned up the kitchen so they—
so he—could start over.

By the time she rejoined him, in proper attire, he was putting the mop and broom away.

"What are those?" He leaned his hands on
the counter and stared down at her fluorescent pink feet.

"My chefy shoes. I told you I ordered some.
They arrived last night." She held up her foot
and rotated her ankle. The pseudo-plastic clog-
style shoes were anything but attractive, but he
recognized them from countless supply cata-
logs as being safely protective in the kitchen.
"They're super comfy."

"Looks like you're wearing stuffed ani-
mals."

"Like I'd take fashion advice from a man
who wears a stovepipe on his head." She knot-
ted her ponytail around the rubber band in
her hair.

"It's a chef's hat or a toque, and I don't wear
one." *Anymore.* "That's for you." He pointed
at the bag by the door. "Try it on. I'll be back
in a minute."

The greetings and familiar voices calling
his name as he headed up to his room surprised him. Maybe the NCN employees were
confused. Could be they thought they were

dealing with David after all. Or maybe they figured Jason was no longer an entity to worry about now that he wasn't officially associated with the network. Either way, he took some comfort in the fact no one seemed to be plotting his demise. Once he was in his room he dragged his suitcase out from under the bed. He flipped the case open.

His hand hovered above the rolled cloth bundle. The monogrammed *DC* embroidered in the top corner brought a smile to his face instead of a pang to his chest. He had no doubt he was rusty. He needed all the help he could get. Given David's spiritual participation in the day already, what did Jason have to lose?

He grabbed the bundle and hurried downstairs. "Hey, Lori. Did Abby say what time dinner was being served?"

Lori pushed her nutmeg-highlighted curls out of her face. "Seven. Wine and appetizers at six thirty. Thank you for the bracelet." She held up her wrist and smiled. "It's beautiful."

"You're very welcome." He hadn't realized how satisfying it felt to give people tokens of his appreciation.

"Is everything okay in there?"

"It will be. Full service, Lori. For the guests

and you and the staff. Alice, too, if she's home by then, please."

"Sure thing. Is, ah, Abby cooking?"

"She is. But don't worry." He hefted the bundle. "She won't be on her own."

He found Abby waiting for him in front of the work counter, the coral-colored chef's jacket he'd had personalized clutched against her chest. "You got this for me?"

"Every chef needs one." He tried not to read too much into the gratitude on her face. His growing feelings for Abby were only going to make things more complicated in the long run. Although...

"Thank you," she said almost reverently. "Do you have one?"

"It's at home."

"Then what's that?" She followed him to the counter as he untied the knot and unrolled the bundle. "Wow. These are beautiful." She ran a finger over the hilt of the knife. "Yours?"

"David's." Speaking his name didn't hurt. Much. "Our grandfather gave us each a set when we graduated culinary school."

"Let me guess. You left yours in New York with your jacket."

"These seemed more appropriate." His fingers tingled as he gripped the hilt. "And who knows, I might need more help than I think. Speaking of help. Are you ready for your first go-around as sous chef?"

"Sous…?" She looked as if he'd smacked her with a spatula. "Uh, yes?"

"Give me that." He plucked the jacket out of her hands, spun her around and helped her slip it on. He buttoned her up, tugged on the collar to make sure it wasn't too tight. "Perfect."

"Five-Alarm Manning?" She poked a finger against the raised stitching.

"A badge of honor." Appropriate given her activities this afternoon. "Now, wear it with pride."

"If anyone asks, I'll say I love peppers. A lie, by the way." She stuck out her tongue and gagged. "Hate them."

"Good to know. Ready?" He headed over to the fridge and pulled out the chicken pieces left over from yesterday, then yanked out two more full birds.

"Just tell me what to do."

"Cut these up."

"Ooh, chicken again. Fancy." She wrinkled her nose but grinned. "I could have managed chicken for them."

"What temperature do you cook chicken to?" he asked.

"Till it's done?"

"That's what I thought. Grab a pair of disposable gloves, Abby. This is going to get messy."

"YOU KNOW WHAT this means, don't you?"

"What does what mean?" Abby carried the last stack of plates and glasses in from the now empty dining room and set them in the sink.

How she could smell the still-baking brownies over the intoxicating aroma of roasted lemon chicken was beyond her. Maybe her nose was just grateful to be inhaling something other than smoke fumes for a change.

"It means I'm officially your secret employee."

"Ah. Hmm." Her grin faltered as she listened to the glug-glug of wine being poured. She wasn't sure she liked the idea of a secret anything, let alone an employee. "That conjures up all kinds of ideas, doesn't it?" she tried to joke.

He'd been pinging about the kitchen like an out-of-control pinball in between scribbling notes on a spattered pad of paper he'd kept at his side all evening. She actually felt like part of a team. She found it much easier to follow his instructions now that he was showing her what to do instead of telling her. One thing was for certain: Jason Corwin belonged in a kitchen.

"Now what are you doing?" she asked as he opened a small square door on the side of the stove and pulled out two clean plates. "So that's what that's for."

"The warming oven?" Jason's perplexed look vanished as he filled their plates. "What else would it be? Doesn't Matilda use it?"

"She could. How would I know? I was banished from the kitchen, remember?"

"Something tells me your banishment will soon come to an end. And now, since we're done serving dinner, it's our turn."

"About time!" Her stomach growled in agreement. She tugged at the stiff collar. As much as she loved the gift, she wasn't used to the clinging fabric.

"You can take that off now."

"Great." She hung up the jacket on a hook beside the cleaning closet. When she turned around, she noticed a tired smile on his face. Until tonight, she hadn't realized how depressed and withdrawn he'd been when he first arrived. From the moment he'd held his brother's knife, he fell into what must have been familiar rhythms and he looked more self-confident, more content with each slice, chop and dice.

It didn't matter how many lessons he gave her. She'd never feel that confident in the kitchen.

"Have a seat, Abby." He held out her stool.

"This is nice."

He'd cleared a space on the worktable, setting out cloth napkins and flatware for the two of them, her now-filled wineglass the final touch to the dining area he'd created for them.

"Normally the kitchen staff eats before service, but we had a few kinks to work out this time around."

"What kinks?" She sipped her wine.

"If you didn't notice, I'm not going to tell you. All that's important is that clean plates came back. There's no better evidence of a successful meal."

"Afraid you'd lost your touch?" She covered her mouth as she yawned. "Sorry. It's not even eight thirty and I'm ready for bed." And he looked ready to go out partying. Where did he get the energy to do this night after night in New York?

"Lightweight. Dinner service would just be starting at JD's." He set her filled plate in front of her before returning for his own.

Now she realized what JD's stood for: Jason and David's. Nice. "People eat that late in New York?" How did they stay awake?

"People eat that late in a lot of places. Did I hear Alice singing your praises?"

"Singing *our* praises, actually. I wouldn't be surprised if you're in the will now." Abby's cheeks warmed when she remembered her grandmother's comments about her plans for Abby and Jason's future. "That scarf you gave her is beautiful. Thank you."

"It reminded me of her." Jason picked up his fork and started to eat.

"You don't strike me as the gift-giving type."

"I'm not." He clinked his glass against hers. "Or I haven't been. Looks like you and this town of yours are having all sorts of effects on me."

"It's the butterflies."

"It's something. What's wrong?" He pointed his fork at her plate. "You're not eating."

"I'm analyzing." She took a deep breath and inhaled the aroma of roasted chicken. She rotated her plate, admiring the cooked bird, rice pilaf with tiny slivered almonds and golden raisins, and blanched and sautéed garden vegetables from every angle. The rim of the plate was pristine, as if the food had magically appeared with the wave of his knife. "How do you do that?"

"Do what?" He drank more wine.

"Make everything so pretty. Like a work of art."

"Practice. We eat with our eyes first. If it doesn't look appetizing, chances are it won't be."

"Does it work the other way? Can a pretty plate hide something horrific?"

"No." A slight bitterness tinged his words. "Trust me. Hopefully you won't have to find that out for yourself."

"I don't know. I don't think I can do something like this." Even the manner in which he'd placed the curled slice of lemon on top of the chicken thigh looked stunning, the image as pretty as a painting. "I mean, who would think rosemary could look like anything other than a tree?" She plucked the branch off her plate and set it on the counter.

"When I grill steaks, I set a soaked branch in the coals. Permeates the smoke. It also makes for a great brush for BBQ sauce."

She pinned him with a vacant stare.

"I told you, it takes practice, Abby."

"Well, if you're out of practice, I'm doomed."

She could only hope her future competition wasn't anywhere near his level.

"Lemon chicken was one of my grandfather's go-to meals when he was in a bind," Jason told her as he sliced through a perfectly cooked baby bok choy. "All he needed was a chicken, a few lemons, capers and olive oil and that was it." He tapped a fork against her plate. "Eat. You look ready to fall over."

"That's because I am." But she did as he instructed and cut into the tender thigh. Her mouth exploded as the tart lemon flavor burst against the brininess of the capers. "Oh, wow, is that yummy. You should do this for a living."

"I'll take that under advisement."

"So what's this you've been scribbling?" She stood up on the rungs of the stool and grabbed for the notepad. "Huh." She took another forkful of rice. Could she just dump the entire plate in her mouth? "So this meal isn't a one-off for you? Got plans for tomorrow? Wow. Spanish omelets with crème fraîche, fruit compote, homemade bread and arugula salad. Fancy schmancy. Is this my next lesson?"

"Possibly. You passed sous chef 101 tonight. Good job, by the way." He clinked his glass against hers as she resumed eating. "I'm thinking we continue along these lines until Matilda gets home."

"Matilda," Abby groaned. "How am I going to explain all this to her?"

"Tell her you had a difficult guest and you did what you had to in order to keep his business. She'll understand that, right?"

"In theory," Abby agreed. "And it feels nice that you trust me enough to help you in the kitchen."

"Once you slowed down and paid attention, you did better. And look. The smoke detector slept through the whole thing. Congratulations."

"So being a sous is a promotion, right? It's not just you ordering me around like a new recruit."

"It's not just that, no." He grinned. "But come to think of it, this might be a good time to discuss my salary."

"Pop a girl's bubble, why don't you?" Abby muttered as she swallowed. "We both know I don't have the money—"

He leaned over and kissed her.

His lips were warm and soft and slightly tinged with lemon and before she could explore further he resumed eating.

"What was that for?" Her appetite vanished. Who needed food when a man could kiss like that?

"Payment for dinner."

She pressed her lips together. Finally. A payment plan she could work with.

She stood up and moved closer to him, kissing him in the same brief, tingling way he'd kissed her. Hoping she had the same effect on him that he continued to have on her.

The kitchen door swung open. "Excuse me," a male voice said.

"Mr. Evans." Abby grabbed her napkin and wiped her mouth. Maybe they needed an Employees Only sign on that door. "Is everything all right with your room? How can I help you?"

"It's Roger, please. I wanted to say thank you. To both of you," said Roger once Jason turned on his stool to look at the interloper. "I take it this is what you meant by starting over, Jason. Dinner was delicious. I should have guessed you'd had a hand in it." His gaze flicked between the two of them, and for an instant, Abby worried as to what he was thinking. But when he spoke again, it was with that trademark—albeit forced—smile she'd seen that evening. "I wanted to apologize for my behavior earlier, Abby. It's been a long day and I was out of sorts when we checked in."

"Apology accepted." Had she misjudged him?

"It's good to have you back in the game, Jason. You haven't lost your touch. The Flutterby's lucky to have you as their chef. In case you were wondering, you've been missed."

"Have I?" Jason's tone retained that chilly note she'd heard when he'd first arrived in Butterfly Harbor. "By whom, exactly?"

"By more people than you'd think." Roger held up his hands as if in surrender. "No hard feelings? What's in the past is past. No need to dwell on it. We can move on from here. Maybe start over."

"Is there somewhere you're suggesting we should be moving to, Roger?"

Abby looked between the two men as if watching a Ping-Pong tournament. What had she missed? Jason's hostility seemed a bit over-the-top considering the man was apologizing. Sort of.

"Forward will do. I'm going to leave a copy of your signed entry form at the desk with Lori, Abby. Have a good night, you two. And, um, carry on." He gave them a grin that seemed more like one of his sneers before he backed out of the room, the kitchen door swinging shut behind him.

"That was weird," Abby muttered.

"Very." Jason pulled the brownies out of the oven. "Even for Roger."

"Oh, yes." She leaned over the counter and inhaled. "Wait. Do I smell coffee in these?"

"You're getting good. Coffee intensifies the chocolate flavor."

She hooked a finger to scoop out a taste only to have him slap it away playfully.

"Dinner first. Then dessert. I thought you could leave the brownies out with the decaf for late snackers."

"Great idea." One she wished she'd thought of.

She glanced around the kitchen as her spirits dipped. "Hey, Jason? I have another question."

"Only one? You must be slipping." He pressed a knife through the gooey brownies.

"Who's doing the dishes?"

"Usually it's the sous chef."

"I was afraid you were going to say that." She already couldn't feel her feet, and that was with her new shoes.

"Tell you what." Jason set the knife down

and took a coin out of his pocket. "I'll flip you for it."

"Wait!" She grabbed his hand after the coin was in the air. "I have a better idea." He caught it in his other hand as she let go of him and leaned in. "After dessert, what say I kiss you for it?"

He topped off their glasses. "Now that sounds like a deal."

"WHEN YOU'RE DONE streaming the clarified butter into the blender, go ahead and chop the tarragon," Jason shouted at her over the roar of the mixer Tuesday morning.

Abby fought yet another yawn as Jason finished slicing up softball-sized tomatoes for his amped-up version of eggs Benedict. Tarragon. The mason jar filled with a variety of herbs glared back at her as she tried to remember which one was which. She flipped off the blender and grabbed for the coffee he'd had waiting for her when she'd stumbled into the kitchen an hour ago.

Outside this room he still wasn't the most social of people; it was obvious he preferred the company of food and knives, but even that was changing. He'd made mention of the fact he planned to go to Luke Saxon's poker game tomorrow evening.

Whoever this Jason Corwin was, inhabiting her kitchen, he was a far cry from the man who had stormed into the Flutterby a little over two weeks ago.

And she thought butterflies were magic. He'd even started sharing memories of his brother during their downtimes. She could see him healing with every passing day.

She ran her finger along the ridge of stitching over her heart. A badge of honor, she reminded herself. He believed in her.

If only she believed in herself. She just might, after she met her competitors and the oversight committee later today. She really wanted this entire weekend over with, especially after Roger Evans's casual mention about her signed contract had had her reading through it again last night. She wanted the pressure gone. She wanted to enjoy her job and not worry if everything she'd built her life on was going to crumble under her feet.

She'd meant to read it, but she'd fallen asleep skimming an article on unexpected uses for prepackaged items. Information like that wasn't something Jason would pay much attention to unless he had a secret penchant for logs of cookie dough and pop-open tubes of pizza dough.

She'd give the contract another once-over before the competition.

Maybe it was time to admit what really bothered her. Jason wasn't going to stay forever. How could he, with everything he had in his life? If his last couple of days in her kitchen were any example, he'd be reinvigorated, reclaim the life he swore he didn't want in New York.

Except she had the unnerving suspicion he did want it.

It wasn't in her to ask him to stay, not when her own future was up in the air. But she was willing to keep him for however long he wanted to be here.

For however long she kept hold of the Flutterby.

She blew out a breath. She really needed Matilda; only then would her life shift back on track.

"You didn't have to do a full breakfast this morning," she told him. "We could have picked up some pastries down at Thistlewood Bakery."

"Save the continental breakfasts for when you need them." He spooned more poached eggs out of the simmering water and into a bowl filled with ice. "This morning, you don't."

"Right."

"I'm heading over to Calliope's later this morning if you want to come with me."

"I have that meeting with Roger and the festival organizers."

"Right. Any requests for dinner tonight?"

"Something that won't make my brain explode when you try to explain it to me?"

He set his spoon down and looked at her. "You're nervous."

Nervous? Of course she was nervous. And scared and worried and... "I should start calling you Sherlock."

"Abby, you've got the basics down. All you have to do is stay calm and go step by step. If you don't take one of your shortcuts, you'll be fine."

"And if I need to be better than fine?" *If?* Absolutely she needed to be better than fine. She needed to be perfect. She needed to win.

"I was hoping to avoid this, but obviously it's time to prove to you what I already know."

He finished stacking the English muffins on a baking rack and set them aside while she scooped the chopped tarragon off the cutting board and dumped it into the blender.

One last whiz of the blades and she set the glass container aside. "What's all this?" He'd piled the work surface with ceramic containers, a cookie sheet and a pizza cutter, and topped it all off with a bag of dried cranberries and an orange.

"You." He retrieved the laminated recipe card from Matilda's stash. "Are going to make those cranberry-orange scones your grandmother loves so much."

"Ah." Her heart thudded against her rib cage. She really wasn't in a mental place to give these a second—or was it a fourth?—shot. She wanted to argue, opened her mouth to, but he pinned her with one of those looks of his, the one that dared her to admit weakness.

She would not fold. She would not falter.

She would not surrender to Matilda's scones. He snatched the card out of reach at the last second and gave her a warning look.

"Step by step. Take your time. The oven's already preheated. I'm going to call Calliope and see what she's got available for me for dinner tonight, so you're on your own until I get back."

Translation: *there isn't much damage you can do before then.*

Oh, he of little faith. Except...darn him, he was right.

By the time he returned, she was placing the last cut scone on the cookie sheet. She admired her work.

"Not bad." Jason rested his hands on her shoulders as he leaned over. "I can see little chunks of butter in the dough."

"That's good, right?"

"Very good. See? It's not rocket science after all. You are missing one thing, however." He tapped his finger against the card.

"Oh, cream." She headed over to the refrigerator as Lori entered, her normally relaxed expression tight with worry. "What's wrong?"

"Matilda just called. The motor home broke down. She and Ursula are stuck in Oklahoma for at least a week."

"A week?" Abby stomach dropped. "Are they okay? Why so long?"

"They have to order parts and there's only one mechanic in town." Lori cringed. "Trust me, she's not happy. She said she'll call back later tonight to talk to you. Ursula was trying to negotiate their hotel rate and she had to intervene before blood was shed."

"Sure, okay. Thanks, Lori." Abby pinched the bridge of her nose and sagged against the counter. "A week. Great."

"Can't you fly them home?" Jason asked.

"You couldn't pay Matilda to step foot on a plane." Abby sighed. What a mess. "And Ursula wouldn't leave her motor home behind for the world. The thing is older than I am."

"Were you wanting to get rid of me that much?"

Jason. She squeezed her eyes shut. Why did her solutions always have to come down to Jason Corwin? She couldn't ask him, couldn't expect him to, but there wasn't anyone else she could count on to help keep her head above water. She needed him. The inn needed him. Again. "I can't ask you to do more than you already have."

"You're not asking, I'm offering." He retrieved the bottle of cream she'd pulled out of the fridge and set it in front of her with a pastry brush. "Unless you haven't been happy with the way things are going around here."

"Aside from my gaining five pounds, I think you know the answer to that." He'd been exactly what she'd needed: teacher, confidant, confidence builder. But she couldn't shake the notion she was buying trouble by having him work here. "It's just, with the competition and everything else—"

"You won't be here to oversee things."

No, that wasn't it. But something…

Abby gasped. The contract. The stipulations she'd agreed to when she'd signed up for the competition. She'd said she didn't employ anyone associated with the National Cooking Network. Except. She pressed a hand to her throat as her pulse double-timed. He wasn't an employee of the network anymore, was he?

"What is it?" Jason asked. "What's wrong?"

"N-nothing." It couldn't be wrong. She couldn't be wrong. She also couldn't withdraw from the competition now that she'd started to believe she could win. If she took the chance and told Jason the truth, he could up and quit on her, raising all sorts of questions she didn't have time to answer. She'd promised herself she'd do whatever it took to save the Flutterby, to keep Gran safe and secure. If that meant being less than honest with Jason about these circumstances, so be it. If it turned out she was wrong? Well, it was always easier to ask for forgiveness than permission, wasn't it? She cleared her throat. "I'm not comfortable having you—"

"Work here for free," he interrupted. "I get it."

Abby gnashed her teeth. His misunderstanding wasn't helping the situation. Or was it? "No, that's not it." Maybe she needed to discuss it with him after all. "It's about the contract—"

"Oh, Jason. Great. I figured I'd find you here." Roger pushed through the door, that overbright grin exposing his back molars. "Working as usual."

Abby resisted the urge to growl. Was anyone going to let her finish a sentence?

"And Abby. Excellent. You've saved me a trip." Jason's former producer rapped his knuckles on the counter. "I'm hoping you can do me a favor. Our emcee canceled on us today and I lucked out with a replacement. I'd like to meet with him over dinner at the Flutterby, if you can manage that? The mayor will also be joining us. I hope that won't be a problem."

"Ah, actually—" Abby had to put a stop to this now. She stood up. Jason pushed her back down.

"No problem at all." Jason's tone sounded

more conciliatory than she'd ever heard him use with Roger before. "We'll make sure dinner is charged to your room. Would that be acceptable to you?"

"Of course." The flicker of annoyance on Roger's face told Abby he'd probably expected her to comp the meal. "We'll be here by six forty-five. Can't wait to see what you come up with tonight."

"Why did you tell him it was okay?" Abby asked once Roger left.

"Why wouldn't it be? Those are paying customers, Abby. Trust me, whoever this new emcee is, Roger can afford to spend some cash on him. Finally, I have the means to start paying you back."

"Paying me back for what?" She wasn't sure she liked the sound of this.

"For all this." He held his arms wide. "I never thought working here, in this kitchen, would help me rediscover why I fell in love with cooking. I was wrong. It wasn't only David. It was me. I wanted this."

Anyone who saw him with a knife in his hand could have told him that, but she appreciated him giving her credit. "You don't owe me anything, Jason. Not with everything I've put you through." Not to mention what could happen if word got out she had a ringer in her kitchen. "And I don't feel right having you continue to work without me paying you." There. She'd said it.

"Fine. Where's Matilda's cash pot?"

"What?" Now what was he up to?

He snatched down the tin marked Tea off the top of the bookcase. He pulled out a couple of singles Matilda kept on hand for petty expenses. "See? Now you've paid me. Problem solved. I'm officially an employee."

Abby's stomach did an odd little dance. How was it he'd made things worse? But given Roger's request, she didn't see another solution. Not without explaining more than she wanted to tell him.

"What about food?" She grabbed the tin and dumped the last of the cash out on the counter. "Do we have enough—"

"Let me worry about that."

"I'm not having you cover our costs." She stared him down. Enough was enough. "We might be stretched thin, but we aren't a charity case. Give me a little while and I'll give you a budget. Then you can go off and wheel and deal Calliope."

"An hour. Perfect." He pushed the brush into her hands and aimed her toward her cookie sheet. "Bet you thought I forgot about these. Now get those scones in the oven and let's get to planning."

CHAPTER TWELVE

"No, Gary. For the hundredth time, I'm not coming back to New York." Jason hefted the bag of leftovers and snacks in his arm as he walked to the sheriff's station. He couldn't remember the last time he'd accepted an invitation to something like this. He couldn't remember the last time he'd been given one. "Where did you get that idea?"

"From you," Gary said with more frustration than Jason had heard in his friend's voice in months. "You just said you were cooking again."

"And enjoying it for the first time in forever." Because cooking at the Flutterby was pressure-free. Because he was doing it both for the love of the food and to help Abby. Because he knew David would approve. He could feel his life falling into place. Different. Surprising. Exhilarating. He could even see a future for himself and… Jason frowned. And what, exactly? "Why would I ruin that by coming back to everything that made me so miserable?"

"Because the board of directors wants you to."

Jason stopped. "Say that again?" He stared out between the trees to the ocean beyond and caught a glimpse of the sunset. He hadn't missed one yet.

"You really haven't been keeping up with the company, have you? Hang on. I'm emailing you the minutes of their latest board meeting."

"You can send me a video for all I care, it won't make a difference." Damned if his cell didn't chime announcing the attachment. Gary must have had his finger hovering over Send the entire conversation. "I don't have time for this. I don't belong there anymore. It's toxic." Only now that he saw what else life had to offer him did he realize that. "Except for you, there isn't anyone I can trust." Everyone in his former life was out for themselves, and most of the time it was at his expense. None of them ever considered the greater good apart from profit margins and bank accounts. Now that he was cooking again, he knew he could start over. Either here or somewhere else. But here certainly held more appeal. Here. Where Abby was.

Abby had never lied to him, never used him or deceived him. She was the most honest person he'd ever met. Other than David, no one had ever understood him or even tried to. That Abby did meant more than he could say or ever repay. She'd helped him find himself. Maybe for the first time. She didn't see him as David's twin, or the cook behind the scenes. She saw *him*.

"So you're going to completely surrender and let your father finish off Corwin Brothers once and for all."

"Dad's going to do what Dad's always done and look out for himself." Still, he didn't like the unease that struck when he considered his father's actions would take David's legacy down with him. "I'll read the minutes, okay? But I'm not promising anything." The last thing he wanted was to poison his time with Abby with his father and the past. But a part of him—the part that would never let go of his brother—said, "They really want me back?"

"It's been discussed. The annual meeting is next month. If there's ever a time to make a bid for a takeover, that'll be it. If you don't have the support of the entire board now, you will soon."

It was bad enough Gary had been pushing him to return to the restaurant. Asking him to reclaim his position as chairman was something else entirely. It would be like stepping backward. Wouldn't it? Plus, he'd be leaving something he only now began to realize he wanted.

"There's been a mass exodus from JD's, Jason. Most of the people who worked for you and David are gone. Edward's either driven them out or fired them. He's changed suppliers and the reviews are piling up on the internet. Horrible reviews. Reservations are down over 50 percent and the bills are piling up. If you wait too long, there really won't be anything left to salvage."

Jason stared up at the sky. He didn't want to know this. "Is there anything you can do to stop the hemorrhaging?"

"Not indefinitely. And not alone."

Damn it. They were talking in circles. "I mean until I look into this a little more. Send me whatever you need me to look at. But I'll need some time. A week, maybe two."

"You're only booked at the Flutterby through next week."

"Nothing says I can't extend my reservation. If anything, you don't need to plan my next escape route." He took a deep breath and stared at the town that had welcomed him with open arms. "I'm not going anywhere for a while. So don't get your hopes up, Gary. It'll take a lot more than frustrated board members and the promise of financial Armageddon to get me to come back." It would take a massive shift in agenda and goals.

"Rumor is you might be making a special appearance during that festival down there."

Jason cringed. There it was. "I should have known Roger wouldn't keep his mouth shut."

"I'd be more concerned with what he isn't saying than what he is. Be careful, Jason. He never does anything without an ulterior motive, and I'd hate for you to get caught in the crossfire."

"Don't worry, I've got Roger's number. I'll be in touch soon." He disconnected before he promised something he couldn't deliver on. For now he was only interested in keeping his word to one person: Abby.

"I HAVE TO ADMIT," Luke Saxon said as he folded his cards and got up to fill his plate for a third time, "you know your poker food."

"Mini hoagies and homemade kettle chips seemed appropriate. Ozzy, I'll raise you." Jason tossed a ten chip into the pot and watched the deputy's eyebrow twitch in the tell Jason had identified three hands ago. Odd how comfortable he felt around these friends. Even odder that he remembered how to play poker, let alone read people.

"Anyone else feel a little strange gambling in a sheriff's station?" Deputy Matt Knight, large and burly enough to remind Jason of a tree, glanced around the office as he stretched out his leg, the metal click from his prosthesis echoing in the room.

"I won't tell if you don't." Jake Gordon, former sheriff and Luke's future father-in-law, sneaked Cash a chip under the table. The dog padded around to Jason, plopped his butt down and blinked pleading dark eyes at him.

"Cash, enough." Luke snapped his fingers and pointed to the oversize dog bed in the corner by a state-of-the-art coffeemaker. "Jake, don't encourage him. I don't want him to be a pest."

Jason swore he heard Cash heave a sigh before he did as he was told and settled in to watch the rest of the game.

"Don't say I never brought anything."

Fletcher Bradley, long and lean with more than a hint of irritation on his face, carried a pink bakery box into the station. "Two of Holly's blackberry pies." He set them out on the counter. "As requested."

"It's your own fault for forgetting dessert," Matt ribbed him. "And don't worry. We haven't played any of your hands."

"Did take a couple of your chips, though." Luke leaned back in his chair to look into his office, where Simon and Simon's sidekick, Charlie Cooper, were holed up playing video games. "Kids, pie's here."

"In a second! We're about to level up!" Simon yelled.

"What kind of video game beats pie?" Matt asked. "I'm sorry, but that is one strange kid."

"Careful, that's my almost stepson you're talking about," Luke said with enough pride in his voice that Jason was reminded of what his younger self had missed.

He couldn't imagine hearing his father talk about him with such affection. Or interest. The last thing Edward Corwin had said to Jason was that he was an even bigger disappointment than he could imagine. Simon was one lucky kid. He wouldn't spend his life trying to please a man who had no interest in being his father.

"But yeah, he is." Luke chuckled. "It's one of the reasons I love him."

"Not so strange you aren't thinking of adopting him," Jake said.

"Not so loud," Luke muttered. "We haven't talked to him about it yet. Holly's figuring out how to tell him."

"Why don't you just ask him?" Jason said. The table fell silent. "Sorry. I guess that was my outside voice. I'm clueless when it comes to kids, so ignore me."

"Clueless has a point," Jake said with a nod of approval. "Ozzy, are you going to bet or what? I'm growing roots in this chair waiting on you."

"Yeah, yeah. Call."

Jason shook his head.

"So why don't you ask Simon?" Matt said as the bet came around to him and he folded.

"What, now?" Luke balked, and if Jason wasn't mistaken, lost some of the color in his face. "Holly would kill me."

"Then tell her I did it," Jake said. "Simon! Front and center, please!"

Jason watched the small boy trudge in, his large glasses taking up a good portion of his face. He had on a worn green superhero T-shirt and jeans that sagged in the behind.

"Grandpa," he whined. "You distracted me and now Charlie's winning."

"I was winning before. You just didn't want to admit it." Charlie slid around the table and stopped between Jason and Matt. A tiny little thing in bright pink overalls, her freckled nose wrinkled as she adjusted her ponytail. "I'm Charlie." She held out her hand to Jason, who, after a moment's hesitation, shook it. "You're Mr. Corwin. I heard Mom and Holly talking about you. Look at all those pretty hearts," she said as she peered at his cards. "Are they all supposed to be in order like that?"

"Fold!" Luke called.

"I'm out," Matt sighed.

"Really?" Jake tossed his cards on the table. Ozzy flushed.

Jason stared at the huge pot in front of him, then looked at Charlie.

She grinned and exposed crooked front teeth. "Mom said she hoped they'd let you win a couple of hands. So you'd feel welcome." She held out her arms as if she'd scored a touchdown. "Welcome!"

"Wait." Matt dragged Jason's cards to the table. "You little cheat," he said to Charlie. "He didn't have a thing."

"Now he does." Charlie grinned. "Oh, look

at all the colors." She leaned over the table and dragged the chips toward Jason. "Don't worry. That's enough for now."

Simon didn't look amused.

"That could be the nicest welcome I've ever had. Thank you, Charlie." Jason handed her a chip. "Your tip."

"You're tipping her for bluffing? Now we know you don't have kids." Jake laughed. "Okay, shuffle up and deal. Simon, what would you say if Luke wanted to adopt you?"

The question came out so fast Jason almost got whiplash.

"Like he'd be my real dad? And I could call him Dad?" Simon looked from his grandpa to Luke. "You want to do that?"

"I do," Luke said. He waited a beat. "But I know how much you loved your real father. I'd never want to get in the way of that."

"But he died. He's not here anymore. That would make it okay, wouldn't it?" Simon looked around the table as if searching for an answer.

Jason shifted in his chair, glancing over when Charlie leaned in and rested her hip against his knee.

"I think it sounds great," Charlie said. "Maybe I should ask my mom for a dad."

"Or maybe you shouldn't," Jake said in such a grandfatherly tone, Jason envied the little girl. Simon and Charlie wouldn't have any crises of self-confidence, any doubt they were cared about. People here loved them. Believed in them. The greatest gift any child could be given.

It's what he wanted to give his own kids when he had them. His hands froze on his cards as flitting images of a little boy and girl with bright blond hair and laughing turquoise eyes drifted through his thoughts.

He twirled one of his poker chips on the table. Well, that was something new.

"It's up to you if it's okay, Simon," Luke said. "Your mom is worried you'll be confused."

"About what?"

"Ah—" Luke hedged. "I'm not exactly sure."

"I'm not confused. You want to be my dad and I want you to be my dad." Simon shrugged. "Works for me. Charlie, you wanna play again?"

"Nuh-uh. I want some pie and I think Mr. Corwin needs my help."

"I think you can call me Jason," he told her. "Now that we're a team."

"Okay, cool." As if his statement gave her

permission, she scooted closer and started arranging his chips. "Can I deal?"

"I'm getting the pie," Fletcher said and Jason could tell he was trying not to laugh.

"So, that's a pile of cash to Jason and one son to Luke, and one possible arrest warrant for Charlie Cooper. Anybody going to beat that?" Matt asked.

Cash let out a gentle woof.

"Fine," Luke sighed as if a bit shell-shocked. "Cash wins. Give him some pie."

CHAPTER THIRTEEN

"ABBY, I MEANT IT. I really don't want to go to the opening of the festival."

"It doesn't officially start until tomorrow. This is an afternoon preview." Abby leaned over the pristine work counter in the kitchen and stretched out her arms to him. "Come on, Jason. I don't want to go alone and I have to get the layout of everything before I compete."

"If there's one thing I've learned about Butterfly Harbor, it's that you're never alone. I don't like crowds."

"But you know a lot of people from town now. And they're only going to ask where you are."

"Tell them I'm working."

"We closed the restaurant for tonight, so I'd be lying." She swallowed hard. "I don't like lying." Except when it was necessary.

"Then tell them the truth."

"That you don't want to be a part of a big food festival?" Abby groaned. "Like that's believable when you cook for a living. Cooked," she corrected herself before he could. "You don't really want Roger thinking you're avoiding him, do you?"

"Why would he think that?"

"You must be, otherwise you wouldn't have sent me out to talk to him and the mayor last night." That emcee Roger had been so anxious to bring to the Flutterby had been delayed until tomorrow. "If you're worried about being recognized, relax. You still don't look like you. Well, the old you. Besides—"

"Besides what?"

"Well." Abby stood up and smoothed her shirt down over her jeans. "I kind of already told everyone you'd be there. They've heard I've been cooking, and since the inn is still standing, they want to meet the man responsible."

"So much for you not wanting word getting around I was helping you."

He was teasing—at least she thought he was—but the statement struck a little too close to home.

"Gran's at Eloise's tonight for dinner and I have to make an appearance with the other contestants. Besides, I need you to help me identify some of the food. I'm betting you aren't the only one who cooks escargot."

"I'll take that bet."

"Snob." She grinned at him. Truth be told, she longed for a break, and while she didn't relish the thought of outing her temporary chef, it was time he realized there was a life outside the kitchen. His poker game last night had been a start; she'd heard through the Holly grapevine he'd played an instrumental role in Luke's plans to adopt Simon. Knowing Jason, however, he wouldn't think himself deserving of any credit.

Meanwhile, Abby hadn't caught a whiff of suspicion from Roger Evans, so any impropriety she'd been worried about in regard to Jason's employment status was a waste of energy. Maybe she could finally relax and focus on the competition.

"For once, can't you have some fun without grumbling about it?" This time she grabbed hold of his hands and squeezed. "For me?"

"Don't you think you've used up your personal pleas where I'm concerned?"

"This will be my last one, I promise. Consider today your graduation into proper socialization practices. Besides, you said you'd be there for me for moral support."

"I said I'd be at the competition for moral support."

"Semantics." Her new favorite word. Still holding on, she tugged him around the table and out the door. "And you're already dressed for it."

"Yeah, jeans and T-shirt make for a perfect uniform."

"They do from where I'm standing." She waggled her eyebrows as they headed for the front door. "Lori, you sure you're okay holding down the fort?"

"It's fine." Lori might have sounded grumbly, but the familiar spark lighted her face as she waved them off. "Like I need to be around an entire park filled with food. Thanks to you—" she jabbed a finger at Jason "—I've had to add another thirty-minute walk to my exercise routine. Go, already. I'll make sure Alice gets to Eloise's okay."

"I've got time to kill," Alice said from her usual chair by the window. "How about some gin rummy? I'll keep score."

"You cheat. Hey, Jason?" Lori called. "Take pictures of Abby's entrance to the competitors' tent? I want to add it to the website and give updates as the weekend progresses."

Great. An internet presence. Like she

needed more pressure. "I can't believe how busy we've been," she said as she and Jason headed toward Monarch Lane. "Between all the rooms being booked and the dining room service, the inn's actually bringing in cash." She'd even managed to write a few checks last night and pay some bills. Things were definitely looking up. Kind of.

EVEN FROM A distance she could hear the rumblings of a crowd. A boost of energy kicked her into high gear and she picked up speed.

"Have you talked to Mr. Vartebetium again?" Jason asked.

"Not since I saw him at the hospital. I'm hoping these three weeks—well, less than that now—will be enough to make a difference and hold off the tax collectors. All that aside, I think, finally, I'm ready." She puffed out her chest and let a confident breath escape.

"For the decathlon? Slow down."

"For this competition to be over with!" As if walking faster would make time speed up. "I met the other competitors the other day. Clara Sterling is from Monterey. This is her third competition. She won some home baking thing last year, so I'm guessing she'll be good under pressure." She couldn't seem to stop herself from babbling. "And then there's Steve Sawyer, whose sister runs a small B and B in Pacific Grove. I heard he's good with a BBQ."

"Shoot," he muttered. "The BBQ. I should have given you the basics—"

"Hey, there's Paige and Charlie. Hi!" She waved at them across the street as they stopped on the corner and waved back. The entire length of Monarch Lane was packed with parked cars and people streaming up and down the sidewalk. All manner of signs and banners welcomed festivalgoers and out-of-town guests as the wafting aromas of hot food roasting and grilling, drifted over them.

Abby couldn't remember the last time Butterfly Harbor had been so full of life. And this was only opening day. "I heard Charlie gave you some poker assistance at last night's game."

"How does word get around this place so fast?" Jason asked. "First Holly, now Charlie."

"We have a special communication system. It helps I'm good friends with her mom. Charlie, aren't you looking cute!"

Charlie grinned at them, her cupcake T-shirt in rainbow hues bright as the summer day. "I've been saving this for today. I'm so excited!" She clenched her fists and bounced on her toes. "Mom says there's going to be all kinds of treats and food to try."

"Yes, it's true. I'm raising a child with a very advanced palate," Paige joked as they resumed making their way to the park.

"Mom makes yummy cheese tarts. They're new. I'm her guinea pig," Charlie told Jason. "They have goat in them."

"Sounds tasty." Abby almost gagged.

"She probably means goat cheese," Jason said. "And I'd love to try them some time. I hear today is all about the wine."

"Yuck. Wine." Charlie stuck out her tongue. "Grape juice that stings."

"Don't ask." Paige held up her hands. "Holly's manning the kitchen today so we can explore the festival. You ready for your final instructions, Abby?"

"Can't you tell?" Abby looked down at her clean jeans, perky peach sandals and matching T-shirt.

"You're also shaking like a leaf. Come on. Kick the nerves," Paige ordered. "You've got the whole town behind you."

"Thanks." Abby managed a tight smile. "That helps."

"Once she gets to cooking tomorrow, things

will shake out." Jason wrapped his arm around her shoulders.

"They asked me to give them a list of my least favorite foods. Why would they do that?" Abby asked Jason.

"Even if I knew, I wouldn't tell you."

"Because that would be cheating." She just had to be in love with a guy with an oversize sense of honor.

She tripped, her heart nearly tumbling out of her chest. Jason grabbed hold of her and pulled her up before she face-planted on the cement. "Thanks," she whispered as the afternoon breeze chilled her skin. She looked up at him. In love? With Jason Corwin?

"It's those shoes of yours." His mouth twisted into that disapproving frown that made her smile. "What?" He glanced behind him as if something was happening there. "What's that look for?"

"Yes, Abby? What's that look for?" Paige chimed in.

Abby's face flushed.

"It j-just occurred to me why they asked me what my least favorite appliance to cook with was." She resumed what she hoped was a straight path. Exactly what she needed. Yet another question she had to have an answer for.

"Was oven or stove an option?" Jason teased.

Paige laughed. "I haven't heard of any fires at the Flutterby lately. Has the crisis passed?"

"We'd better hope so, or this will be a very short competition." Oh, boy. Abby swiped a hand across her suddenly moist forehead. Did she have the absolute worst sense of timing or what?

"I think you're going to win, Abby!" Charlie jumped around and walked backward. "So does Simon. In fact, we're going to make sure you do."

Paige and Abby both came to a halt.

"What does that mean?" Paige asked her daughter.

"Nothing." Charlie smiled mischievously. "Oh, there's Simon…and Luke. See you later, Mom!"

"Now I'm terrified." Abby turned wide eyes on Paige. "Tell me you can find out what she's talking about."

"Sure. We both know Charlie's an open book when it comes to her plans with Simon. I'll get back to you." She moved off to join Luke and the kids.

"Okay, I give up. What's the story with those two? They seem to scare the heck out of most every adult I've met in town."

"Let's just say Simon is one comic book away from becoming a mad supervillain." Who knew what fresh ideas that kid had come up with this time? "Really? Darn it." She planted her hands on her hips and stared at the throng of people flooding Skipper Park.

"What's wrong?"

"Oh, only that Gil was right." Her heart swelled with pride and gratitude. "This festival's turning out to be a really good idea. Look at all these people."

"Yes, look at all of them." Jason didn't sound nearly as thrilled as Abby felt. Well, too bad. It was time for him to get social.

She lost count of the number of bright white tents zigzagging through Butterfly Harbor's largest park. She could see the metal beams of a makeshift stage at the far end of the perimeter. She'd heard the committee yesterday discussing the pros and cons of seating before they decided to use hay bales instead of folding chairs.

Picnic tables had been set up and scattered about the park, some under trees for shade, others in the bright sun for added warmth. The weekend forecast was promising one of the nicest temperature runs in a long while, as if Mother Nature herself approved of the festivities.

"Mmm, smell that?" Abby took another deep breath and inhaled the aroma of smokers running on high, the salty brine of boiling seafood and the telltale kick of hops from a family-brewing company. Add that familiar tinge of fresh ocean air as she and Jason pushed their way through the crowd, and she couldn't fathom a more perfect day.

The beer and wine were definitely flowing, the congenial crowds cheering as bottles were opened and everything from bar snacks to gourmet appetizers was served to hungry drinkers.

Music from the band was beating away in the distance and the tinkling of butterfly wind chimes added to the carefree atmosphere.

"Hey, Abby." Jason squeezed her arm. "Don't look now, but you have a fan club." She found the Cocoon members, minus her grandmother and Eloise, heading toward her, wearing bright coral T-shirts with Go Five-Alarm Manning! emblazoned on the front along with her face.

"That's not unnerving at all," she whispered, then smiled when she heard Jason chuckle.

"That makes having come here worth it."

"Benny, Myra, hi!" Abby couldn't help

laughing as the group of elderly Butterfly Harbor residents encircled her. From what she remembered, they traveled in the same pack they had in high school. "And Elliot, Harold, Delilah. Marty! Oscar? Even you're here. What's all this?"

"This is us showing our support!" Delilah, all of five foot nothing with hair taller than her closest friend, puffed out her ample chest and twirled, showing off the one hundred twenty-fifth anniversary banner displayed on her back. "Abby Manning's going to win this for Butterfly Harbor!" Her cheer drew additional cries of support.

"Please, no more pressure." Abby was touched, if not a bit overwhelmed. "There's no guarantee I'll win."

"Of course you'll win," Harold McKreevy stated in his typical former-college-professor tone. All that was missing was a pair of Benjamin Franklin spectacles perched on the tip of his nose. "There's no other choice. Victor's hoping to be discharged in time to see you compete in the final round."

"I thought they were going to move him to a transition facility before releasing him." Why didn't Abby know about this?

"Victor Vartebetium?" Jason muttered

under his breath. "Now who sounds like a supervillain?"

Abby elbowed him in the ribs.

"We've made up dozens of shirts," Marty told her and hefted the large shopping bag in his hands. "We're handing them out to everyone in Butterfly Harbor. We're all behind you, you know. Make us proud."

"Oh." Tears burned her eyes. "You guys are amazing. Thank you."

"Abby, there you are." Gil Hamilton pushed through the crowd, a haggard expression on his face. "NCN would like to take those photos with you and the other contestants. Please. Come with me."

Her stomach jumped as if she'd swallowed a handful of crickets. "Would you guys keep an eye on him for me?" Abby jerked her thumb in Jason's direction.

"Sure will," Oscar said with more than an appraising look in his overprotective gaze. "You'd be this New York chef we've been hearing of. What's this about some scandal you've got back home? Nothing that's going to impact our Abby, is it?"

"No, it's not, Oscar," Abby jumped in as she felt Jason stiffen beside her. "If it wasn't for Jason, I wouldn't be in this competition, period. So behave." She pointed at each of them. "All of you."

"Go on. I'll be fine," Jason said. Abby left them, a little uncertain at first, but then she heard him say, "So, Oscar. I've heard for an amateur at the barbecue, you're quite the Picasso of pork?"

CHAPTER FOURTEEN

"WHERE'S THE OVEN?" Maybe it was the morning sun in her eyes, but as Abby scanned her designated cooking area on the raised stage in Butterfly Harbor's aged baseball field, she didn't see a sign of her nemesis of an appliance.

Pots and pans? Check. Two containers of metal and wood utensils. A mini fridge, two hot plates, a blender, food processor, hand mixer, waffle... "There's no stove or oven."

"Maybe your reputation precedes you." Jason took hold of her hands and pushed them down to her sides to stop her from fidgeting with her collar. She'd left her chef jacket at the Flutterby. There she might be Jason's sous chef, but here, she was all amateur.

Probably the most amateur.

They'd set her up on the far end of the stage, next to the bulky man who was Steve Sawyer. Hefty and friendly, Steve had that green-around-the-edges look of a man who'd spent a little too long at one of the brewery tents. He gave her a weak wave and pushed his sunglasses higher on his nose.

Clara, on the other hand, looked as if she'd stepped out of a 1950s family sitcom. She wore a white-and-pink-checked summer frock— Abby wouldn't deign call that throwback outfit a simple dress—and flipped-up hairstyle. She waved to the crowd and glided across the stage like a former beauty queen. Next to her I-can't-believe-it string of pearls, Abby felt underdressed.

Abby lifted a hand to her throat, the absence of her parents' rings striking fast and sharp. She hadn't realized until this moment how much she could have used the added support.

"You keep doing that." Jason dragged her hand down again, a frown forming. "Why do you—" He seemed to cut himself off as he stared at her.

"Have they introduced the judges yet?" Abby looked around him to where Roger and his crew were putting the cameras and lights into place. "And where's this emcee Roger keeps raving about?"

"Abby, where's your necklace?"

"What necklace? Oh, hey, that's Raymond Benedict, one of the judges. I read about him.

Does he really spearfish his own meals and cook them on the beach?"

"Your parents' rings." Jason spoke slowly. "You showed them to me the first day we met. I don't remember seeing them since."

"They're at home. I didn't want to lose them." Her voice broke.

"Don't do that." Jason's whip-fast order shocked her. "Whatever else you do, don't ever lie to me, Abby. I've had enough of that to last a lifetime. Where are they?"

"I—" She couldn't pull it off. Even if she had the fortitude to try, he was right. She owed him the truth. "They were all I had that was worth anything." Abby tried to shrug it off. "I sold them to pay for the entry fee."

"You sold—"

She hated the sympathy she saw as he put the pieces together. "Please, let's not discuss this now. You told me the only way you'd teach me was if I paid the entry fee. So I paid it. And now look. We're here! Speaking of here. I think the rest of the judges have arrived."

"I don't care about the judges—" Jason started as he glanced in the direction of her gaze. She felt an odd tension in his hands before he released her.

Roger's assistant Emily escorted two more

individuals, both women, to a table near the stairs that led to the stage. On the table were monitors for them to view the contestants up close.

"I'm going to need some help here, Jason." Abby nudged him with her elbow.

"Magdalena Hernandez is the shorter of the two," he said. "Her show focuses on Mexican and South American cuisines. She was nominated for a television award last season. And that's Bobby Palmer."

"That name I know," Abby said.

"She did a series of specials focusing on cooking for the troops overseas, brings a bunch of celebrities over with her to meet those serving. David and I went to cooking school with her before she broke out on her own. You'd like her. She's spunky."

"Spunky." Abby grinned. "I love how your vocabulary's been expanding since you've been here."

"Never really understood its meaning until I met you. And what do you know." The humor faded from Jason's voice faster than it disappeared from his face. "Gary was right. Roger's up to his usual tricks. I'm betting that's our new emcee."

Abby peered beyond Roger to the younger

man coming up behind him. Shorter than Jason, more compact, but definitely in good shape, he had longish blond hair and a dimpled smile that spoke more of Hollywood pretty boy than food show chic. "Who is that?"

"Marcus Aiken."

Abby's stomach stopped jumping. "That's Marcus Aiken? He doesn't look anything like he did from your competition."

Even without touching him, she could feel Jason's tension rise.

"Yeah, sorry. I did watch. But that was a while ago, Jason. Water under the bridge. What happened to him?"

"He's Roger's new poster child for success, I'm betting," Jason muttered. "Hence the makeover. Now it's as if he should be singing lead for a waning boy band."

Abby's ears began to ring. "I don't understand why Roger would have chosen him over you."

"That's because you don't have a devious bone in your body," Jason told her. "Roger, however, could give master classes. Don't worry about it. It'll be fine."

"But that's the guy who exposed you as a cheater. If it hadn't been for him—"

"If it hadn't been for Marcus Aiken blowing

the whistle on me, I'd still be in New York, a miserable, lonely, grieving man." Jason shook his head. Just like that, the irritation she saw on his face vanished. "If anything, I owe him."

"You're not angry?"

"What good is getting angry going to do me?" He took hold of her arms and switched places with her so she couldn't see around him. "Other than playing into Roger's hands? I was as much, if not more, to blame for what happened. You're right, Abby. What's past is past. I'm not letting this get to me, and you're not to let it get to you."

"I don't like either one of them."

"Marcus is okay. He's young. Eager. And maybe a little gullible when it comes to his career. He's also one heck of a talent. I only hire the best." Jason brushed a finger down her cheek.

"Can I at least hate Roger? Maybe slip a vial of bedbugs into his room later today?"

"That would finish the Flutterby once and for all, so no." He pressed his lips to hers. "But I thank you for the offer. Now. I'm going to go sit with your grandmother and Holly and watch you kick these cooks' butts in round one. Don't let anything distract you. Focus on one step at a time. And if you get flustered,

I'll be right over there." He pointed to where Alice was sitting, a wide-brimmed bright yellow hat perched on top of her head, her arm linked with Holly's as they waved at her. Holly shifted to let Eloise join them. "You can't miss us."

Abby took a deep breath as he walked away, a sea of coral-colored Five-Alarm Manning! shirts glowing at her from the stands.

"Abby, before you go." Gil jogged over from where he'd been schmoozing with the judges. "I wanted to wish you good luck. And that I'm sorry if you ever thought I had less than the best intentions for you with this contest."

"Apology accepted." It made her sad, however, that she wasn't sure which Gil offered it: the Gil she'd known growing up or the mayor determined to keep hold of her vote. "Thanks." Whether he meant it or not, she'd take it.

"Contestants, please take your places!" Roger's voice blasted through, of all things, a bullhorn. Abby gave Gil a quick smile and climbed the stairs to her station. She heard cheers and cries of support and some people chanting her name, but instead of the encouragement bolstering her, her head began to swim. Her ears buzzed. Nausea swirled in her stomach as everything she'd tried to learn the last two weeks formed an impossible lump in her brain.

She needed to focus on the items around her, to see what she had available. She caught sight of a flash of color in the front row.

Calliope Jones gave her a nod of support and, after holding her hand in front of her mouth, blew against her palm.

A pair of monarch butterflies flitted in her direction. Abby could almost hear the beat of their wings as they broke against the ocean breeze. As they reached her, the tension in her body eased.

For the Flutterby, they seemed to whisper. *For Gran.*

For Jason.

She stretched out her hand and one of the butterflies perched on her index finger, its tiny legs tickling her skin.

Her mind cleared. Her skin cooled and the second butterfly came to claim its mate and the two of them flew off, leaving a calmness in their wake.

"Now that's the way to start an event in Butterfly Harbor!" Roger shouted into his microphone, facing the main camera. The deafening cheers and cries from the audience unlocked the band of tension around her chest.

Abby breathed easier. She was ready.

"Tell me we got that on tape?" He dropped his mic and looked toward his crew, who gave him a thumbs-up. "Okay, great. Ladies and gentlemen, contestants, judges. Welcome, everyone, to the inaugural By the Bay Food Festival amateur cooking competition!"

Abby applauded with everyone else as Roger recited the disclaimers and how the day's event would proceed. Voice-overs would be added during the editing process before the program aired in six to eight weeks. She tuned out, choosing instead to memorize where everything was. Not the setup she would have organized, but Jason had taught her to be adaptable in the kitchen.

A large cardboard box sat on the edge of the counter to her right, and when she checked the other stations, she saw they had identical ones.

A cameraman passed in front of her as Roger introduced each contestant. Her hometown crowd let their support be known and she couldn't help but laugh at the added shouts and comments coming from the Cocoon Club. Roger continued his intros to polite applause. Abby looked toward Gran and Jason, the latter of whom held up a bottle of water and gestured toward hers.

He was right again. The second she drank the cool liquid she felt better. The way things were going, she would have to get "he was right again" tattooed on her forearm. Okay. She wiped her sweaty palms on her thighs as Roger introduced the judges and then, finally, rattled off Marcus Aiken's bio—without any mention of Jason, thankfully—before announcing the former sous chef as the emcee for the event.

Maybe his being here was a coincidence. Except Jason didn't think so. Which asked the question, why was he?

"Thank you, Roger!" Marcus took the microphone and picked up where the producer left off. He climbed the stairs and stood at the edge of the stage near Abby's station. "Contestants, you'll have ninety minutes to put your own spin on a comfort food classic. The meal must be served hot to our judges, so make sure you time things accordingly. Here's the twist. As you can see, none of you have an oven or stove. This meal must be made only using the kitchen appliances currently at your station. You can use any of the ingredients found in your refrigerators or in the box behind you. When you've completed your meal, please take it down to the table right here in front and we will serve it to your judges. Keep in mind, this round is worth thirty points, five of which will be awarded for presentation, so make those plates as appealing as possible. Clock ready?" Marcus pointed to the large digital clock above the computer screen at the back of the stage. "And, go!"

The audience erupted as Abby dashed over to unload the box. She took mental inventory before heading to the refrigerator to do the same. Comfort food. Okay, she knew comfort food. Hot. Warm. Melty. Creamy. All the terms that came to mind circled around each other as she started grabbing items to fit the description. No, not cheese. Too easy. *Think outside the box.* She wanted rich, she wanted homey, but not elegant. That didn't fit. The familiar blue tube of biscuit dough wedged in the corner of the fridge called out to her. "Ah, man, that's good. Come here."

Calm, she told herself. Reasoned, patient. Step by step. She couldn't let herself think what her competitors might be planning; she could only focus on what she could do, what she could control. When she couldn't find a tablet or notebook, she grabbed a pencil and started scribbling notes on the side of the box, mapping out her plan before grabbing a large sauté pan and the waffle iron, which she plugged in to heat.

Jason had been right. The noise of the crowd faded into the distance. She could hear her heart pounding as the adrenaline kicked in. Within minutes she was used to the camera. She peeled and diced carrots, celery, baby potatoes and onions, tossing them into the pan with some olive oil and butter. The pan smoked and she caught the instant blast of burning onion.

Stifling the panic, she yanked the pan off the hot plate, dumped out the contents and wiped the pan out with paper towels, wincing as the heat singed her fingers.

She could see Jason in the crowd instantly. His eyes narrowed in warning. She could hear his voice in her head. *Carefully. Slow and steady. Take your time.*

The clock ran down. She'd already lost six minutes.

Back on track, she turned the hot plate on, this time remembering Jason's comment that electric was more difficult to control and settled for medium heat. Now, when the vegetables hit the skillet, they settled into a gentle sizzle that had her senses singing in approval.

No time for more mistakes. She checked her

list, set a saucepan on the second burner and got started on the sauce: after butter and flour cooked down, she added double the amount of cream and as it thickened, added chopped thyme and rosemary before she married the sauce to the finished vegetables, removing both pans from the heat.

She checked the clock. Forty minutes had passed already? Grabbing a clean cutting board and knife, she diced up the two chicken breasts, which she threw into another pan, then hit it with some white wine to grab all those brown bits Jason made such a big deal out of.

She popped open the biscuit tin and opened the smoking waffle maker, buttered it liberally, then stretched out each piece of dough into one of the sections. Within seconds, she had mini chicken potpie turnovers cooking in the waffle iron.

Fifteen minutes left. The pies would be a good size, but they would need something more. The plates she'd been provided were plain, square and white. Nothing fancy. Great. Setting them out on the counter, she raided the fresh vegetables and made a quick salad in a bowl, refraining from dressing it to keep it from getting soggy.

She ducked down and peeked under the

top of the waffle iron. It wasn't browning as quickly as she'd like, but there wasn't a temperature control. Nothing she could do except wait.

Lemon juice and olive oil, a couple of cloves of garlic and she had her dressing. Season at every step, Jason had reminded her over and over. She added salt and pepper to the salad.

Eight minutes.

Sweat poured down the sides of her face. Waiting for the pies, she piled up her used pots and pans, organizing them off to the side for whoever needed to clean up after her. Courtesy in the kitchen, she remembered. By the time she returned to the waffle iron, the biscuits were perfect.

Time to plate.

She saw Clara speed past her with two plates, off to deliver her entries to the judging table with Steve right on her heels.

Three minutes.

It was missing something. A punch of color. Ah! She'd seen...

She dived back into the fridge and pulled out the container of edible flowers, choosing the four best-looking ones and setting one beside each of the pies.

The audience counted down from twenty.

She got her first plates on the table by her name, and, as the audience yelled, "Five… four…"

She placed the last two—one of which was for the emcee—and scribbled "Petite Chicken Pies" on her card. The crowd exploded into applause.

Abby managed to make it to her station on wobbly knees. The adrenaline that had sustained her through the round drained out of her and she gripped the edge of the table. Dragging in deep breaths, she crouched down. When she popped up again she immediately looked over to Jason. He was on his feet, staring at her station with concern on his face, but his face broke into that smile she loved so much when she met his gaze.

For a moment, that smile of his was worth more than the prize money. For a moment, win or lose, she was happy.

The buzzer sounded.

"Contestants, your time is up!" Marcus strode to the table, a camera right behind him. "All I can say is I'm glad I'm not one of the judges. Ladies and gentlemen, we'll announce the winners soon. Keep your eyes pinned on that screen right up there!" He made a motion for the camera to follow his lead as Roger ordered his crew to clean up the kitchens and set up for round two later this afternoon.

Abby smoothed her hair and headed for the stairs. By the time she joined Jason, Eloise, Gran and Holly, she'd been congratulated by practically everyone she'd ever known in her life; her back and shoulders were stiff and sore. Her feet were numb. She felt like she could take on the world.

"I have no idea how you ever did this," she whispered to Jason as he folded her into his arms with a hug so tight she couldn't breathe. Almost. She gave herself a good thirty seconds to enjoy the embrace before she sagged onto the bench next to Gran as Eloise squeezed her hand.

"Good show, Abby."

"Thank you." The pride on her grandmother's oldest friend's face felt like another badge of honor.

"I am so proud of you," Gran said and hugged her side. "You were so focused. I couldn't believe it was you. Not a flame in sight."

"None of us could." Holly leaned across Gran and pushed a bottle of water into Abby's hands. "Mini potpies were genius. Those are so going on the diner's menu as soon as I talk to Paige and Ursula."

"As long as I don't have to make them," Abby said as she finished the bottle. Jason sat beside her and without a word, slipped his fingers through hers. "That's the most exhausting thing I've ever done."

"And that's only round one," he reminded her.

"Does anyone see Simon?" Holly frowned and got to her feet, looking toward the judges' table. "I told him and Charlie to sit in the front row. Where—" She let out a curse Abby had heard her use only once and that was during labor. "He's in big trouble. Both of them." She climbed through the people nearby with murmured apologies.

"I don't even want to know," Abby said as she leaned into Jason. "You have my undying admiration. You and David."

"Nice to know we're appreciated. Alice, you doing okay over there?" Jason asked.

"I'm fine," Alice said as she fanned herself. "But I don't know if I'm going to make it through round two. I'm knackered."

"Would you like me to drive you home?" Jason offered. Abby squeezed his hand. That he treated her grandmother like a queen softened her heart.

"I'm about ready to call it a day myself," Eloise said. "The sun's brutal. But we'll be with you in spirit."

"I appreciate that." She probably would worry less if Gran was back home.

"March! Both of you." Holly had her hands pressed against the backs of Simon and Charlie as she resumed her seat. "You, there." She pointed Simon to the space between her and Eloise. "Charlie...yeah, okay. You can sit with Abby and Jason. Lucky them, you criminals."

"What did you do?" Jason whispered as Charlie wedged herself between him and Abby.

"Simon crawled under the judges' table. He was coming out when Holly saw us."

Abby spotted Roger leaving a rather intense conversation with a clearly irritated Marcus, proving she and Jason weren't the only ones in the anti-Roger brigade.

The recorded sound of a drumroll exploded out of the speakers.

"Here we go," Charlie squealed and grabbed hold of Abby's hand.

The monitor buzzed to life. The crowd roared.

"Second place!" Holly whooped.

"Only one point off first," Jason said as Abby skimmed the display. Twenty-eight out of thirty points. Clara had squeaked past her with her chicken meatball spaghetti. Steve wasn't that far off the mark, only two points behind Abby with his sausage-and-pepper hoagies.

Once the audience quieted, Roger took over the announcements again.

"Well, everyone. That ends round one. Round two will commence at two this afternoon. Contestants, please return to the stage by one thirty. Until then, enjoy the festival!"

Abby glanced at her watch. "Do I have time for a nap?"

"Can we get ice cream?" Charlie asked as she dived toward Simon and Holly.

"Wuss," Jason joked as the crowd broke up and her group meandered down the path to the other side of Skipper Park. He draped an arm over her shoulders and drew her against him. "I'm proud of you, Abby. You did great. What do you want to do to kill time?"

"Eat?" She laughed.

"I have to get to the diner," Holly said. "It's been nonstop since yesterday morning. Excellent for the cash register, not for Paige and

Twyla's nerves. Congratulations." She grabbed Abby into a big hug. "You proved me wrong. Good for you. Take care of her, okay?" She gave Jason a gentle punch on the arm. "Kids, let's go!"

"Aw, Mom, can't we stay?"

Holly shook her head.

"We can keep an eye on them," Jason offered.

"We can?" Abby squinted at him. "I mean, sure, yeah. We can do that." He was really embracing her attempts to help him socialize.

"You sure?" Holly didn't look convinced. "Luke said he'd stop by the diner later, but I have no idea what time."

"It's not a problem. But before you go, there's something I wanted to ask you. Give us a second?" Jason moved off with Holly before Abby could answer.

"I think I may have entered an alternate dimension." Abby winked at her godson and Charlie. Despite his protests to the contrary, Jason had become quite the social butterfly in the last couple of days.

"You two behave," Holly called out a moment later to her son and Charlie. "No more spying."

"'Kay!" Simon yelled. The second his

mother turned her back, he said, "Come on, Charlie! Race you!"

"And there goes any hope of relaxing," Abby commented just as Jason returned. Before she could think it through, she kissed him square on the mouth. "You've come a long way. Thank you. For everything."

"It's only round one, Abby," Jason reminded her and whistled for Charlie and Simon to return. "I saw an ice cream booth with our names on it. Let's go."

"Yes!" Charlie gave a significant fist pump as Simon stuffed what looked like a phone in his pocket.

"Don't get used to it." Abby laughed as she waited for them to catch up. Only then did she realize they—or rather Jason—had an audience.

But when she caught Roger and Marcus looking in their direction, they immediately walked away. Whatever they'd been discussing, she wasn't sure she liked it.

She wasn't sure she liked it at all.

CHAPTER FIFTEEN

JASON LET ABBY into the Flutterby ahead of him, or rather, he guided her inside. Contrary to her insistence that they attend Calliope's celebration dinner at Duskywing Farm, Abby was dead on her feet.

"I just heard!" Lori darted around the desk. "You took first place in the second competition! That's amazing."

"It's a minor miracle," Abby said as she returned Lori's enthusiastic hug.

"Don't shortchange yourself," Jason said. "You're in the lead going into tomorrow's final challenge. That's nothing to sneeze at."

"The only reason I won this round was because Clara overcooked her steak," Abby said. "Which she wouldn't have if it hadn't been for that bee."

"You owe your winning to a bee?" Lori didn't look convinced.

"Apparently Clara has a phobia," Jason explained as Abby struggled not to laugh. "After today, I'm betting the feeling is mutual. I've never heard anyone shriek that loudly before."

"She was flapping her arms so hard we thought she'd take off." Abby shook her head. "It'll make for great television. We shouldn't be laughing. Karma's going to kick me for sure."

"Well, whatever the reason, I'm glad you won." Lori headed to the desk.

"I need to check on Gran." Abby gestured down the narrow hallway.

"This came for you." Lori turned to his mailbox and pulled out his key and an envelope. "We don't get many registered letters these days. I almost didn't know what to do."

"Thanks." He read the return address and repressed a sigh. Since he'd agreed to read all the documentation surrounding Corwin Brothers, Gary's campaign to get Jason to come home to New York had kicked into high gear and forced Jason to turn off his phone. "Hey, I'm going to be fixing a light supper tonight if you and the rest of the staff want to join us. Say, six?"

"Sounds great." Lori beamed as he walked toward the kitchen.

When Abby joined him a few minutes later, she groaned. "Why are you cooking? How can you be cooking? Wait." She sat on her favorite stool and examined the ingredients on the counter. "What are you making?"

"Gazpacho and grilled cheese sandwiches."

"How can you make grilled cheese without those plastic-wrapped slices?"

Because he suspected she could barely focus, he chopped up half a jalapeño and dumped it into the food processor. "That's not cheese. And since when don't you trust me?"

"Snob. And don't ruin my childhood for me." Abby yawned, then perked up. "What's this?" She picked up his letter. "Registered? Looks important."

"Gary thinks everything's important." He should have left the envelope with Lori or put it in his pocket, but he'd been anxious to get cooking.

"Don't you care what's in this?"

"Not as much as you, apparently." Jason scoffed. "It's the same old stuff he's been talking to me about for a while, Abby."

"I can read it to you."

"If you want to open it, open it. There's nothing in there that's going to change anything."

"You really don't mind?"

Jason shrugged and tried not to lose his concentration as she ripped open the envelope.

"This is signed by the entire Corwin Brothers board of directors." Abby's eyes went wide as she read. "Jason, they want you back."

"I know." He bit into a chunk of celery. "I told you, it's nothing new."

"No, Jason, I think it might be. The board has already notified your father they're taking a new vote next week. You're the de facto chairman."

Jason swore and set his knife down. "Meaning they aren't going to give me a choice. Great." He held out his hand so he could read it for himself. "Doesn't mean I'm going to take it." A feeling of vindication swept over him. "Doesn't mean I want to take it."

"You don't sound as convinced as you did a few days ago." Abby rested her chin in her palm and watched as he pocketed the letter. "Don't tell me you're not curious about what this could mean for your company."

"It means they're tired of losing money and I'm a better bet than my profit-obsessed father."

"Because you're the brand. You and David. Maybe this is the opportunity you've been waiting for. You said you and your brother wanted to take things in a different direction—"

"I'm taking things in a different direction

already." Jason picked up his knife again. "I don't need to be chairman of anything to do what I'm doing now."

"Lurking in my kitchen until my regular cook comes home? Yeah, that sounds productive."

"There you go again, trying to get rid of me."

"That's not what I'm trying to do. But I don't want you ignoring something potentially wonderful because you're afraid it isn't going to work out."

"That's the second time you've called me a coward, and I like it even less this time." He shoved his knife through the red peppers with more force than necessary. "Then again, you have a point. Maybe I don't want to get my hopes up. Maybe I don't want to open that door because I know it's going to get slammed in my face."

"Or maybe you're afraid you'll get everything you want."

He didn't hear her get up, didn't notice her walk around the counter, but when she touched his arm, yet another door he didn't expect opened. He set his knife down and gripped the edge of the countertop and asked what he'd been building up the courage for. "What if all I want is you?"

"Me?" There it was, that uncertain squeak of disbelief he'd come to love. When he glanced at her, her cheeks had gone pink, her eyes glassy bright. "You want me? Why— how—when—"

"I do love seeing you flummoxed." He turned toward her and cupped her chin in hand. "Speechless is even better." He brushed his lips against hers and embraced that mind fog that descended whenever she looked at him. Kissed him. "I want you to listen to me, Abby. All I care about for the next few days is watching you win that contest. I want you to get that money and save your inn and give your grandmother the security you've been fighting for. I want to watch you win every battle you've taken on. Better yet, I want to fight by your side."

"I'd like that." She wrapped her hand around his wrist. "More than anything I want you to stay. Here. With me. But—"

"I love you, Abby." His lungs suddenly emptied. His shoulders straightened. Who needed alcohol when he had Abby around?

"Oh." She squeezed her eyes shut. "Crispy crickets, Jason, when did you start saying the right thing at the right time?" She leaned in and wrapped her arms around his neck as he drew her closer to him. "I love you, too."

"I hear a *but* in there."

"You do, yes." She stepped back and stared into his eyes, nose to nose, determination shimmering in the turqoise depths that had entranced him from the day he'd met her. "I do love you, but I don't want you to turn away from something you might regret later on. I don't want you to fight only for or with me. I want you to fight for yourself. I want you to at least think about going back to New York, seeing what the offer is, what you can get out of it. If there's a way to make this work between us, we'll find it, but I don't want you to look at me one day and think you should have made a different choice. I don't want to be your fallback plan."

He stroked his hand against the base of her spine, pressed his forehead against hers. "If I promise to think about it, will that be enough to get you to back off at least until after the festival and you're on solid ground again?"

"Assuming I win," she added.

"Abby?"

"Fine. I'll stop pestering you about New York until we're on the other side of the Flutterby issue. Now, are you going to teach me how to make your famous grilled cheese sandwiches, or will I have to read about it in your new cookbook?"

His gaze narrowed. "What new cookbook?"

"A conversation for another time." She grinned and jumped out of his arms. "Show me what you got, Super Chef."

"I THOUGHT IT was time I introduced myself."

Water sloshed over the edge of Abby's cup as she spun around.

"Sorry." Marcus Aiken aimed one of his trademark heart-stopping smiles at her as she faltered. "I didn't mean to scare you."

"It's fine." As much as she wanted to be rude to the chef who had hurt Jason's chances for success, her years of customer service kicked in and she offered her hand. "Abby Manning."

"Pleasure. I, well, I wasn't sure if you would even want to speak to me." His handsome features shifted into uncertainty. "Word is you've been seeing Jason Corwin."

Seeing? Her cheeks warmed. "We're… friends. He's been a big help getting me ready for this competition." A competition that would be over in a matter of hours.

"Jason's always been an excellent teacher. I miss working with him."

"I guess we've all done things we wish we could do over." Her words hovered on snarky before she reeled in her animosity. "He told me he's not angry with you anymore. In case you ever want to apologize for taking advantage of his grief."

Marcus flinched. "Believe me, I wish I'd done a lot of things differently during that time."

Sympathy sneaked in. Here she'd expected Marcus to argue, to protest, even to defend himself and insist he could claim the high ground.

"Maybe I should talk to Jason directly," he continued. "He should hear the tru—" His gaze shifted uneasily past Abby's shoulder as Roger Evans joined them.

"I almost didn't recognize you without your coach, Abby." Roger winked at her over his coffee cup. "I hope everything's okay with him."

Unease prickled the back of her neck. "Why wouldn't it be?"

"Oh, just rumblings around the industry. Nothing serious, I'm sure. Will Jason not be joining you today?"

"He had some errands to run." Something he hadn't been particularly forthcoming about, but she'd lay odds he'd sneaked off to Calliope's farm again. "He'll be here later."

"Well, we're set to start in an hour. Tick tock. Marcus, would you excuse us for a moment? There's something I need to discuss with Abby privately."

"Yeah, sure." Marcus moved away with what Abby likened to a silent warning on his face. "I'll see you onstage, Abby. Good luck."

"Thank you." Darn it, she really didn't want to like the guy, not after what he'd done to Jason, but she couldn't shake the feeling there was more to the man than what headlines and gossip had conveyed. "What did you need to talk to me about, Roger?" Abby sipped her water to have something to do.

She frowned when Roger took her arm and steered her into the far corner of the contestants' tent. "You're doing a wonderful job in this competition, Abby. Far better than I expected."

"Um, thanks?"

"Funny thing. And I'm sure you heard about this, but part of the reason we're taping this event is to find some new talent for the

National Cooking Network. It's been tough, given recent events, keeping shows on the air."

"Maybe you should stop booting people off without giving them a chance to explain themselves." She could only imagine how much goodwill the network might have garnered if, instead of kicking Jason to the curb, they'd offered their support and understanding.

"I like that about you, Abby. You speak your mind. And you'll defend the people you care about to the death. I don't see that type of loyalty much these days." He moved to stand beside her as Clara shifted into focus, today's '50s dress a mix of ocean blues and greens. "Now, that girl there." Roger gestured toward Clara. "She's a star in the making. She'd be a perfect addition to the network and, if you don't mind my saying, my list of discoveries."

"I'm sure she would." Tension percolated in her stomach. Where was he going with this?

"And Clara wants it. Wants it really bad. I'm guessing you don't?"

"You'd be correct." All Abby wanted was that prize money so she could get her life back, get the inn in the black and settle Gran once and for all. The very idea of events like this becoming a regular occurrence made her want to run screaming from the tent.

"It's too bad Clara's in third place going into this final leg," Roger said. "There's no way we could justify giving Clara her own show if she doesn't win something of significance."

Abby's stomach pitched. "I wasn't aware this contest was that big a deal."

"It is, it is. It's my baby, and getting the network to fork out so much cash wasn't easy, but I told them it was an investment. An investment I intend to grow over the next few years. And it wouldn't do anyone any good if in the inaugural year it was discovered a contestant lied on her application."

Abby felt the color drain from her face. "I'm sorry?" She couldn't believe she got the words out.

"I'm betting you are about now." Roger smirked. "See, when you signed that contract, you stated you didn't employ any member of the NCN family. But that's not exactly true, is it? Not with what I saw the other night in your kitchen."

"Kissing one of your ex-employees doesn't violate that contract." The plastic cup in her hand cracked and water dribbled over her fingers.

"That isn't what I'm talking about." He got out his phone and showed her a photo taken from the porch outside the kitchen, of her and Jason exchanging money from Matilda's cash jug. "He's cooking for your guests, Abby. He's been teaching you how to cook, and while that doesn't necessarily constitute professional training, it's definitely something to think about. It certainly makes me wonder if there's been another violation of the rules."

"You canceled his shows," Abby reminded him. "He doesn't work for you any—"

"Whether his shows are on the air or not, he's still under contract with NCN. And before you try to explain your way out of this, you signed that contract the very next day after Jason arrived at the inn. A reservation, I should note, that was made weeks before. You can't convince me you didn't know he was coming just in time to participate in the festival. And if you can't convince me, you won't convince anyone else."

"Why don't you give me the chance to tell you and we'll see about that?" She crushed what was left of the cup and tossed it into the trash. "Point me in the direction of your boss and I'll happily discuss it with him or her. Or maybe I'll withdraw from the competition all together."

"You don't strike me as someone who

makes empty threats, Abby. You're forgetting I've become fast friends with your mayor, and he let slip just how unstable the Flutterby Inn's future is. You won't withdraw. Not when you need that cash to save your precious inn. But even if you did pull out, that doesn't give me what I want."

"You don't strike me as a man who beats around the bush, Roger." Abby was more than happy to throw his own words back at him. An angry fire of humiliation burned low in her belly. "What do you want?"

"I want Clara to win. I want her to shine."

"Which means I have to fail." Her mind raced, dread swirling as she comprehended his meaning. "You want me to throw the competition."

"Your words, not mine."

"So, lose on purpose or you'll what? You'll expose me on national TV? What would that do to your reputation as a producer, having to expose one of your contestants because of a clerical error that, by all rights, should have been caught before the start of the competition?"

"Oh, you misunderstand me, Abby. It's not you I'd be concerned about. Tell me something." Roger shifted in front of her and stared with snakelike eyes into hers. "Do you think Jason can withstand another scandal? Because that's what this would be if his involvement came to light. No one would care that *you* lied on an application. But with this particular man's history of cheating and aversion to the truth, a man who chose to disappear rather than own up to what he did and who, from what I've been told, is poised to reclaim his struggling company... Well." Roger shrugged. "That just puts a whole new *public* spin on things."

"You'd blame everything on Jason when I'm the one who signed that contract?" Was he serious? This couldn't be happening. Not over a cooking competition. "But it's not true. Jason didn't know anything about what I signed."

"Ah, there's the kicker, Abby." Roger pointed a finger in front of her face. "This isn't news to you. You aren't surprised I'm even mentioning this, so I'm guessing you knew what you'd done was wrong."

Suspecting and knowing were two different things. Worrying and hoping...hadn't done her any good. "None of that means Jason's to blame."

"It doesn't matter if he's to blame or not. The public will believe what they're led to believe. Perception of wrongdoing is enough to ensure Jason never spends another day in New York, let alone becomes chairman of Corwin Brothers. I'd be surprised if he's ever let back into a kitchen."

Abby swallowed hard and, despite her best efforts, she looked away. A flash of movement exposed Marcus standing on the other side of the tent, not quite close enough to hear the details, but the quizzical expression on his face told her he understood something was amiss. "You'd go to all this trouble just to make Clara a star?"

"Clara happens to be convenient. It could easily have been Steve, but the frat brother vibe isn't working. He's a goof. Clara's a multimillion-dollar brand waiting to happen. Just like Marcus was before her and the others before him. It's Jason's own fault he never learned to play the game. Not that David did, but at least he understood how things happen in this business. And that's what all this is, Abby. It's business. Fame, fortune—it's all tied to celebrity these days, and celebrity is what people like me create." He glanced at his watch. "You have a little time to think about all this. But just so you're aware, I've already drafted a press release outlining Jason's role in your deception. While you might be able to salvage something, I'm not entirely sure Jason will. It's one contest, Abby. And you'll walk away with some, if not enough, prize money to fix whatever's broken. Unless of course you don't care about Jason and his future. In which case I'll take my chances and hope Clara wins fair and square." She was a little surprised he didn't slither away.

Abby's entire body trembled. Her hands shook as she touched her neck, feeling the absence of her rings, apart from Jason the only things that could have given her comfort.

"Abby?" Marcus approached with a new cup of water and pushed it into her hands. "What's going on? I only heard bits and pieces. What did he say to you?"

She tried to smile and play off her conversation with the man who could ruin Jason once and for all. Everything Jason had done to rebuild himself, rebuild his life, and now it was all at risk because of her stupid, selfish, impulsive actions.

"Nothing important," she managed to say. The water splashed over the edge of the cup again before she could drink it. "He's really a piece of work, isn't he?"

"Like a lot of slimy producers, I'm betting

he has a special place reserved for him in the underground afterlife." Marcus attempted a laugh. "Are you sure you're okay to compete?"

"Of course. I'm just going to get some air before we start. Ah, thanks for the water."

Her mouth went dry as she exited the tent. She refused to acknowledge Clara when her fellow competitor called out to her or when Steve insisted the three of them get their picture taken. She couldn't stop, not to think, not to play along like nothing had changed. She hurried down the worn path toward a bench beneath one of the park's giant oaks and, bending over, tried to breathe.

Her lungs burned. She needed that money. She had to save the Flutterby. Save Gran. But if she won, if Roger went through with his threat, he'd destroy any chance Jason had at recapturing everything he'd lost.

Except... Abby straightened, a sliver of hope shooting through her. Hadn't he said last night he wasn't sure he wanted to resume his position at Corwin Brothers? Maybe that was her out. Maybe he'd already made the final break and her choice wasn't as difficult as she was making it out to be. Maybe—

"Abby!"

For an instant, she thought Jason's voice

was in her head, but then she saw him sprint around the side of the tent and race toward her.

"Someone said they saw you coming this way. You need to get ready. What's wrong?" He bent down in front of her and captured her hands, squeezing them tight. "You're white as a sheet. You feeling okay?"

"Nerves." He looked so concerned, so…energized. "Where have you been?"

"Errands, I told you." He grinned and touched her cheek. "I also did what you suggested and called Gary. I told him I'd only consider coming back if the board agreed to implement the local farm–friendly campaign David and I talked about. If they want me that badly, they're going to have to agree to take the company in a new direction. The direction you helped me find. He took the offer to the board."

If he went back? Hope faded. "And?"

"They agreed. More than agreed, they love the idea and are already putting a new marketing strategy in place." She'd never seen anyone smile so widely. "The chairmanship is mine if I want it."

It was as if a knife sliced her heart in two. "And of course you want it," Abby whispered.

"That's great, Jason." She swallowed the tears in her throat.

"It can be everything David and I wanted. I can keep him alive, Abby. Thanks to you." He pressed his mouth to hers. "Because of you, I'm getting that second chance."

"I'm proud of you, Jason." She held him and squeezed her eyes shut as he hugged her. "I only want what's best for you."

"Best for us. You're going to be a part of this, Abby."

"One hour at a time, okay? This is a lot to take in." She pushed herself to her feet and he stood. "Let's get through today and see where things stand. I have a competition to finish."

CHAPTER SIXTEEN

"READY? AND BEGIN!"

The audience cheered as the contestants got to cooking.

At least that's what she was supposed to do. Abby had no memory of Jason escorting her to the stage or her climbing the stairs. She barely remembered what had been arranged for her in this final round.

But she was on the stage now. She was supposed to be cooking *now*. She had to decide between her future or Jason's *now*.

She unloaded the mystery items from the miniature picnic basket and tried to control her shaking hands. Her stomach twisted in a completely new way as she stared down at the blue cheese, jalapeños and kiwi—all items she'd listed as her least favorite foods.

She had to turn these *things* into something edible? How did she check for quality control when she couldn't stomach tasting any of them? She couldn't help it. She looked in Jason's direction, but as she scanned the crowd, the sea of coral shirts and familiar faces smiling at her made her breath catch. Calliope, Simon and Charlie. Luke, Matt and Ozzy. Even Gil looked far more encouraging than he had yesterday. How could she let them—how could she let the town—down?

Losing having done her best was one thing; she could live with that. But purposely throwing the competition? How was she supposed to look in the mirror every day when throwing the competition could cost her grandmother her home? All the effort Jason had put into getting her ready for this—she owed it to him to do her best.

Unless her best was going to cost him his future.

"Come on, Abby!"

She hiccuped a sob as she recognized Mr. Vartebetium's voice from the crowd. She looked down and found him front and center surrounded by the rest of the Cocoon Club. She didn't want to see or hear encouragement. She didn't want to have to choose...

"Head in the game, Abby!"

She jumped at the sound of Jason's voice, looking over as he pointed to the clock, concern and irritation marring his face.

Jason.

"Is there a problem, Abby?" Roger called to her from the edge of the stage.

"No." She didn't even try to mask her hostility. "No problem at all." She had time to consider, time to think, but meanwhile, she had an entry to create. Somehow she'd make something edible out of these items, beginning with adding bacon to the mix. Bacon made everything better. Strawberries from the fridge along with a good dose of tequila would turn the gross kiwi into something drinkable.

With only thirty minutes on the clock, she put her head down and got to work. The second she dropped her first batch of bacon-wrapped blue cheese–stuffed jalapeño poppers into the mini fryer, she knew one thing for certain.

This competition was hers to win or lose.

The first batch of poppers done, she set them on a cooling rack and dusted them with salt—always season after frying. Jason would not get out of her head. The second batch went in as she set out dishes and concocted a dipping sauce.

Once the plates were arranged and the poppers were ready for service, she added the tequila to the blender and then poured the contents into shooter-sized glasses.

"You've got this, Abby!"

She couldn't listen. She didn't want to hear. Maybe second or even third place would give her enough money to stave off the taxes, or maybe Roger was bluffing. Maybe he wouldn't—

She found Roger standing on the stairs near her. He inclined his head, his eyes like steel as he flicked his gaze toward Jason, waving the paper in his hand ever so slightly.

The press release.

She swallowed around the bitterness and got back to her task.

She finished mixing the sauce, mayonnaise with a kick of Sriracha and some lemon juice to balance out the heat. She grabbed for the sweet paprika as an added kick, her hand knocking the bottle next to it onto its side. Her heart beat so hard she was afraid it would explode out of her chest.

She stared at the label. It was like a sign. Confirmation and yet…once she did it, there was no going back. She had to stop thinking and act. Make a decision. Save the inn or protect Jason?

She grabbed the toppled bottle and shook a liberal amount into the sauce.

Her entry completed, she carried the first two plates to the judging table, then the second, her muscles twitching as she passed Roger on the stairs.

"Well?" he asked her on her return trip.

She didn't answer—couldn't answer. No words would have come out anyway, only a strangled scream, and she'd be damned if she'd give him the satisfaction. Instead she concentrated on every ounce of loathing she felt for him as she walked past.

"And count it down with me, folks," Marcus yelled into the mic. "Five, four, three..."

Abby ripped off her apron and threw it onto the table, turning away from the crowd before they could see her cry. It was over. For better or worse, good or bad, she was done. Whether she'd take Jason or the Flutterby down with her remained to be seen.

She swiped her cheeks dry and faced the audience again, new tears flowing as they cheered her name. Abby left the stage, her vision blurry, and almost tripped on the last step. Marcus caught her arm, keeping her on her feet.

"Abby, are you okay?"

"I'm fine." She drew in a shaky breath.

"What did Roger say to you in the tent?"

"Nothing that matters anymore," Abby whispered. "He won. But then, as Jason told me, Roger always wins, doesn't he."

"Abby—" Marcus tried to keep hold of her but she pulled free and beelined for Jason, Holly and the rest of her friends. She didn't stop for congratulations, didn't want anything except Jason's arms around her. Maybe that would be enough.

"You did it." Jason grabbed her shoulders and ducked down to look into her tearstained face. "I'm so, so proud of you."

There it was. The hug she'd been waiting for. The hug she'd needed. But even now, as Marcus announced the judging was underway, she doubted the comfort would last.

"Abby, my girl." Mr. V spoke from behind her and she turned, finding the frail old man standing short and proud and leaning on a shiny new walker. "What you did for me, for my Maisy and the Flutterby—" he pressed a hand against his heart "—it means the world. Win or lose, you've made this old man very proud."

"I'm afraid—" The words caught. Just as she knew they would. "What if—"

"We will face whatever happens together. As we always should have." Mr. V squeezed her hand and gave her a sad nod. "Whatever's meant to be will be. That you fought so hard is all that matters."

Except she hadn't fought. She'd surrendered.

"Sit down before you collapse," Holly ordered as she maneuvered around the crowd and pushed a bottle of water into Abby's hands. "I swear, if that flighty bumble head wins this thing, there's no justice." She grabbed Abby's face in her hands and said, "You are amazing, my friend."

She wanted to argue, wanted to tell everyone they were wrong about her. But how could she regret giving Jason not only what he wanted, but what he needed? He wouldn't be whole without cooking, without his business and company. It was the only way to continue to tether himself to his brother.

Who was Abby to sever that?

The minutes passed and Abby pulled herself together in time to be called back in front of the cameras with Clara and Steve.

The drumroll sounded. The crowd fell silent. Abby heard Marcus's voice as if from a distance. She angled her chin up, locked her jaw and focused on remaining calm, collected and supportive as the winner's name flashed on the screen.

She didn't have to look. Not when the crowd deflated. Protests and cries sounded before smatterings of polite applause made its way through the stands. Abby clapped, and despite feeling a wave of sympathy for the triumphant Clara—who knew what Roger had in store for her—offered her competitor a congratulatory hug.

The minutes seemed endless as the checks were handed out. Eventually Abby returned to Jason and her friends, but there wasn't anything left to be said.

"Second place?" Luke said as he wrapped her in a brotherly hug. "That's just wrong. You did amazing, Abs."

"Thank you," Abby whispered, her hands crushing the check in her hand.

"It's not fair!" Simon hollered only to be hushed by his mother. "She should have—"

"But why?" Charlie asked Jason, her confused little face scraping against Abby's heart. "I thought she did good."

"She did great." Jason smiled at Charlie as he pulled Abby into his arms and pressed his lips to the top of her head. "I'm so sorry, Abby."

"It's okay." She'd find a way to live with the regret if only to keep a smile on Jason's face.

"You did your best—that's all that matters."

Marcus and the rest of the NCN crew began talking about air dates as Clara claimed her oversize check, guffawing and giggling as if she didn't have any idea the quagmire of muck she'd be wallowing in under Roger's tutelage.

"I want to go home," Abby whispered against Jason's chest. "Can we go home now?"

"You bet. Holly?"

"Yeah, go. We'll do dinner another time. We'll find another reason to celebrate soon." Holly reached across Jason and took Abby's hand. "You have nothing to be sorry about, Abby."

Abby watched Mr. V wobble out of the baseball field among his friends.

"Abby, congratulations on second place." Roger offered his hand. "It was close, and I bet the judges are still trying to cool their mouths down after those poppers of yours. Maybe that extra dose of cayenne in the sauce was a bit too much. But all in all, excellent effort."

"Thanks." If she could have loaded the word with poison she would have. Fifteen thousand dollars. Anyone else, any other time and she would have been celebrating as Holly suggested. Instead, it felt as if this little slip of paper was the final nail in the Flutterby Inn's coffin.

"Since when do you use cayenne pepper?" Jason asked as the stands emptied out. "You hate spicy food."

"I thought it was paprika," she lied. "They were right next to each other. I guess I picked up the wrong one. I must have gotten flustered again."

"You didn't look flustered."

"Yeah, well. Things aren't always how they look."

The continued congratulations and shouts of support bolstered her a bit as they made their way to Jason's car. "Right now all I want is a long hot bath, a bottle of wine and a stupid reality show to watch." She sank back in the passenger seat as Jason maneuvered the car out of the parking lot.

"I think we can arrange that." Jason entwined his fingers with hers. "I know you're disappointed, Abby, but you gave it everything you had. Holly's right. You don't have anything to be ashamed of."

Didn't she? She stared down at the check. She'd have to make sure it did the most good, and that would entail a long sit-down with

Mr. V. If anything, perhaps they could use the money to hire a lawyer to help with the tax issues. But she already knew the truth. Mr. V didn't have it in him to fight any longer.

That meant, starting tomorrow she'd look for another solution. For tonight, however…

"What's Gran going to say?" She stretched her neck from side to side and stared out at the people filling Monarch Lane as they turned onto Great Copper Way.

"She'll be as proud of you as the rest of us are. Buck up, Abby. We'll put our heads together and come up with something."

"Yeah." At least Jason's future was in place. Whatever else happened, she had that to be proud of.

When Jason stopped in front of the inn, Lori's voice erupted from the front porch in a tone that terrified Abby to her core. She quickly climbed out of the car. "Abby! I've been trying to call," Lori shouted. Her assistant manager raced down the stairs, her strained features draining the color from Abby's.

"Gran," Abby whispered. "Is it Gran? What happened? Where is she?" Last she'd heard, Eloise was going to pick Alice up for bridge at her house with Myra and Delilah.

"Myra called a couple of hours ago. Alice is okay, but she had a spell of some kind."

Abby's mind emptied. A spell? Her grandmother didn't have spells. But she'd been warned about them. She spun to find Jason, but he was right behind her. "I'll drive."

"Call me when you know something!" Lori yelled after them.

"My phone." Abby dug into her back pocket. "I thought I had it set on vibrate...the battery's dead." She pressed it against her forehead until it hurt. Could today get any worse?

"Where am I going?" Jason asked as he shot out of the parking lot.

"Down to Monarch Lane, make a right at the end and south on 101. Southern Memorial. There are signs."

"Got it. Here." He handed her his phone. "Use this. See if you can find anything out before we get there."

"Yeah." She couldn't focus, couldn't concentrate. This wasn't like her. She was always in control, always knew what to do. Especially when it came to Gran. "I can't remember the number." Her throat tightened, but she refused to shed another tear.

"Hey." Jason squeezed her arm. "She'll be okay, Abby. We've got this. I'm right here. I'm not going anywhere. Now relax. Stop thinking of the worst case and focus on putting a smile on that pretty face of yours."

He really was getting good at saying the right thing. "Okay." She nodded and her mind began to clear. "Yeah, okay." The number came to her and she dialed, switching the phone to her other ear and trying not to be grateful that she wasn't alone.

Jason was with her. That's all that mattered.

"GRAN." ABBY GRIPPED the door frame to steady herself before she stepped inside the emergency room. "Gran, I'm so sorry. My phone—" She came up short when she realized they weren't alone. "Oscar. Eloise. Myra?" Some of her grandmother's Cocoon Club friends were settled in chairs around her grandmother's bed. They were still wearing their Five-Alarm Manning shirts while Alice was sitting in bed as if she were holding court. Given the cards and plastic chips on the table, bridge had given way to poker.

"There you are." Alice sighed and pressed a shaking hand against her heart. There was a large bandage on her forehead and the beginnings of bruising around her eyes and nose and her left arm was in a sling. She'd been hooked up to a rainbow of cords and monitors that were beep-beeping happily. "Buttered biscuits, but I was getting worried. How did the competition go?"

"I came in second." In her panic over Gran, she'd almost forgotten.

"Second? After who? That whippersnapper of a girl?" Alice frowned when Abby nodded. "This world doesn't make sense to me sometimes. You did good, Abby. Everyone's so proud of you."

What Abby wouldn't give to never hear that phrase again. "What happened, Gran?"

"Your grandmother's wiped me out of half my Social Security check, that's what's happened," Oscar grumbled. The grizzled, stooped man shifted in his chair and gathered up the cards. "A card shark, I tell you."

"Eloise?" Abby tried again. "Why is Gran here?"

"She tripped on one of the area rugs in my front hall." Eloise pushed up out of her chair and patted Abby's shoulder. The former schoolteacher always had a calming aura about her. "Cracked her head something good on the table by the door. The doctors ran tests. She has a mild concussion, and as you can see, she took a bit of a beating. Given her age, they want to keep her a couple of days. We're just waiting for her room assignment."

"Did they call your doctor?" Abby leaned around Eloise to ask Alice, who either didn't hear her or pretended not to. "I'm so glad you were with her." Clearly Alice was moving toward the phase where her being alone could be dangerous. All the more reason to keep her in familiar surroundings. Abby's chest constricted. Where were they going to go? "She's really okay?"

"That depends," Eloise said.

So much for relief. "On what?"

"On whether you two are going to tell us what's really going on," Myra said and then cackled as Oscar lost another hand to Alice. "Too much whispering between this one and her doctor. Secrets, I tell you, and I won't have it. Not now that you're in the fold again."

Abby sighed. Even after their talks, her grandmother still hadn't confided in them about her diagnosis. Not even in Eloise. Given the look Abby was getting from Alice, she shouldn't be thinking about outing her.

"Well, here's the patient I've been looking for." Jason strode in, most of his upper body and face obscured by the biggest flower bouquet Abby had ever seen in her life.

"Jason." Abby pressed her fingers to her forehead. "I totally forgot—"

"Sorry I'm late, but I had a stop to make." He shifted the wheeled table to the side and set the deep, wide sea green vase down, plumping up the daisies interspersed with roses and lilies. "You have some explaining to do, young lady."

"Oh. My." Alice touched trembling fingers to her lips. "Oh, lilies. My Bob used to bring me lilies every year on our anniversary. How do you know these things?"

"Magic." Jason dropped a kiss on her grandmother's cheek. Abby almost whimpered. Why did this man always make her want to cry? "You know what else is magic?" Jason asked Alice. "Talking to your friends. It's done wonders for me. Just ask your granddaughter."

"Now's not the time to be lecturing me, young man," Alice stated. "What's this nonsense about her coming in second?"

"Gran—"

"Hush," Myra ordered and pointed a stern finger at Abby. "I want his take as well. We all know Abby had more going for her on that stage than those other two. I'm betting it was rigged. They didn't want the hometown girl stealing the spotlight."

Abby's fingers tingled as she clenched her fists. Leave it to Myra to land on the truth with one leap.

"Sometimes it's how things go," Jason said. "But Abby has her family and friends to support her. That's always a good thing. Right, Alice?"

"Like a dog with a bone," Alice grumbled. "The two of you."

"How is it the city boy knows what's going on and we don't?" Myra asked. "Alice Manning, you'd best remember who you're talking to and come out with it before I lose my temper." Given her penchant for red hair coloring, her threat carried significant weight.

"See?" Jason said. As he moved away, her grandmother's lifelong friends encircled her, a hand grasping her blanket-covered leg, another taking her hand, and Oscar, for all his curmudgeonly habits, patted her foot. "Now watch what happens."

He drew Abby into the hall as she heard the word *Parkinson's* escape her grandmother's lips for the first time since she'd been diagnosed.

"Dr. Reed," Abby muttered when Jason turned to face the man waiting for them. Tall and a bit on the chunky side, the doctor had a round face that contorted into an understanding smile. "Is she okay?"

"She's fine, Abby. She never lost consciousness, but with head injuries, we like to be sure. At this stage, it's as likely she tripped."

"You mean it wasn't Parkinson's related?"

"We can't say for sure, but I'm betting if she'd confided in her hostess for the day, Eloise would have removed those rugs. You know I treated Eloise's sister for years."

"Eloise's sister had Parkinson's?" Abby felt a new surge of hope and support. How had she never known this? Did Gran know? She had to know, but why hadn't she said anything? "Hopefully Gran's learned her lesson about letting people help her."

"And the sling?" Jason asked.

"A precaution," the doctor said. "She landed pretty hard on her left shoulder. Nothing's broken, but I'd feel better if she kept it immobile for a few days. Eloise saw the whole thing, so we were able to get an accurate account. I promise, Abby, she's fine. You can take her home soon."

Alice wouldn't stay fine. As she and Gran had discussed the other day, she was only going to get worse. And without their home... "Thank you, Doctor." Abby hugged her arms around her waist and ducked her head, waiting for him to leave before she looked up at Jason. She didn't know what to say, didn't know how to say it. She opened her mouth, but no sound came out.

Jason wrapped an arm around her shoulders and pulled her into him. "When are you going to realize you aren't alone in this, Abby? Tiny as you are, you can't spread yourself so thin."

"Listen to the boy," Eloise said as she joined them in the hall. Her tangerine-colored hair glowed beneath the fluorescent lights and accentuated every earned wrinkle in her face. "Why didn't you tell us? Why didn't you tell me?"

"She didn't want anyone to know." But Abby realized now she should have told her. "It's not embarrassment. She doesn't want to be a burden." Not to anyone. Not to Abby. Not to her friends. But it was obvious Abby had run out of time. She had to tell Gran the truth about the Flutterby.

"Alice Manning of all people should know the people you love are never burdens," Eloise scoffed. "I've known that woman most of my seventy-nine years. A more stubborn individual hasn't been seen in these parts save for one person—me. And I'm laying down the law here and now. She's stuck with me. You both are. We'll sit her down and explain what's what as soon as she's feeling up to it, but until then, you do what you need to, young lady. And that includes letting us know when you need something."

Abby smiled, exhaustion and relief creeping over her. "Yes, ma'am."

"Now, your gran would like to order pizza for dinner, so we're all going to hang out here, play some cards and make sure she and you understand you're not in this fight alone." She pointed through the door. "Now march. Both of you."

"ON THE BRIGHT SIDE, it looks as if your grandmother and Mr. Vartebetium will be settling back in at the Flutterby about the same time," Jason said. "Gives you a chance to figure things out."

As it was close to ten, Abby bypassed the Flutterby and Lori and went straight to her cottage. What was there to figure out? Without the fifty thousand dollars, her choices had gone from promising to nonexistent. Maybe things would look better in the morning. Abby unlocked her front door and clicked the light on.

"Since when are you the optimist?" She realized she sounded cranky, but that's what happened when anger, frustration and Roger-defined secrets and lies bored down on her.

"Turning people into optimists must be your superpower." He followed her into the kitchen. "Any idea what happens now?"

"I'm betting Mr. V will call a staff meeting and break the news he's selling to the highest bidder." She dived into the fridge. "Wine or beer?"

"Beer sounds good, thanks. You don't think he'll give you the rest of those three weeks to come up with something else?"

"That time hinged on me winning, something that didn't pan out. As nice as the check they presented me with was, it won't go very far." Especially not after taxes. Taxes. Again. She handed him a beer and poured a large glass of wine. Then hugged the bottle in her arms as if it were a security blanket.

"You should eat something. I can cook."

"Food really isn't on the top of my list right now." But that didn't stop her from ripping open a bag of BBQ chips and diving in wrist deep. "Thanks for the offer, though."

He was trying so hard to be supportive and she loved him for it. But right now, all she wanted to do was rage, to punch something. To scream out all the fear and frustration. If only she could rewind the day and start over. But what would she have done differently? Told Roger to shove it? Sacrifice Jason's future for her own, a future that hadn't been written in sand, let alone stone?

Instead, she'd settle for falling into mundane TV and empty calories.

"Let me know if you change your mind." He found a bowl and took the bag from her to make for easier access. "Couch and TV time. Any preferences?"

"Anything but NCN. And I can't promise not to pass out on you."

"Understood. Good grief, Gary." He pulled his phone out of his pocket and stared at the blinking screen. "What is going on with him? I told him I'd call in the morning. He's left like six messages."

"Must be important." Given the decisions Jason had made regarding the company, she wasn't surprised. His life was about to get very busy. Busy enough for her to wonder how he planned to fit her in. Or if he planned to.

"It's after midnight in New York," Jason muttered. "The restaurant better be on fire. I'd better—"

"Yeah, of course. Gimme." She hugged the bowl against her chest and headed into the living room. "Better bring another bag. I'll probably inhale this one."

She settled on the couch and clicked on the TV, Jason's voice fading into the background. Her eyes drooped.

"Abby." Jason jostled her shoulder.

"I'm awake." She shot upright. Her brain was muddled, foggy. "What is it? What's wrong? What did Gary want?"

"I need your laptop." There was an odd expression on his face, one she couldn't define beyond guarded.

"Right there." She gestured toward the end table. "What's happening?"

Jason held up a finger. "Hang on, Gary. I'm bringing it up now. He told me to check Roasted&Skewered.com. One of those food industry gossip sites."

"What for?" She rubbed at the grit in her eyes.

"Probably something to do with my father." He frowned at the phone. "What? It has to do with me?" He dragged the laptop over and sat next to her, waiting for the page to load. "Gary, give me a sec." He set the phone on the coffee table. "What the hell is this?"

She covered her mouth and scanned the headline: Celebrity Chef Jason Corwin Caught in New Cheating Scandal. "Oh, no." She almost retched.

"This is crap!" Jason scrolled through the article to the video.

Oh, no. No, no, no. "Jason, don't—" She flailed her hands to get him away from the tabloid website.

But it was too late. He clicked Play.

"While details are still sketchy at this time, *Roasted&Skewered* has learned exclusively that celebrity chef Jason Corwin, who only a few months ago was caught cheating during a televised cooking competition, is embroiled in yet more questionable dealings in the food competition world. An unnamed source at the National Cooking Network tells us that a participation contract signed by a local hotel manager was done so with fraudulent intentions by not naming Jason Corwin as an employee of her establishment, nor did she admit on her application that she'd received personal training by Mr. Corwin.

"While Jason Corwin's whereabouts have remained unknown for some time, it appears as if this once hot kitchen commodity and television personality was planning a less than ethical comeback to the food world, which included reclaiming his position as chairman of Corwin Brothers, a possibility that certainly seems up in the air now given these new developments. It was rumored that returning Mr. Corwin to the board would help save the struggling company that Jason Corwin and his late brother inherited from their grandfather. Corwin Brothers was formerly one of the most respected and highly valued companies in the food industry, with multimillion-dollar deals and endorsements. It's widely believed Jason Corwin's lack of business acumen and dedication to his brother's vision began the company's downward spiral, a spiral Edward Corwin, the brothers' father, has been trying to stop—"

Abby slapped the laptop shut. Her entire body felt as if she'd been dipped in a vat of ice. Roger had lied to her.

Jason's voice was no less chilly. "Do you know what they're talking about? What contract?"

"The one I signed to participate in the contest." Abby swallowed hard and tried to keep herself from getting sick. "But he told me, he promised me—" Why would Roger have done this? What did he have to gain? "Jason, I didn't realize, not at first—"

"Stop." He held up his hand and picked his phone up, all the while staring at Abby with something akin to disbelief. "Gary, I'm going to have to call you back." He set the phone down again. "Start from the beginning. What exactly did the contract say?"

"What didn't it say? It was all so—" No. No more excuses. She took a deep breath but couldn't calm her racing heart. "I had to check off all these boxes. About my amateur status, that I hadn't had any professional training— and I took that to mean an actual education," she added when the heat flared in his eyes. "I guess I was wrong about that. I answered those questions in good faith with what I knew then. And yes, there was a question about whether I employed anyone from the National Cooking Network, which of course, at the time I submitted my application, I didn't."

"Why didn't you say something when you realized the truth? They might have—"

"I didn't think it mattered! When I started to worry about it, you said your shows had been canceled and besides, it was only cooking lessons." Could she explain and justify herself in the same breath? Did any of this make sense? "I figured I was in the clear. And then Roger—"

"Roger," Jason spat. He stood up and began to pace, the anger radiating off him warming her still chilled body. "I should have known he had a hand in this. It's his style. How does he fit in?"

Abby's mind wouldn't stop spinning. "The date on the contract I signed is the day after you arrived in Butterfly Harbor. I still don't know how he found that out—"

"It's Roger. He always gets what he needs."

"I told him it was a coincidence. That you weren't an employee, not officially, and that was true, but then you started working in the kitchen and he showed me a picture of us that day you took money out of Matilda's cash jar. He said given your history, no one would believe anything you said. From there, it went downhill. He gave me a choice. Either throw the competition or—" She hesitated.

There wasn't any way Jason was going to believe she'd done this to protect him, not with the fallout that was happening right now on the internet, and besides, if he had any hope of salvaging his company, the less he knew, the better.

"He told me to throw the competition or

he'd expose me on national television," she lied. "I couldn't let the Flutterby or Butterfly Harbor take that hit. I had no idea he'd leak this to the media. He didn't have any reason to." Tears burned her throat like acid. Why had she believed anything Roger had said? "He'd already won. His precious Clara is going to be the next NCN star. He said it was all he wanted."

"This was all about the Flutterby. God, Abby, I expect my father to come at me from behind, not you!"

She jolted. He honestly thought she was capable of the same malicious behavior as his father? "Jason, I'm sorry—"

"You could have told me. You should have, and you would have if you'd been on the up and up." He sounded so tired, so defeated. "Instead you've been lying to me from the moment I got here."

"No!" Abby jumped to her feet. "No, Jason, that's not true. You knew I only got into this to save the Flutterby, and maybe I didn't fill you in on all the details—"

"Maybe you didn't? The other day in the kitchen." Realization dawned on his face. "You didn't want to pay me. You didn't want me as an employee." He seemed to be fitting the jagged pieces together. "You knew about this then. You suspected you'd done something wrong and you still stayed quiet and hoped no one would find out. You lied to my face. Even knowing how much I was struggling to put my life back together and move beyond my own mistakes, you didn't tell me. You didn't warn me."

"I didn't think I had to. I mean, yes, I wondered if I was putting *my* situation in jeopardy, but I never once thought *you'd* be dragged into this. I figured if anyone was held responsible for that contract it would be me. You have to believe me, Jason! I didn't think any of this would affect you." This entire conversation was like an avalanche she couldn't stop as her words tumbled over themselves.

"How could it not affect me? You used me, Abby. You lied to me—maybe not at the start. I knew why you had to do this, but you've lied to me every day since."

Exhaustion dried up her tears and cut through her desperation. "In hindsight I should have told you, but I was afraid you'd take off and I'd be stuck." He wanted the truth? Better late than never. "It wasn't as if we were on the best of terms starting out, and by the time I had something to worry about, it was too late. I didn't have another choice, Jason! I had to win."

"Except you didn't win, did you? And thanks to you and your lies, I'm right back where I started. No, that's wrong. I'm even worse off. What a mess. I'm going to have to put Gary into major damage-control mode in the hopes we can salvage something before this story blows wide." He paced in front of the window, the color on his face hotter than a wildfire in summer. "When the board hears about this, if they haven't already, and the rest of the media picks up on me cheating again, that site is right—they're going to rescind the offer and my father's going to step right in and destroy what's left of Corwin Brothers. It's like David dying all over again."

"You can't think this is what I wanted." Abby's heart broke at the thought of him losing his brother a second time. Was he right? Was this all her fault? "Jason, I know how hard you've fought to get back what you have, to find who you are again." How had this all gone so wrong? How had she not seen… "You're the last person I wanted to get hurt in all of this."

"You could have fooled me. You should have trusted me, Abby. Right from the start."

"I did what I had to do. With what few options I had then. You of all people should know about hindsight, how easy it is to see that you should have done things differently. The Flutterby is all I have to protect my family. Tell me you wouldn't have done the same if our places were reversed. If you had the chance to save Corwin Brothers, or another chance to save David, tell me you wouldn't have done the same thing."

He stared at her, those intoxicating blue eyes of his bright in the dim light of her living room. For a moment, she thought maybe she'd gotten through. That he understood. That he could forgive her.

"I can tell you one thing, Abby," he said finally. "I wouldn't have used the one person who was on my side from the start, and I sure as hell wouldn't have told them I love them. You know what it took for me to decide to go back to New York, to even think about opening those doors again. To fight for my company, and all the while this was hanging over my head like some giant invisible guillotine."

"I never would have—" His words stung. She'd never felt so low.

"Stop. Just stop. I can't believe anything you say right now."

"Jason, please. You're wrong about all this. Let's talk this out. I love you. I—" She would not break. She would not cry. Not as he turned his back on her. Not as he walked to the door. Not as she feared she'd never see him again. "I don't want to lose you."

"Lose me?" He looked over his shoulder at her, the icy fury in his eyes knocking her back a step. "Abby, I don't think you understand. Hearing all this? Knowing you lied to me? You never had me."

He closed the door behind him.

CHAPTER SEVENTEEN

"Ah, Abby. Wonderful." Alice beamed at Abby as she stepped into her grandmother's private hospital room. She stacked a second empty lime gelatin container on her table. "Eloise and I were just chatting—" She broke off as she took in Abby's red-rimmed eyes and strained face. "What's the matter?"

"Gran, I need to talk to you about some things." Abby hugged her arms around her torso and squeezed. Maybe she'd run out of breath before having to deal with her grandmother's disappointment.

"Why don't I go get some coffee," Eloise said. She stopped next to Abby and touched gentle fingers to her arm.

Abby gave her a weak smile.

"Come. Sit." Alice patted the bed. She reached her grandmother and the tears returned. Tears that had refused to fall. Tears that had lodged painfully in her throat as she climbed the stairs to Jason's room this morning before being told by Lori that he'd checked out late last night.

She'd had so much to gain it didn't seem possible she'd lost everything. It was as if she'd been catapulted into someone else's nightmare and she couldn't wake up. She didn't even have Roger left to rail at. He and the rest of the NCN gang had left early this morning to finish the festival in Monterey.

"What's all this?" Alice grabbed hold of Abby's hand and tugged her onto the thin mattress.

"Gran." Abby sobbed, unable to keep it inside any longer. "I've been trying so hard..." How did she tell her grandmother she'd failed? That she'd broken the promises she'd made to always keep Gran safe? "I don't know what to do."

"Hush, now." Alice's soft command only added to the weight on Abby's heart. "Come here." She held out her uninjured arm. Abby couldn't resist. She lay beside her, curling into her grandmother in the same way she had when she was a little girl. When her grandmother and grandfather could fix everything. Except Gran couldn't fix this. Abby closed her eyes as Alice's fingers stroked her hair. This was what she'd needed. "Now tell me what's wrong. Is this about your young man?"

"No," Abby whispered. She didn't want to think about Jason. *Couldn't* think about him or that shocked look of betrayal that would haunt her. But how could she not when all that rang in her ears was the disbelief and disappointment he'd thrown at her? "Not only. There's more. So much more."

"Then out with it. It's not doing you any good keeping it inside. If anything, it's breaking your heart."

It took her a good while to find the words let alone the courage to come clean. When she did, the dam cracked. "It started a couple of weeks ago when I visited Mr. V in the hospital." The rest of the story spilled out, the floodgates open. Her panic, her determination, the stress of the contest, of paying the bills and keeping the secret about the Flutterby tumbled out of her, and as she released the details, the pressure on her chest loosened.

Despite the regret and grief, she felt better for having purged herself of what had been happening the last few weeks.

Her grandmother listened, still stroking her hair in the same controlled motion that made it impossible for Abby to understand what she was thinking or feeling. She only needed to know Gran, as always, was there.

"I'm so sorry, Gran. I've tried everything I can think of, but there's no way to save the Flutterby now. Mr. V's going to have to sell, which means we have to move. But I'll find us a place." She clenched her fists. "I'm not going to let you go to a care facility or home. I don't care what I have to do, where I have to work, but—"

"Hush, Abby." Alice's hands stilled. "That's a discussion for another time. I don't know what got into you that you didn't think you could come to me with all this."

"You sound like Jason." Abby caught her lip between her teeth and struggled against a new wave of pain. "I lied to him, Gran. About so many things, and now he's suffering the fallout that should have been mine. He's so angry."

"What's that?" Alice tucked her chin into her chest as Abby shifted her head. The stern look on her grandmother's face surprised her. "Even knowing you lost on purpose to protect him?"

Abby hesitated.

"Abigail Marie Manning!" Sometimes her grandmother's strength and vehemence astonished her. "You didn't tell him? What is wrong with you?"

"It wouldn't have made a difference, Gran." It wouldn't have changed anything. He'd still have to scramble, to try to fix what she'd destroyed. Besides, she wasn't sure he would have believed her. How could she expect him to? "He's gone."

"Gone? Gone where?"

Abby almost laughed. In spite of everything else she'd told her grandmother, Jason's leaving was what outraged her? "Off to New York, I assume."

"And what are you going to do about it?"

Do about it? What right did she have to do anything about it? She'd done the one thing she knew was unforgivable in Jason's eyes: she'd betrayed him. "Right now there's nothing I can do." Maybe in time… Abby pushed herself up and wiped her face clean of the tears. "It's my own fault, Gran. Some mistakes can't be undone." No matter how much she wished otherwise.

A KNOCK SOUNDED on the glass door of JD's as Jason locked up. "We're closed!" he called over his shoulder. He froze as he recognized that black hoodie. What the— He twisted the lock and wrenched open the door. "What are you doing here?"

"I come in peace." Marcus Aiken raised his hands as if in surrender. "I know I have no right to ask, but someone suggested I talk to you. May I come in?"

Jason sighed. When was Gary going to stop meddling? It was bad enough he was playing Abby advocate, not that there was much time to talk about anything other than Corwin Brothers business the last few days. "I was just going to fix myself something to eat. You want?"

Surprise flashed on Marcus's face before he nodded and stepped inside. "Who am I to turn down a Jason Corwin dinner?" He glanced around the empty restaurant. "New business hours? I thought JD's used to be open until 1:00 a.m.?"

"We're working out some new kinks." Jason locked up again and headed into the kitchen. "Thanks to some detrimental reorganizing by my father," including getting rid of most of the JD's staff who had remained loyal to Jason, "ten is as late as we can manage right now." At least Edward had left the decor alone. From the elegant teakwood bar to the thin arches over individual seating areas, the draped tables were perfectly arranged for tomorrow night's pretheater service.

"Does that mean things are settled with the board of directors?" Marcus followed Jason into the spacious, orderly stainless steel kitchen that lacked that punch of character Jason recalled from the Flutterby. "They came around after all?"

"After I pretty much promised them my firstborn." Jason pulled out the beef patties he'd made earlier in the evening and slapped them on the grill top. The normally satisfying sizzle didn't make a dent in his sullen mood. Nothing had in the week he'd been home. Nothing felt right. Nothing felt complete. The New York scene bored him. The office bored him, but the work had to be done. "The formal vote isn't until tomorrow, but one thing riding out a national scandal does is prepare you for the next one. Apparently the board decided I couldn't do a worse job than my father, so."

He shrugged. "In the meantime, I've been spending most of my days using what capital we have left to buy ourselves out of the contracts he got us into." He'd spend a small fortune when all was said and done, but he would, once and for all, cut his father out completely. The future was too bright to put it at risk again. He was scheduled to meet with the CEO of Lansing Hotels, the same man David had been on his way to consult with the night of the crash. Apparently David hadn't been their focus: he had. It was Jason's cooking that interested them, his point of view, his dedication. And they were definitely encouraging about his farm-to-table idea, especially when it came to their smaller hotels.

If only all of this didn't sound so lonely.

"Since you're here." Jason tossed two russet potatoes at Marcus. "Make yourself useful. Fryer's over there."

"Some things never change." Marcus took off his hoodie. "At your beck and call once again."

"Last I heard you were over at Clementine's," Jason said. The modern bistro had been getting good word of mouth since it opened late last year, mostly due to Marcus's unique and enthusiastic take on classic fare. "Your night off?"

"No." Marcus grabbed a knife and hacked off the ends of the spuds. "I quit. Before I went out to California. I am officially unemployed."

Jason turned from the fridge. Now, that he hadn't expected. "Except for your contract with the National Cooking Network. You've got a couple new shows in the pipeline, from what I hear."

"Maybe, maybe not. Depends on how my meeting with the network president goes tomorrow morning. After what went down in Butterfly Harbor, he needs to be made aware of just how dangerous Roger is."

"You're not going to convince the network brass Roger was behind that leaked story." But Jason would go to his grave knowing he was.

"Honestly? Falsely ratting you out to the press is the least of his sins, Jason. You never made a deal with that particular devil, did you?"

"He did his best, but no. That's where it helped being behind the scenes most of the time. He ran David ragged, though, and made some inroads, I suppose." Jason set the vegetables and condiments on the counter. Where was this going, exactly?

"The man should come with a warning bell. It took me a while, but I finally woke up. That's why I'm here." He took a deep breath. "It's time to come clean with you."

"Clean about what?"

"What really happened during that competition you went into for David." Marcus set his knife down and gripped the edge of the counter. "Roger told me if I sabotaged your meal during the competition and then told on you, he'd give me my own show. I'd be his new go-to for emceeing and any other specials he produced. His new star."

"And you agreed?" Was there anyone who hadn't betrayed him? "David and I gave you your first job. We even helped you pay off your tuition bills." Hadn't their support brokered any goodwill or loyalty?

"Yeah, well, it's a little hard to shine in a room full of stars. And Roger can read people." He snapped his fingers. "He saw I wasn't happy, that I was ambitious. And way too cocky. I wanted to get to the top, but wasn't interested in paying my dues to get there. I also didn't want to be under your and David's thumbs for the rest of my life."

"You wouldn't have been." Jason couldn't believe this. Yet another person who had lied to him. Someone else who had used him. "But I guess it's too late to convince you of that. Come on." He waved his hand. "You're in this deep. Might as well come out with the rest of it. What did you do to me at the competition?"

"Replaced the all-purpose flour you were supposed to use for the popovers with pastry flour." Marcus flinched and returned his attention to the potatoes that could now be considered slivers. "When they didn't rise, I made the suggestion you use what I cooked. I am so sorry, Jason. I know I have no right to expect your forgiveness—"

"*You* made the suggestion?" Jason frowned. Truth be told, he didn't remember a whole lot about that night. Only that he'd defended himself against the indefensible. The evidence was right there. In full color on the internet. "I don't remember it that way."

"Of course you don't. You're not a cheater, Jason. I've never met anyone with more integrity than you. Everyone knew your mind wasn't in the game. How could it be when David hadn't even been gone two months? That made Roger's plan all the easier," Marcus said. "Even Shelly Sengal went to the producers and suggested they postpone the telecast, but Roger and your father convinced the network brass—"

"Wait." Jason's voice snapped like a whip. "What does my father have to do with this? He was there?" That he definitely didn't remember. "During the competition?" That wasn't right.

"Sure." Marcus nodded. "He was in the sound booth most of the time. I saw him myself talking off and on all night with Roger. You didn't know your dad and Roger are friends?"

"No." Suddenly so many things made sense. Beginning and ending with that *Roasted&Skewered* story. "No, I did not."

"Well, like you said. Competitions have never been your forte."

"Don't make excuses for me, Marcus. And while I'll happily give you grief for putting the plan in motion, the outcome doesn't change," Jason said. "Your idea, Roger's or even mine, when push came to shove, I lied. But." He gave Marcus a few extra seconds to suffer. "I appreciate you telling me the truth."

"Yeah, well, Abby was the one who suggested I talk to you about it. I didn't buy into it at first, but after what Roger pulled on her, and what she did for you at the festival, I couldn't very well not follow through."

Jason's ears roared. He could smell burning meat on the stove, he couldn't seem to move. "What do you mean, what Abby did for me?"

"Ah, man." Marcus squeezed his eyes shut. "I've probably said too much already."

"Oh, no. Don't you dare back down now. What do you think you know about Abby?"

"That depends," Marcus hedged. "What do you think you know?"

"That she fraudulently signed that contract and then threw the competition to protect herself." And the inn. And Alice. And Mr. V... "He was going to out her and the entire town on TV."

"That's what she told you?" Marcus looked as if a feather could have pushed him over. "No, no, no. I was there, Jason. I heard most of what he said to her. I heard enough to know it wasn't Abby that Roger threatened. It was you, Jason. She threw that competition to protect you."

Jason opened his mouth to demand more information, only to have it slam shut again as the smoke alarm blared.

"Come on, David!" Jason blasted and grabbed the mop. "Stop it, already! I get the message." He rammed the handle at the detector until it dropped from the ceiling.

Marcus stared at him as Jason waved his way through the smoke and threw the burgers in the trash. He aimed his metal spatula at his former sous chef and pinned him with a deadly stare. "You. Start over. From the beginning. And don't leave anything out."

"WHAT DO YOU mean your parents' rings are gone?" Holly set a pot of tea on Abby's coffee table and sat next to her on the sofa.

"Someone bought them during the festival. The rings, the necklace, poof." Abby rested her cheek in her hand. "Gone." Just like Jason. She hadn't gotten up the courage yet to tell Gran. Not when she was still fending off Alice's "call Jason" mutterings.

"You're running low on chocolate chip cookies," Paige said as she carried a plate in from the kitchen. "I'll make you some more."

"Don't." Abby sighed. "I've already gained five pounds thanks to this stupid thing." She pounded a fist against her heart. "Has the gossip died down yet?"

"About you being in cahoots with a scheming, conniving chef out to redeem his good name?" Paige waved away her concern and stuffed a cookie in her mouth. She claimed a spot on the floor. "Please," she said and spit crumbs before she swallowed the cookie. "Anyone who met Jason knows that's all baloney."

"Not all of it."

"You did what you needed to do, Abs." Holly patted a hand on her knee. "No one blames you for it, especially now that we all know the Flutterby is up for sale."

Abby couldn't have cried any more if she'd wanted to. "I guess I should start finding another place to live for me and Gran." She looked around her tiny cottage before glancing out the window. A vegetable garden would have been nice.

All three of them jumped at the knock on the door.

"Luke?" Abby asked Holly.

"He's camping with the kids and my dad, remember?" Holly got up to answer the door. "Eloise, Alice." She waved them inside. "What are you doing out and about in the dark?"

"Getting my exercise," Alice said. The bruises on her face had faded and the bandage on her forehead was smaller, but the sling still managed to turn Abby's stomach. "Eloise and I have something we need to discuss with Abby."

"We don't want to intrude," Holly said. "Come on, Paige."

"No, no." Alice motioned for them to stay in place as she sat in the chair opposite the sofa. "Goodness, Holly, you're family. You, too, Paige. Stay where you are. Abby, you've been fretting something awful about where we're going to live when Mr. Vartebetium sells the inn."

Abby pinched her lips shut. Guilty. Lately, her grandmother wouldn't hear of her carrying the bulk of responsibility any more. If anything, Alice had commandeered just about all of Abby's decision making for fear she'd dig herself into an even deeper hole.

Poor Mr. V had been inundated with Alice's previous experience of managing the inn. The two of them had been holed up in his office nearly every day since he'd come home. On the bright side, Alice's attitude about, well, about everything, had drastically improved. Abby couldn't remember the last time she'd found her grandmother staring out at Gramps's bench.

"Your grandmother and I have come to a decision," Eloise said, holding her oversize red purse on her lap. "Alice is going to move in with me."

"What?" Surely she couldn't have heard that correctly.

"Not only me," Alice said. "Oscar's moving in, too. And Myra. It'll be like we're all twenty again. Back when your grandfather began courting me."

"That house of mine is too large for one

person," Eloise explained before Abby could comment. "And as I told you, I took care of my sister for a number of years. She had her own set of rooms, even bigger than what your grandmother has now, and it's already equipped for assisted living. Handicapped railings, wider doorways, smooth floors. It's the perfect solution. For both of you."

"But what about money?" Abby said. "Gran—"

"I've already worked out a budget. Between your grandfather's pension and the Social Security I've been able to save thanks to you getting us free board at the Flutterby, I have more than enough to play with."

"The rent will be minimal, Abby," Eloise added. "And I'd only need a little help covering the uptick in utilities."

"And when I need more care, we'll cross that bridge then," Alice said. "So you can mark me off your worry list."

"Gran," Abby whispered. Holy hamburgers, she did have more tears after all. "I don't want to mark you off my list."

"I think this sounds wonderful," Holly said. "It'll do wonders for all of you, and it's relatively close to where Abby can live."

"From where Abby can what?" Why did she feel as if she was always playing catch-up?

"Show her," Paige prompted as she shifted to her knees.

Holly held up a set of keys. "We were saving it for a surprise. And I lied earlier. Luke and my dad and the kids, along with Fletch..." Holly waggled her eyebrows in Paige's direction.

"Stop that." Paige pointed a sharp finger at her. "He's not my type."

"He's a man in a uniform," Alice said. "He's any woman's type."

"Don't you start," Paige moaned.

"Anyway," Holly said. "All of us have spent the last few days making over Luke's parents' old house. I know it's a little ways out of town and it still needs some work—"

"It needed a lot of work, from what I remember," Abby said as Holly pulled out her phone and tapped open her photos. "Oh," Abby gasped. The house was almost unrecognizable. What she remembered as a run-down, graying ramshackle structure had been given a facelift. Bright yellow paint with crisp white trim, something reminiscent of the Flutterby, shone back at her; the rotting stonework had been replaced, as had the trellis along the base of the structure. She didn't see a hint of the sadness and violence she knew had once taken place there. "It's beautiful."

"Calliope even came by and burned about ten sage bundles," Paige said with a grin. "Got rid of all the bad vibes on that property. Even Luke likes it now."

Luke. Abby couldn't believe it. That house, that property, had been hell for him growing up. He'd always sworn he'd burn it to the ground given the chance. Instead, he'd transformed it. For her. "I can't take this," she said.

"Why ever not?" Alice demanded. "Seems the perfect solution to me."

"I won't have a job, I don't even know if I can find one here in town—"

"Calliope said to come by the farm when you get a chance. She has some ideas on that front. And given Luke considered it lost property anyway, we're not in any rush to start collecting any rent. The place is yours for as long as you want it."

"Everyone's solving all my problems." Abby looked around the room at the people she loved most. Her smile dipped.

There was one person who was missing.

And there wasn't anyone who could solve that problem for her.

CHAPTER EIGHTEEN

"HELLO, DAD." JASON leaned back in the conference chair and watched his father stride into the boardroom.

"Jason." With his usual show of nerves, Edward Corwin buttoned his tailored suit jacket and straightened his burgundy silk tie. A small man, Jason realized now, not in stature, but certainly in standing. If ever an honest thought passed through his father's mind, Jason would have been shocked. A nice enough presentation, Jason supposed, but when had his father started looking like an understudy for a mob boss? The permanent scowl of disapproval on his round face, the telltale suspicious, calculating eyes, but beyond that…nothing. "I wasn't aware you'd be here."

"Where else would the chairman be except in the boardroom?" Jason tapped a finger on the button under his desk and watched as the man he'd thought of as imposing for most of his life took a seat at the opposite end of the table.

How many years had he looked up to this man, waiting for a sign, any sign, that Jason mattered to him?

"Jumping the gun, aren't you?" Edward said. "I believe I still have the opportunity to make my case to the board before the final vote."

"The board agreed to move the meeting up once they were presented with new evidence about my previous ousting." *Ousting* seemed more in line with having been set up, rather than removed.

"New evidence or new scandal? I'm surprised they'd even let you in the door given what transpired in California with that butterfly girl."

Butterfly girl. Jason's lips twitched as he pictured Abby with butterflies flitting around her beautiful blond hair. "You seem awfully up-to-date on what's been going on in my life, Dad. I didn't realize you were so interested."

"Only insomuch as it affects Corwin Brothers. It's only a matter of time," Edward said and stood, "before they come crying to me. I was making a difference in this company. I was making a—"

"You were making a joke out of your father's legacy along with your son's," Jason interrupted. He didn't care what his father thought of him or even what he'd done to him, but for Edward to do this to David—that could never be forgotten, and certainly not forgiven. "Nothing you've done since taking over Corwin Brothers has been for the good of anything other than your own pocketbook. By the way, my first action was to hire an independent auditor and investigator to go over the company's and your finances and accounts. They'll also be looking into any company you've done business with both before I was ousted and since."

"They won't find anything," Edward blustered, but for the first time in Jason's life, he saw a flicker of fear on his father's face. "As if you know anything about running this business. That was your brother's job."

"Yes, it was." Jason could accept the pang of grief with little more than a twinge now. "And he excelled at it. But now I'm going to excel at it. While you and your friend find yourselves out in the cold."

"What friend?"

"Roger Evans. You know, I've always found it fascinating, considering how hard you pushed me and David to get our own TV show, how little time you spent in a studio. It could be why I always enjoyed it," he lied.

"What's that got to do with anything?"

"It's just interesting that you were so concerned about me—for the first time in my entire life, I believe—that you were at the competition you cornered me into. Front and center. Watching every moment." He clicked on one of the computer screens on the wall as the tape he and Marcus had requested from NCN ran.

"If you'd been around the studio more, you'd probably have realized how many cameras are running. This one's a particularly good shot. No, wait. Don't go." Jason turned up the volume just as Edward demanded Roger do whatever it took to get Jason out of the competition. "I think the wagging finger gives it an extra something, don't you?" Jason clicked to the next screen. "And here you are again. This would be you in the sound booth watching me refuse to admit to cheating. I can't tell you what that smile on your face means to me."

"Proves nothing."

"On its own and to anyone but me? You're right. It doesn't." How he'd wanted to be wrong. "But with the sworn affidavit from

Marcus Aiken admitting to setting me up and being paid off by Roger Evans, it adds up to something more. Then there's the matter of that Butterfly Harbor debacle. It didn't take much to get Roger to admit he'd called you about Abby's contract issue. Did you know cell reception can be pretty crappy out there? Well, either that or Roger was just that stupid, because he called you from the Flutterby Inn the night he arrived in Butterfly Harbor. Stayed on the phone for a good fifteen minutes. What were you talking about, Dad? Contracts, perhaps? And the perception of wrongdoing?"

Edward held his arms stiff by his sides, his gaze skittering across the screens before Jason turned them off. He shifted his gaze to his son. "It's none of your business what two old friends discuss."

"I was hoping you'd say that," Jason said. "Because Roger came clean almost immediately. It probably helped that the person asking him about it was the president of NCN. He's been fired, FYI. He's done. For good. And so are you."

"It should have been you."

"I'm sorry." Jason turned his head and cupped his ear. "I didn't quite catch—"

"It should have been you on that plane." Edward slammed his fist on the table so hard, the floor vibrated. "David was the star. David had the talent. It should be David sitting in that chair, not you!"

It wasn't a fact he could argue. How could he, when the same thoughts had haunted him since David's death? It was another thing entirely to hear it from your only living relative.

"You really hate me that much?" Jason felt he'd prepared himself; he'd thought he knew how much his father loathed him. But he hadn't. And he couldn't. Not without asking the one question he should have asked decades ago. "Why, Dad? What did I ever do except whatever I could to get your attention after Mom died? An ounce of affection? A compliment, a kind word of encouragement. You couldn't even bring yourself to dole out punishment. Just tell me, what did I do?"

Edward smoothed the front of his jacket, and calmly, coolly replied, "You were born."

"That's it?" Could it really be so...simple? All the guilt, all the self-loathing and doubt he'd heaped on his own shoulders because he thought he'd been unworthy of his father's love, vanished. "That's why you hate me?"

"I don't hate you, Jason." Edward looked at

him as if he were nothing more than a piece of lint on his jacket. "I didn't want two sons. I wasn't supposed to have two sons, and I couldn't love you both."

Jason felt the shackles break free. "Six minutes."

"What are you talking about?" Edward snapped.

"That's what David always said. 'Six minutes, Jason. Be grateful for them.' And now I am. Thank you, Dad. For proving to me once and for all blood doesn't mean you have to love someone. And as much as I am happy to forget you exist from this moment on, I will never forgive you for what you and Roger did to Abby."

"What's that butterfly girl got to do with any of this?"

"It's because of her that I'm here, Dad. You see, Abby's the one who taught me how to fight for what I believe in, for what I need in my life. So when you go home tonight, and when those investigators come knocking on your door, I want you to think about me and my butterfly girl and know that she's the reason every day of your life will be spent alone. Now, if you'll excuse me." Jason hit the button under the desk again and the faces of all the board members, along with Gary and the president, CEO and VP of programs from the National Cooking Network, flashed onto the screens. "I'm about to close on that deal David started before he died. And then I'm going to go home. To my butterfly girl."

"Abby, where have you been?" Mr. V tottered out of his office and waggled a finger at her as she closed the lobby door behind her. "I thought you said you'd be home by two?"

"Sorry, Mr. V." Abby sighed. "Oh, hello." She plastered on her polite customer service smile for the man and woman behind Mr. V. "I thought your meeting would be over by now. I was just taking some more of Gran's boxes over to Eloise's." Alice hadn't wasted any time making a new start. Maybe it was for the best. Her grandmother certainly seemed to be thriving under the watchful eyes of her friends from the Cocoon Club.

Abby wasn't ready to meet the new owners, not even after more than a week of preparation. She'd procrastinated until she hoped they'd be gone, stopping for a long lunch at the diner with Calliope. That the Flutterby was now a part of some hotel conglomerate undoubtedly more focused on profit than service broke her heart. But at least the inn would stay open. At least they'd paid almost double Mr. V's previous offer, eliminating his having to accept Gil Hamilton's suggested enterprise.

"You must be Abby Manning." The sprite of a woman who looked like a pixie with close-cropped blond hair and a smile slightly too large for her round face offered her hand. "Bethany Cabot. We have heard so much about you. It's an absolute pleasure."

"Thanks." She couldn't keep the confusion out of her voice. "I didn't think Mr. V—"

"Not from me," he said. "Although I've given them an earful as well."

The middle-aged man beside Bethany smiled. "Spencer Marshall." He shook her hand. "We'd like to arrange a time to speak with you later, to discuss terms and whatever future plans you see for the Flutterby." He reminded Abby of a sportscaster with his too-perfect hair and polished smile, but she got a vibe of honest professionalism off him. "There will be some changes, of course, beginning with the restaurant, but I think the new head chef would like to discuss that with you himself."

"New head…future…terms?" She was behind on things again, wasn't she?

"He's getting to know Matilda," Bethany said. "Such a character. But you go on. We've already checked in, so we'll settle in our rooms, maybe catch the sunset."

"We hear it's spectacular," Spencer agreed.

"I guess I'll—" Abby headed toward the kitchen, wondering why Lori wouldn't meet her quizzical gaze. She pushed through the dining room and heard voices chiming from the kitchen. Okay. She straightened her shoulders and took a deep breath. She could do this. She could start the farewell process and begin her new life.

The smoke alarm screamed.

"Matilda!" Abby dived into the kitchen. "What's going—Jason?" She stared, her face flashing hot and cold as he turned those heavenly blue eyes on her, the ones she'd tried to forget. "What are—"

"What?" He grinned.

"Turn that thing off!"

"Oh, right." He pushed a button. "Sorry. It's new. Upgrade." He jumped down off the counter. "I was showing Matilda how we met."

"There was more smoke involved," Abby told her cook, who ambled around the counter and out the door, clicking her tongue in that way she had when she approved of people.

The silence hurt Abby's ears. "What are you doing here?" she asked again.

"Didn't they tell you? I'm the new head chef."

Her spirits dipped. "What about Matilda?"

"Who do you think is going to be my sous chef? You? I'm sorry, Abby, but that won't be possible."

"Wait, Jason." She grabbed his arm and spun him around. She touched his cheek. "You shaved your beard." When she pulled away, he moved in and pushed his cheek into her hand. She couldn't stop staring at his bare, handsome face. The ghosts, the depression, the anger—they were all gone.

"I did. New start. All around. You lied to me."

She frowned. So much for hoping they'd moved beyond that. "Yes. And I'm sorry for it."

"You should be sorry. Throwing the competition to protect me at the expense of the Flutterby? Not your smartest move."

"You know?" Hope swirled around her heart. "How did you—"

"Doesn't matter. But I'm the one who owes you an apology." He caught her face between his hands and brought them nose to nose. "I'm sorry about all those things I said. The accusations I slung. You didn't deserve them. Even if you hadn't done what you did to protect me, you did it to save your home. Your family. Of all people, I should have understood that."

"I didn't think you'd believe me. Jason, I—"

He kissed her. Probably to shut her up. "I love you, Abby Manning. And if you'll have me, I want to come home."

"Home?" She couldn't believe her ears. "But what about New York? What about the restaurant—"

"I'll have to go back occasionally—frequently at first to make sure my new vice chairman doesn't get overwhelmed."

"New vice chairman?"

"Marcus Aiken. He's also taking over JD's while I start Corwin Brothers' new venture. What do you think?" He hugged her against his side as he waved an arm around the kitchen.

"What do I think about what?"

"Lansing Hotels and Corwin Brothers are officially partners. Smaller, farm-focused restaurants in at least 50 percent of their properties. We're calling this one—our anchor restaurant—Flutterby Dreams. Providing we get the right manager for the inn, of course."

"Of course." She nodded, her mind spinning. "I think Lori—"

"I think Lori deserves a promotion for sure, but I told Lansing there was only one woman for the job when it came to the Flutterby. The whole deal hinged on it." He kissed her again, something she refused to ever get used to. "What do you say? Will you stay on and run the new Flutterby Inn? With me? Forever?" He opened his hand and a chain dropped down, still looped around his finger.

Her parents' rings twirled in front of her face.

"Jason." She'd never loved a person more in her life than at this moment. "When—"

"One of those errands during the festival. I rendered you speechless. I love it. But I'm waiting for an answer, Abby. Will you?"

Abby grinned. "Yes. But only on one condition." She slipped her hands around his neck and raised up to brush her mouth against his. "Never ask me to cook again."

His lips curved up to form a bright smile. "Deal."

* * * * *

LARGER-PRINT BOOKS!

**GET 2 FREE
LARGER-PRINT NOVELS
PLUS 2 FREE
MYSTERY GIFTS**

Love Inspired

SUSPENSE

RIVETING INSPIRATIONAL ROMANCE

Larger-print novels are now available...

YES! Please send me 2 FREE LARGER-PRINT Love Inspired® Suspense novels and my 2 FREE mystery gifts (gifts are worth about $10). After receiving them, if I don't wish to receive any more books, I can return the shipping statement marked "cancel." If I don't cancel, I will receive 4 brand-new novels every month and be billed just $5.49 per book in the U.S. or $5.99 per book in Canada. That's a savings of at least 19% off the cover price. It's quite a bargain! Shipping and handling is just 50¢ per book in the U.S. and 75¢ per book in Canada.* I understand that accepting the 2 free books and gifts places me under no obligation to buy anything. I can always return a shipment and cancel at any time. Even if I never buy another book, the two free books and gifts are mine to keep forever.

110/310 IDN GH6P

Name _____ (PLEASE PRINT) _____

Address _____ Apt. # _____

City _____ State/Prov. _____ Zip/Postal Code _____

Signature (if under 18, a parent or guardian must sign) _____

Mail to the **Reader Service:**
IN U.S.A.: P.O. Box 1867, Buffalo, NY 14240-1867
IN CANADA: P.O. Box 609, Fort Erie, Ontario L2A 5X3

**Are you a current subscriber to Love Inspired® Suspense books
and want to receive the larger-print edition?
Call 1-800-873-8635 or visit www.ReaderService.com.**

* Terms and prices subject to change without notice. Prices do not include applicable taxes. Sales tax applicable in N.Y. Canadian residents will be charged applicable taxes. Offer not valid in Quebec. This offer is limited to one order per household. Not valid for current subscribers to Love Inspired Suspense larger-print books. All orders subject to credit approval. Credit or debit balances in a customer's account(s) may be offset by any other outstanding balance owed by or to the customer. Please allow 4 to 6 weeks for delivery. Offer available while quantities last.

Your Privacy—The Reader Service is committed to protecting your privacy. Our Privacy Policy is available online at www.ReaderService.com or upon request from the Reader Service.

We make a portion of our mailing list available to reputable third parties that offer products we believe may interest you. If you prefer that we not exchange your name with third parties, or if you wish to clarify or modify your communication preferences, please visit us at www.ReaderService.com/consumerschoice or write to us at Reader Service Preference Service, P.O. Box 9062, Buffalo, NY 14240-9062. Include your complete name and address.

LISLP15

WESTERN WP PROMISES

YES! Please send me **The Western Promises Collection** in Larger Print. This collection begins with 3 FREE books and 2 FREE gifts (gifts valued at approx. $14.00 retail) in the first shipment, along with the other first 4 books from the collection! If I do not cancel, I will receive 8 monthly shipments until I have the entire 51-book Western Promises collection. I will receive 2 or 3 FREE books in each shipment and I will pay just $4.99 US/ $5.89 CDN for each of the other four books in each shipment, plus $2.99 for shipping and handling per shipment. *If I decide to keep the entire collection, I'll have paid for only 32 books, because 19 books are FREE! I understand that accepting the 3 free books and gifts places me under no obligation to buy anything. I can always return a shipment and cancel at any time. My free books and gifts are mine to keep no matter what I decide.

272 HCN 3070 472 HCN 3070

Name	(PLEASE PRINT)	
Address		Apt. #
City	State/Prov.	Zip/Postal Code

Signature (if under 18, a parent or guardian must sign)

Mail to the **Reader Service:**
IN U.S.A.: P.O. Box 1867, Buffalo, NY 14240-1867
IN CANADA: P.O. Box 609, Fort Erie, Ontario L2A 5X3

* Terms and prices subject to change without notice. Prices do not include applicable taxes. Sales tax applicable in N.Y. Canadian residents will be charged applicable taxes. This offer is limited to one order per household. All orders subject to approval. Credit or debit balances in a customer's account(s) may be offset by any other outstanding balance owed by or to the customer. Please allow 4 to 6 weeks for delivery. Offer available while quantities last. Offer not available to Quebec residents.

Your Privacy—The Reader Service is committed to protecting your privacy. Our Privacy Policy is available online at www.ReaderService.com or upon request from the Reader Service.

We make a portion of our mailing list available to reputable third parties that offer products we believe may interest you. If you prefer that we not exchange your name with third parties, or if you wish to clarify or modify your communication preferences, please visit us at www.ReaderService.com/consumerchoice or write to us at Reader Service Preference Service, P.O. Box 9062, Buffalo, NY 14240-9062. Include your complete name and address.

WPBPA16R

REQUEST YOUR FREE BOOKS!
2 FREE WHOLESOME ROMANCE NOVELS
IN LARGER PRINT
PLUS 2
FREE
MYSTERY GIFTS

⋇⋇⋇⋇⋇⋇⋇⋇⋇⋇⋇⋇⋇⋇⋇⋇⋇⋇⋇⋇⋇⋇⋇⋇⋇⋇⋇⋇⋇⋇

H E A R T W A R M I N G™
⋇⋇⋇⋇⋇⋇⋇⋇⋇⋇⋇⋇⋇⋇⋇⋇⋇⋇⋇⋇⋇⋇⋇⋇⋇⋇⋇⋇⋇

Wholesome, tender romances

YES! Please send me 2 FREE Harlequin® Heartwarming Larger-Print novels and my 2 FREE mystery gifts (gifts worth about $10). After receiving them, if I don't wish to receive any more books, I can return the shipping statement marked "cancel." If I don't cancel, I will receive 4 brand-new larger-print novels every month and be billed just $5.24 per book in the U.S. or $5.99 per book in Canada. That's a savings of at least 19% off the cover price. It's quite a bargain! Shipping and handling is just 50¢ per book in the U.S. and 75¢ per book in Canada.* I understand that accepting the 2 free books and gifts places me under no obligation to buy anything. I can always return a shipment and cancel at any time. Even if I never buy another book, the two free books and gifts are mine to keep forever.

161/361 IDN GHX2

Name _____ (PLEASE PRINT)

Address _____ Apt. #

City _____ State/Prov. _____ Zip/Postal Code

Signature (if under 18, a parent or guardian must sign)

Mail to the **Reader Service:**
IN U.S.A.: P.O. Box 1867, Buffalo, NY 14240-1867
IN CANADA: P.O. Box 609, Fort Erie, Ontario L2A 5X3

* Terms and prices subject to change without notice. Prices do not include applicable taxes. Sales tax applicable in N.Y. Canadian residents will be charged applicable taxes. Offer not valid in Quebec. This offer is limited to one order per household. Not valid for current subscribers to Harlequin Heartwarming larger-print books. All orders subject to credit approval. Credit or debit balances in a customer's account(s) may be offset by any other outstanding balance owed by or to the customer. Please allow 4 to 6 weeks for delivery. Offer available while quantities last.

Your Privacy—The Reader Service is committed to protecting your privacy. Our Privacy Policy is available online at www.ReaderService.com or upon request from the Reader Service.

We make a portion of our mailing list available to reputable third parties that offer products we believe may interest you. If you prefer that we not exchange your name with third parties, or if you wish to clarify or modify your communication preferences, please visit us at www.ReaderService.com/consumerchoice or write to us at Reader Service Preference Service, P.O. Box 9062, Buffalo, NY 14240-9062. Include your complete name and address.

HW15